TO HAVE
AND TO HIDE

PATCHWORK MYSTERIES

TO HAVE
AND TO HIDE

CAMY TANG

Guideposts

New York

Guideposts.org
(800) 932-2145
Guideposts Books & Inspirational Media

Cover design by Wendy Bass
Cover illustration by Joyce Patti
Interior design by Lorie Pagnozzi
Typeset by Aptara

Printed and bound in the United States of America
10 9 8 7 6

To Mom and Dad, who have always encouraged
me to follow my dreams

PATCHWORK MYSTERIES

Family Patterns
Time to Share
Muslin Mystery
Timeless Treasures
Homespun Holiday
Pieces of the Past
Threads of Truth
Secret in the Stitches
Bound in Love
Yesterday's Secrets
Squared Away
Mystery on the Midway
A Quilt of Memories
The House on Lookout Mountain
To Have and to Hide

TO HAVE
AND TO HIDE

 CHAPTER ONE

S arah Hart smiled as she swept aside the playful streamers falling from the decorative crown over Roseanna Walsh's front door. She knocked briskly on the glossy white-painted wood, shivering a little in the October air.

Sarah's best friend Martha Maplethorpe grinned at her as they heard the girlish giggling and chatter filtering through the door. "Sounds like the party's already started."

"Wait for me," came a huffing voice behind them.

Sarah turned to see Angela Miller, a friend from church, hurrying up the walk toward them.

"We're only a couple minutes late," Sarah assured her.

They saw a figure through the glass panes on the door a split second before it opened to Roseanna's round figure and wide smile. "Come on in! Everybody's in the living room."

"We're not the last ones, are we?" Angela asked.

"No." Roseanna stepped aside so they could enter the front hall of the Georgian colonial home. "We're still waiting for the bride."

"Caitlin isn't here yet?" Martha asked.

"She called me half an hour ago to say she was on her way," Roseanna said. "Maybe she had car trouble? Although I hope not. It's getting a bit cold to be stuck changing a tire." Roseanna glanced out the door before she shut it, then said to Angela, "Aunt Imogene isn't with you?"

Angela shook her head. "No, she's not coming."

"Imogene Dowling?" Sarah said. "She's my next-door neighbor. I didn't realize she was your aunt. I would have volunteered to bring her."

"She's not really my aunt," Roseanna said. "She and my mom were cousins."

"Imogene is my aunt," Angela said. "She and my mom were sisters. But Roseanna and I grew up like cousins."

"I can't believe I've gone to church with you all these years and didn't know you were cousins with Roseanna," Martha said to Angela.

Angela shrugged. "Since Roseanna and I go to different churches, there's hardly ever a situation where we mention it to other people."

"Why isn't Aunt Imogene coming?" Roseanna asked Angela.

"I was on my way to her house when she called to tell me that Uncle Elmer tripped on his way down the front steps.

She thinks he sprained his ankle, but she wanted to take him to the emergency room just in case."

"Poor Elmer. This will cut into his fishing time." Sarah shifted the covered pie dish in her arms while keeping hold of the gift bag slung over her wrist.

"Oh my goodness, and here we are just standing here talking. Let me help you." Roseanna took the covered dish and headed through the open doorway on Sarah's left into the spacious dining room. As Sarah entered the room, she smelled roast chicken wafting from the open doorway that led into the kitchen at the other end of the dining room. A fire had been laid in the large fireplace, with colorful autumn leaves artfully arranged around a pumpkin on the wide mantel.

The long, elaborately carved dining table groaned under the weight of food ranging from appetizers and salads to breads and pies. With the efficiency of a general, Roseanna had told each guest what type of dish to bring, whether appetizer, side dish, or dessert, while she took care of the main course.

"Gracious, Roseanna." Martha laid her bowl of green salad on the table. "There's enough to feed an army."

"You know people in Maple Hill." Roseanna laid Sarah's lattice-top apple pie down on the other end of the table, next to an orange chiffon cake. "I told each person to bring a dish to feed eight to ten people, but everyone brought a dish big enough to feed twenty."

Sarah eyed her twenty-four-inch pie plate. Guilty as charged.

"Where do we put our gifts?" Martha held up her pink frilly gift bag.

"This way." Roseanna led the way back into the central hall and straight through into the open doorway to the living room, where several women were gathered. Some perched on the edges of antique Victorian chairs while others tried to find a comfortable spot on the narrow Regency couches. But the laughter echoing off the silk wallpaper showed the women cared less about the comfort of the furniture and more about spending time together.

An end table was buried under bridal shower gifts, so Angela, Sarah, and Martha laid theirs on the Turkish carpet underneath, where other gifts already rested.

The doorbell rang, and without waiting for Roseanna to answer it, the door opened. A slender girl rushed inside with the scent of crisp fall air and a hint of smoke from burning fireplaces.

"Hello, Caitlin." Roseanna gave her a light hug. "Caitlin, you know my cousin Angela Miller—you met her at the family party last week."

"Hi again," Caitlin said with a smile.

Roseanna continued, "And you've met Sarah Hart and Martha Maplethorpe, haven't you? They're friends of your father."

Caitlin turned to Sarah with bright green eyes, the same color as her father's though her eyes were shaped just like her mother Jeannie's. "Hi, Sarah. I didn't really know you well while I was growing up, but Dad said that recently you've been getting close."

Sarah smiled. That was a good way to put it. It seemed a little silly to say she was "dating" Liam. "I hope we'll get a chance to know each other better soon," Sarah said. "This is my friend Martha. I don't think you've met."

Caitlin shook hands with Martha, then turned to Roseanna. "Sorry I'm late." She pulled her colorful wool cap from her head, loosing a riot of long, red-gold curls. "I couldn't get my car trunk to close for some reason. It kept popping open every time I slammed it shut."

"Is everything okay?" Roseanna asked.

"Oh yeah, I finally got it to latch." Caitlin gave Sarah a grin. "But I also knew you couldn't start without me."

"Well, you're just in time." Roseanna took Caitlin's coat. "The chicken has only a few more minutes in the oven before we can all start eating. Then we'll do the gifts, and then I'll give my special gift to you."

"Special gift?" Caitlin's green eyes lit up like emeralds. "Roseanna, you shouldn't have."

"Of course I should have." Roseanna's brown eyes crinkled as she smiled. "I'll be your mother-in-law in a month, so that gives me license to spoil you silly."

Liam had told Sarah that while Caitlin and her fiancé Travis were both from Maple Hill, they had become close while working in Concord, so Caitlin hadn't really gotten to know her future mother-in-law until recently, when she had become engaged. Sarah hoped Caitlin would eventually become as close to Roseanna as Maggie was with Sarah.

Sarah asked Caitlin, "So have you decided where you and Travis are going to live?"

Caitlin described their cozy cottage just outside Concord, and only three hours away from Maple Hill. "It was a great price, even though Travis's commute into Concord is going to be a little long."

"How about your commute?" Angela asked. "Where's the hospital where you work?"

"It's just outside Concord, so my commute will be only about fifteen minutes."

The five of them wandered toward the living room, where the bride was greeted with a friendly chorus of voices. Angela bustled after Roseanna, who greeted a few other women on the other side of the room.

Tiffany Henderson, Caitlin's maid of honor and a nurse at Bradford Manor, approached them. Sarah liked Tiffany for the gentle care she had given Sarah's late father, but the sight of the nurse sent a pang through her. How she missed Dad, especially at happy gatherings like this. He loved hearing about who was getting married, who attended the party, how people were doing.

"Hi, Mrs. Hart, Mrs. Maplethorpe. Caitlin, come meet some of Travis's cousins."

As Tiffany took Caitlin to a group of young people in the far corner, Martha touched Sarah's arm. "Are you okay? For a moment you looked sad."

"I'm fine. I'm just missing Dad." Sarah took a deep breath. "But I don't want to be a downer at a happy gathering like this."

Martha squeezed her hand before they started making their way through the living room, saying hello to friends. Kathy Earhart, Vanessa's young assistant at the Wild Goose Chase fabric store, laughed with Alana Marquez and Missy Johnson. Alana had helped Sarah with her late husband Gerry's funeral years before, and Missy's grandmother Myra had shown Sarah a quilted dress back in April. All three women attended Congregational Church with Caitlin and Liam.

Sarah and Martha sat next to Karen Bancroft, one of the waitresses at The Spotted Dog. "So Liam let you escape today, did he?" Martha asked with a wink.

Karen laughed. "Considering that as of tomorrow, I'll be working a lot more hours for the next few weeks, he owed me at least one afternoon off."

"Where exactly is Liam going?" Martha asked.

"He's going to a Christian men's retreat in some mountain cabin for about seven days," Sarah said. "From there, he's going to drive to an invitation-only event at a publishing house, and from there to a weeklong booksellers' convention. But he'll be back a week before the wedding."

"Poor Caitlin, to think she has to plan everything without him," Karen said.

"What do you mean, 'poor Caitlin'?" Martha snorted. "I wish my father had been out of town while Ernie and I planned our wedding. Then I wouldn't have had to hear him sigh and moan over every single penny we spent."

Sarah chuckled. "Actually, most of the preparations are done by now, according to Liam. And he's had the retreat and the business trips planned for a while. Caitlin knew when she set the wedding date, and she made sure Liam was okay with it. She said she didn't mind he'd be gone for so long just before the wedding, if he didn't."

"Do you know anything about the special gift Roseanna has for Caitlin?" Karen asked.

Both women shook their heads. "It must be fantastic. At least, Roseanna seems very excited about it, and she never does anything halfway."

Roseanna called them to the dining room to start eating, and once Sarah and Martha were back in the living room with their heaping plates, Tiffany Henderson sat down next to them. "Hi ladies—whoops!" She caught her sweet roll before it fell off her overloaded plate.

"I don't think you got enough food," Sarah teased.

"I could eat a house," Tiffany said. "Who knew being a maid of honor took so much work?"

"You've done a great job."

"Thanks, Mrs. Hart." She pushed a lock of straight brown hair over her ear, and the silver bracelet on her wrist gleamed.

"That's lovely. Is it new?" Martha asked.

Tiffany held it out so they could see. "My boyfriend just gave it to me for my birthday."

The silver bracelet shone with a glossy patina, indicating exquisite purity and a high price tag.

"How beautiful," Martha said. "So modern. Did he get it in Concord? Or Boston?"

"No, he got it at the jeweler's shop right here in Maple Hill."

"Really? I thought Les McLean retired this year."

Not to mention this very trendy piece didn't seem like something Les McLean would have at his staid jeweler's shop, which had been open in Maple Hill for over fifty years.

"Mr. McLean let his grandson Aiden take over the shop, and it's gotten really busy the past couple of months," Tiffany said. "Aiden has been bringing in some really neat pieces. Travis and Caitlin got their wedding bands there too."

Jason had asked Sarah earlier this week about helping him find something nice for Maggie for Christmas. Maybe the "new and improved" McLean Jewelers was just the place for him to go.

Roseanna got everyone's attention and they played a couple of shower games that had them all laughing. Then came time to open gifts. The gaily colored packages were being transported from the table to the area around Caitlin, although Roseanna objected, "Just a few at a time. Don't crowd her."

Caitlin and the rest of the women oohed and aahed over the gifts. Martha had given her a delicately crocheted lace shawl made of fine mohair yarn, and Sarah had made a small quilt in the Courthouse Steps pattern. Caitlin also got kitchen towels and pretty sleepwear sets.

After the last package was opened and the giver thanked, Roseanna rose to her feet in exultation. "And now, Caitlin, for my gift to you." She reached behind her chair for a large box covered in white embossed wrapping paper with an elaborate silver bow. Sarah leaned forward in her seat.

Caitlin opened the package carefully, then gave a small gasp. "Thank you, Roseanna. It's extraordinary."

She lifted out a quilt which had been folded so that an intricately embroidered patch lay on top, with "Caitlin Connolly m. Travis Walsh, November 2011" stitched in flowing letters. Sarah caught her breath at the clusters of embroidered flowers in lots of colors that decorated the edges of the patch. She knew Roseanna enjoyed doing fine embroidery, but Sarah had never seen any of Roseanna's work until now. It was breathtaking.

Just as interesting as the patch was the quilt. When Caitlin unfolded it to see the front side, the scent of lavender tickled Sarah's nose. She saw that it was a Double Wedding Ring pattern. Each ring was a different color, red or pink or green, and each ring had been pieced from many different fabrics, ranging from solids to prints to stripes. The colors created the impression of a flower garden on the white background of the quilt top.

"I know this quilt," Caitlin said in surprise. "It used to belong to Mom."

Roseanna nodded. "Your father took it out of storage and intended to give it to you for your wedding, but I convinced him to give it to me first to attach the patch on the backing."

"It was Jeannie's quilt? I didn't realize she used to quilt," Sarah whispered to Martha.

"I don't think she did," Martha said. "Maybe it was given to her."

The quilt was passed around, and as Sarah touched the hand-quilted top, she realized the quilt was very old. Perhaps not a hundred years old, but not made recently either. It was also a difficult pattern that had been constructed very well.

If Jeannie had made it, she would have been young, in her teens or twenties, and she would have had to have been very proficient in quilting.

Sarah flipped the quilt over to gaze at the patch again, and caught her breath at the lovely embroidery. It had been appliquéd on the bottom right-hand side of the quilt's backing, and positioned exactly an inch from each edge.

As they passed the quilt to Tiffany, sitting on the other sofa, Martha turned to Sarah. "What are you going to wear to the wedding?"

Sarah thought about her wardrobe. "Actually, I don't know. The silver and gray dress I wore to Jason's and Jenna's weddings got a terrible rip at the waistline when a relative stepped on the skirt at Jenna's reception."

"You can't fix it?"

"The rip isn't on a seam, so I'm afraid any repair would make the fabric pucker."

"Well, you'll have to buy something, then." Martha grinned. "I suppose I could make some time to shop with you."

Sarah smiled. "Such a sacrifice."

"Anything for my friend. I'll pick you up Monday morning at ten o'clock."

On Monday morning, Sarah flipped through her closet again. Her clothes were by and large comfortable and neat, and she had never owned many fancy dresses. She had that black crepe skirt...but it was too light and summery for a late fall wedding. Besides, she also didn't have any appropriate tops to pair it with, so she would have to go shopping either way.

Also the black crepe skirt was only so-so. She wanted something extra special. She wanted something that would make Liam's eyes light up when he saw her.

The doorbell rang downstairs. She glanced at the clock—only nine. Too early for it to be Martha. The bell rang again as she was heading down the stairs. Who would be so insistent?

She opened the door to Caitlin's white face. "Caitlin! What's wrong?"

"I think it's ruined!" Caitlin held out a large open box, and inside was her mother's quilt, darkened with muddy water. "Dad said you restore antique quilts, so when this happened, I couldn't think of anywhere else to go."

"Oh goodness. Come in." Sarah led the way to the dining room where she quickly laid out some old towels on the table. "Lay it down here."

"Do you remember how my car trunk wouldn't latch on Saturday? It popped open when I was driving to Dad's house today and the box fell out—upside down—into a puddle."

Sarah carefully lifted the quilt from the box.

"I don't know why I didn't bother to put the cover back on the box after the bridal shower." Caitlin wrung her hands. "I liked looking at it, I guess, every time I opened the trunk. I was going to take it to our new house today."

"Don't worry. It's only a little wet and dirty. We can clean that up with a little tender care, and it'll be good as new."

But as she unfolded the quilt, she realized the part that had landed flat in the puddle had been the corner with the embroidered patch. While the quilt was cotton, Roseanna had used silk embroidery floss and fabric for the patch. The delicate weave of the fabric and the extreme cold temperature of the water was making the fabric tighten and shrink slightly, which would normally not be much of a problem in a garment. But because of the embroidery, the fabric was starting to wrinkle. There was also a large mud stain.

She would need to take extra care that the patch wasn't ruined.

The tightening silk was causing the patch to pull away from the stitches on the edges where Roseanna had sewn it to the quilt, and Sarah worried the silk would continue to pull away and rip if she tried to rub the mud stain out without first taking the patch off.

"I'll need to remove the patch," she told Caitlin.

"That's fine, as long as you can put it back on," Caitlin said. "I hope you can fix it. I remember Mom telling me that one of my great-aunts made this quilt and it's a family heirloom. I'll die if I've ruined it."

"It'll be fine," Sarah assured her.

"I hope I didn't interrupt you this morning. I was panicked, plus I'm late for a nine o'clock premarital counseling session at church."

"Oh, don't let me keep you. I'll take care of this and call you when it's fixed."

"Really? Oh, thank you so much," Caitlin said. She leaned in and gave Sarah a quick hug. "I hope we get a chance to spend some time together before the wedding. Dad has told me so much about you."

Sarah waved good-bye as Caitlin drove away, then hurried back inside to take care of the quilt.

She got a bowl and filled it with lukewarm water, then went into the laundry room to get a bottle of baby shampoo from under the sink. She squirted some into the bowl and headed back through the kitchen.

Sarah went to her sewing room and got her seam ripper, a measuring tape, a small goosenecked table lamp for extra light, and a cloth rag. She set the lamp up on the dining room table and started carefully ripping out the stitches that held the patch to the backing, starting from the bottom left corner and working her way around all four sides. When she was done, she picked up the patch carefully so as not to rip the silk by accidentally pulling at an embroidery thread.

But as she took the patch up, she saw something written on the quilt backing itself, underneath the patch.

"Liam Connolly" had been written in faded black ink on the cotton fabric in a flowing cursive hand. Then beneath it were embroidered letters:

"M. Fiona Hamill."

CHAPTER TWO

Sarah could only stare at the names. *Liam Connolly M. Fiona Hamill.* On a Double Wedding Ring quilt. Liam had married a woman named Fiona Hamill at some point. Sarah's insides felt hollow.

Who was Fiona Hamill? Why hadn't Liam told Sarah about this? It seemed odd. Secretive.

Caitlin had said one of her great-aunts had made this quilt, which was her mom's. It was completely confusing that Liam's name was there with another woman's name on Jeannie's quilt.

There had to be a logical explanation for this. Maybe she should call Liam.

But Roseanna had made the patch and had deliberately put it over Liam's and Fiona's names. Did Liam know Roseanna had done this?

Did Liam have the names covered over on purpose?

Sarah shook her head. This was all speculation. Her imagination was running wild. She should just call Liam to ask him about this.

Her fingers hesitated as she reached for the telephone. Liam had always been friendly and warm, but he tended to be a very private person, so she hadn't pushed to know more about him than he was willing to tell her.

Did their months of growing closer to each other give her the right to know his secrets? Especially when she had inadvertently stumbled across them? He hadn't told her about this at all.

He had left early this morning for the retreat center in the mountains and would be almost there by now. He had mentioned that there was no cell service at the retreat center—a reason it had been chosen. If she wanted to catch him before he was unreachable, she would have to call now.

Her fingers shook as she dialed his cell number, but the call went straight to voice mail.

She had to admit feeling a bit relieved. She decided to leave him a voice mail message, however.

"Hi, Liam, it's Sarah. Could you please call me when you get this message? I have something I discovered and…" She swallowed again. "I just have something to ask you. I hope you're having a great time at the retreat. Bye." She hung up.

The retreat center had a landline telephone, but it was mostly for emergencies because they didn't want the "outside world" to intrude. Liam had been looking forward to this retreat for so long, especially because he hadn't been able to go during the other years his church had held the event. Sarah didn't want to pull him from something that meant so much to him.

She would just have to wait until after the retreat to ask him about Fiona Hamill.

Sarah turned her attention to the damp, muddied patch, which she had laid on a dry towel. She had to work fast to prevent the mud from staining.

She got the cloth rag she had brought from her sewing room and dampened it with the water in the bowl, then gently dabbed it over the patch and the silk embroidery, checking to see if the color bled anywhere.

The patch was truly a work of art, done in freehand embroidery with a multitude of colored silk flosses. Roseanna had made sunset-colored roses, pink foxgloves, pale blue-violet forget-me-nots, and sunny yellow buttercups in clusters around the edges. The embroidered names flowed in elegant script across the middle, with the wedding date in smaller letters beneath.

There was the faintest hint of pink when she dabbed some red embroidery floss, but otherwise the colors didn't run. Sarah had a feeling that Roseanna used only the best quality embroidery threads for her needlework, and they tended to be safely colorfast.

She picked up the patch and did a quick measurement of the dimensions. Nine and a half inches by nine and three-quarters of an inch. Sarah then gently immersed the patch in the bowl of water.

The water turned murky from the mud, and she swirled the water slowly. Then she took the bowl to the kitchen, removed the patch, and poured the water into the sink. She refilled with more lukewarm water and shampoo, and then again settled the patch in the water. She repeated this a few more times until the water didn't turn murky when she put the patch in.

There were still some mud stains on the patch, so she went to her sewing room and rooted around in the closet for a small, very soft brush she used for cleaning delicate fabrics. She went back to the kitchen and delicately dabbed at the stains with the brush, making sure the bristles didn't snag any of the embroidery threads. Then she poured off the water and refilled the bowl with soapy water before settling the patch back inside.

She peered at the patch, drifting in the water. It would be fine for a while. She would just let it soak. She hoped she had gotten all the stains off—it looked like she had, because she had caught it when the stain was still fresh. She would let it soak and then look at it later under brighter light, just to be sure.

Now for the quilt. She headed back to the dining room and studied the cotton backing.

The patch had taken the brunt of the mud stains, and the cotton backing looked like a thick, sturdy material. Sarah went to the hallway closet to retrieve a three percent hydrogen peroxide solution and another set of cloths.

She dabbed at the stains with a cloth dampened with the hydrogen peroxide, and it started bubbling gently on the surface of the quilt.

When it stopped bubbling, she wiped the areas with a cloth dampened with cold water, then repeated the process. It took several applications, but the mud faded. She put the goosenecked lamp closer to the quilt to make sure, but it looked like the stains were gone.

She breathed a sigh of relief.

Sarah peered more closely at a corner of the quilt that had flipped over, exposing the pieced front side. The fabrics were all cotton, no polyester-blend fabrics, and the backing fabric was a cotton that Sarah didn't often see in modern quilts. The binding had been hand-sewn on one side, but it looked as if it had been machine stitched on the other side. She peered at the Double Wedding Ring design and traced the circular edges of the pattern. It looked machine pieced, but by a master quilter—she knew this pattern was difficult, and yet the edges were beautifully round, the joins sharp and perfect.

She didn't think it could be more than a hundred years old, but it hadn't been pieced in the recent past, that was for sure. It may not have been new when it was given to Liam at his wedding.

The thought made her hesitate. Roseanna had said Liam had taken the quilt out of storage, and since it was a Double Wedding Ring quilt pattern, Sarah had assumed it had been given to him and Jeannie as a wedding gift.

But with his and Fiona Hamill's names on the quilt, Sarah guessed he had not gotten the quilt at his wedding to Jeannie. Who had given it to him? Who had made it?

With Liam out of touch right now, Sarah considered calling Caitlin, but she shrank from asking her. She didn't know Caitlin very well, but she didn't want to bring Caitlin's attention to the quilt. She didn't want to risk Caitlin asking her why she wanted to know who had made the quilt. Sarah couldn't lie to her, but she also couldn't tell Caitlin about Liam's and Fiona's names, at least not before speaking to Liam first.

Well, if she couldn't talk to Liam, then Sarah needed to speak to Roseanna. To find out why she had hidden the names behind the patch, and to find out what she knew about Fiona Hamill and Liam.

Sarah dialed Roseanna's number, but got only her answering machine. She left a message, and the doorbell rang as she hung up.

Without waiting for Sarah to come to the front door, Martha bustled into the house. "Ready to go?"

"Martha, have I got something to show you."

Her friend gasped when she saw the names on the quilt. "Liam married Fiona Hamill?"

"Did he ever mention anything about her to you?"

"Of course not. He'd be more likely to tell you about it than me." Martha stared at the name. "Fiona Hamill. You know, I think I've heard that name before. It sounds familiar."

"Really? How?"

"I have no idea. We've lived in Maple Hill our entire lives. I'm sure there are lots of people I've forgotton. But I do remember that name."

The two of them stared at the quilt as if it would give up its secrets to them if they intimidated it enough. But then an echo of Martha's words made Sarah say, "You're not quite right, you know."

"Don't tell Ernie that."

Sarah chuckled. "I mean about us living in Maple Hill our entire lives. We both spent time away during college. But then I took two more years and got my master's degree in history in Concord. I was home only once a month or so."

Martha's eyes lightened. "That's right. I'd nearly forgotten about those years. Maybe I heard about Fiona Hamill during the time you were gone."

"If you remember Fiona, I wonder if Ernie would too. He's always kept up with local news."

"That's a great idea. He's home right now, tinkering with Duncan's car."

"Is it okay?" Sarah hoped Martha's son's car didn't have anything seriously wrong with it.

Martha picked up her purse where she had left it on a chair. "When Duncan came by with Lexie the other day, Ernie said the engine sounded funny, but it doesn't sound any different to me."

Martha drove them to her Cape-Cod-style home. She parked the car in the driveway and they walked into the detached garage in back of the house.

Ernie loved working on cars and often helped Sarah with hers. Because his Parkinson's made his hands shake occasionally, he couldn't participate in his favorite activities as often as he used to.

Ernie was bent over the engine of his son's Jeep, fiddling with something Sarah couldn't see. He straightened when he saw them, and his dour face lightened. "Back so soon?"

"We didn't go shopping," Martha said.

"And here I thought I'd have to prepare myself for an astronomical credit card bill."

Sarah snickered while Martha gave him a stern look, ruined by the smile tugging at the corners of her mouth. "We were going shopping for Sarah, not for me."

Ernie's black moustache twitched. "And that makes a difference?"

Sarah hesitated, but then asked, "Ernie, do you remember a woman named Fiona Hamill?"

He leaned a bony hip against the front of the car as he thought. "The name sounds familiar."

"It's familiar to me too," Martha said. "But not Sarah. We were thinking I might have heard about Fiona during the years Sarah was getting her master's degree in Concord."

"That would be around..."

Sarah thought back. "Nineteen sixty-eight to nineteen seventy. I finished my degree that winter."

Ernie scratched at his thick black hair. "We'd just gotten married. I was working two jobs back then, at the maple syrup factory and driving the tow truck for the local garage, trying to recover from the amount of money we poured into that furniture store we started the year before."

"I was so disappointed that store only lasted a few months," Martha said, "but I guess it wasn't meant to be. After we closed the store, I got that; so I was working as a secretary for Doc McLean," Martha said.

Ernie snapped his fingers. "Now I remember. Fiona Hamill used to live in Maple Hill, but she disappeared."

"Disappeared?" Sarah asked. "What happened?"

He shook his head. "It was so long ago, I don't quite remember. I think she just vanished one day."

"Now that you mention it, I do remember something like that," Martha said. "But we didn't know the Hamills, so we didn't talk much about it."

Ernie said, "One of the guys I worked with at the factory, Walt Bitty, was dating a girl who was a maid at the Hamills' estate. Everyone asked him about the disappearance because of his girlfriend, but he didn't know much beyond what was in the papers."

"What was the girlfriend's name?" Sarah asked.

Ernie shrugged. "I'm sure he told me, but I don't remember. It was forty years ago."

"I wonder if she's still in Maple Hill," Sarah said. "I wonder if we could find her."

"How did you hear about Fiona Hamill?" Ernie asked.

Sarah briefly told him about the quilt. She added, "I'd appreciate it if you didn't say anything to anyone about this. I feel a little uncomfortable investigating Liam's past behind his back this way."

"I think Liam should have told you about Fiona," Martha said.

"Now, there might be a perfectly innocent explanation for their names being on the quilt," Ernie said. "Maybe it was a mistake."

"Maybe. I'd like to find out more about Fiona Hamill." Sarah thought about what Ernie had told her. "If this did happen during those years I wasn't in Maple Hill, that only complicates things."

"How so?" Martha asked.

"Liam told me he came to Maple Hill in 1975. He married Jeannie in 1976, and Caitlin was born nine years later in 1985. So why would his name be on a quilt, paired with a girl from Maple Hill, when at the time he was still in Ireland?"

Sarah was anxious to get back to cleaning the quilt, rather than go shopping, which Martha understood all too well. She drove Sarah back to her home and left her to examine Caitlin's quilt.

After soaking the patch for a few hours, Sarah nailed muslin to a small piece of plywood for a blocking board. Then she took the patch out of the soapy water and rinsed it in a bowlful of water with a tiny bit of white vinegar to dissolve any soap residue, then in a few bowlfuls of plain water. To dry, she rolled it in a towel. She pinned the patch to the muslin on the plywood, making sure the patch was blocked to the same dimensions it had been before she had washed it. She left it there to dry.

She lay the quilt on her quilting table with the pieced front on top, and switched on the lamp so she could get a better look at the Double Wedding Ring pattern.

Whoever had pieced this had done a wonderful job making the rings perfectly circular, not an easy feat. Each ring was made of segments, and the quilter had alternated solid fabrics with prints. Each ring, in turn, had its own color scheme, so the quilt was a beautiful rainbow. The diamond in each double join of interlocking rings was made of four squares sewn together, two black and two gray, which nicely muted the riot of color in the rings. The rings had been pieced together with the white background fabric, then the white edges of the quilt had been bound with strips of the gray fabric that had been used in the diamonds.

Sarah peered closely at the segments of the rings. There were literally hundreds of different fabrics. Even the solids were of different saturations, or perhaps slightly different hues. The gray and black diamonds, on the other hand, repeated throughout the quilt, unifying it and tying all the rings together.

The quilt had been hand-quilted in the ditch in the seam of each segment, and there was also quilting in the center of each ring and in the elliptical "melons" where two rings overlapped. As Sarah looked closer, she realized that a different quilting pattern had been used in the center of each ring, while the quilting in the melons was always the same— two simple arced quilting lines.

Sarah looked at the center of each ring to pick out the quilting pattern. She found a rose in one center, a flowing vine in another. The quilter had gone on to put a unique pattern in the center of each ring, the shapes done in freehand running stitches that were fine and exact.

Something about the arc-shaped quilting lines caught her eye, and she took out a magnifying glass. Yes, she was right. While the quilting in the center of each ring had been done by a master quilter, the quilting in each melon had been done by an amateur. The stitches were not as even or as tiny. They weren't crooked or sloppy, but they had not been done by the quilter who had done the centers of the rings.

How strange. She studied the center quilting patterns again, tracing shapes and lines and stitches. Often it was difficult to tell for sure that such-and-such a section had been done by one quilter, and another by a second quilter. But Sarah was fairly certain that the same quilter had created all the center quilting patterns, while another quilter or perhaps several other quilters, none as skilled as the first, had stitched the arc-shaped quilting lines in the melons.

Regardless of how many people had done the quilting, it came together into a magnificent whole. The color and fabric choices, the quilting pattern in the center of each ring— all made for a truly amazing quilt.

Sarah turned it over carefully, noting how heavy it was. The sight of Liam's name and Fiona's made her uncomfortable. She avoiding studying those first, and instead examined the outer edges. Where the binding was sewn to the backing, the thread had come loose and there was a small hole where the binding had pulled away from the backing.

It was an easy fix. Sarah went to get a needle and thread, then adjusted the quilt so she could better sew the binding to the backing again.

But as she was adjusting the backing, she noticed that the batting of the quilt looked strange. She peeked into the hole between the backing and the binding, and realized that the batting layer was made of polyester.

The fabrics of the quilt were all heavy cottons, no polyester- or rayon-blend fabrics, and even the thread was a hundred percent cotton. She had initially thought the quilt had been made in the early 1900s, but this was polyester batting, which wasn't available until after 1960.

However, it wasn't any of the newer types of polyester batting sold in stores now. This polyester batting seemed thicker, denser. She realized that the batting must be quite old also, although not as old as the batting in an antique quilt, which would have been made from cotton.

So despite the all-cotton fabrics, the quilt had been made sometime after 1960, but probably not many years after that.

After fixing the hole and examining the rest of the backing, she took a deep breath and turned her attention to the names on the bottom right-hand corner.

Liam's name was on top, written in flowing script in a black ink pen. The ink had faded and the edges of the lines were a little blurry with age.

Centered almost directly beneath his name, perhaps four inches below it, was Fiona's name, embroidered in black thread. The embroiderer had not been as skilled as Roseanna, who had used both thick and thin satin stitches to mimic calligraphy on her patch. Fiona's name was traced in a simple backstitch, but still in the same type of flowing script. Her name was about three inches from the bottom of the quilt, and the right ends of both names were about four inches from the right edge.

Was Liam's name smaller than Fiona's? Sarah measured the height of the letters, but found Liam's name, on average, was only a scant eighth of an inch smaller than Fiona's.

Why was Liam's name written but Fiona's embroidered? Beneath Fiona's embroidery, Sarah could see the faint outline of black ink. Her name had also been written on the quilt in ink and then embroidered over with thick black embroidery floss. Maybe the quilter had intended to embroider Liam's name also, but hadn't had time to finish.

Caitlin had said this was her mom's quilt, but Sarah wondered if perhaps this quilt had been given to her by a relative from Liam's side of the family. If so, maybe the Liam Connolly whose name was written on this quilt wasn't her Liam but an ancestor, and the quilt had been passed down from the generation before.

She felt a lightness in her chest as she pondered that possibility. If the quilt had been made around 1960, it could certainly have been for one of Liam's family members. And perhaps that family member had died and Liam had gotten the quilt. What a simple explanation.

Except for Fiona Hamill. It was too much of a coincidence that another Liam Connolly had married another Fiona Hamill, and that this quilt went to a Liam who lived in Maple Hill where another Fiona Hamill had lived—and had disappeared.

Sarah stared at the names for a moment before getting out her camera to begin taking pictures of the quilt. She would take a large overall view, but she would also take close-up shots of each ring and the names.

Liam, she wondered out loud, *Who gave you this quilt?*

CHAPTER THREE

Agusty October wind buffeted Sarah's car as she drove up the gravel driveway toward Bradford Manor. The charge nurse had called her that morning to gently tell her that she had three weeks to pack up the last of her father's things from his room. A well of sadness pooled in Sarah's heart as she got out of the car and headed between the white columns at the front of the building to enter the main lounge.

An old man in a wheelchair played the piano on one side of the room, and Olive Cavanaugh, Jason's old Sunday School teacher, waved Sarah over to where she was sitting next to the birdcage.

"How are you, Olive?" Sarah asked as she approached the spry woman in her wheelchair.

"Oh, just making sure the birds don't fight with each other. You know how rowdy they get when someone starts playing the piano."

"With you policing them, I'm sure they don't dare step out of line."

Olive's mischievous expression softened, and she asked in a low voice, "How are you doing?"

Sarah couldn't answer at first, because the heartache closed off her throat. But then she took a deep breath and replied, "I'm okay, all things considered. I know things will get better eventually." It was like when she lost her mother, and then when she lost Gerry. Losing someone never got any easier.

"Remember the good memories of him," Olive said. "I know I have a bunch from just the time we've spent here. Your father was a wonderful man."

"Thanks, Olive."

"You're here to collect his things?"

Sarah sighed. "Yes."

Olive sighed also, and her fingers bunched in the rather thin crocheted blanket covering her legs. "Take your time. These things always take time."

Sarah supposed she was right. "I'll see you later, Olive."

With a halfhearted smile, Sarah headed toward her father's old room.

She paused before opening the door. Then she took a deep breath and turned the knob.

The nurses had cleaned up the place a bit, but the plant on the windowsill and her father's baseball glove on the dresser made it seem like her father would wheel into the room at any moment. Sarah inhaled deeply and breathed in a trace of her father's scent in the air. She fought a tightening in her throat, and instead headed to the dresser.

She started sorting through the drawers. She found the quilt she had made for her father out of his old shirts, and with a flash, remembered Olive's thin crocheted lap blanket. Olive had been good friends with Dad, and perhaps she would appreciate this quilt to use. Yes, she would do that. What was more, she knew Dad would approve.

It also reminded her of the quilted baby blanket she had found in the wall of her grandfather's old house, now Jason and Maggie's home. She had given it to Dad last year when she discovered the truth about what had happened to his mother Molly Drayton.

But as she cleared out the drawers, she couldn't find the quilt. What could have happened to it? Had Jason or the twins taken it home with them?

"What are you doing?" demanded a deep, rough voice from the open doorway.

Sarah turned to see a man on a walker, glaring at her. "Excuse me?"

"Why are you going through his things? He just died."

"I'm his daughter."

For a moment, the man stared at her with an intense expression she couldn't quite understand. Then suddenly his face closed. "Well. He's gone."

She didn't know how to respond at first. The man's unfeeling words pierced her. "I'm . . ." She swallowed against her tight throat. "I'm glad God took my father home with him." While the words felt stilted, saying them out loud gave her a warmth in her core that reminded her that Jesus had her father with him, and she didn't need to worry. It gave her a comfort she didn't expect to feel so soon after his death. "Did you know him?" she asked. "I don't think I've seen you here before. Did you just move in?"

"Six weeks ago. I'm highly forgettable."

It was almost like a challenge. "What's your name?" she asked.

"Leland Mercer."

"I'm Sarah Hart."

Leland's eyes swept the room. "Cleaned out already. Like he never existed."

His words were hopeless and sad, and Sarah ran her hand over the shirt quilt, missing her father all over again.

Leland's gaze fell on the quilt. "Missing the other one?"

She looked up at him. "My father's baby quilt. Do you know where it is?"

At Leland's silence, Sarah frowned.

"Do you have it?" she asked.

A militant spark came into his dull brown eyes. "He gave it to me."

Somehow she doubted that. She remembered seeing it only a few days before he passed away.

"Mr. Mercer." Tiffany appeared. "Time for your therapy." She peeked into the room, and her eyes softened. "Hi, Mrs. Hart."

"Hello, Tiffany." The nurse had always been so good to her father, and the sight of her cheered Sarah's spirits.

"Is Mr. Mercer giving you a hard time?" Tiffany winked at her. "He likes to pretend he's a grouch, but underneath, he's a teddy bear."

"I am not," Leland protested violently.

Tiffany only grinned. "Catch him on another day, Mrs. Hart," she said. "He might actually say hello to you." She led the grousing old man away toward the therapy rooms at the back of the building.

Tiffany was so good with all the residents at Bradford Manor, but Sarah wondered if the nurse was mistaken about Leland's soft inside. Would he have taken her father's quilt? It was the most precious thing Dad owned because it was tied to his beloved mother. Sarah was a bit annoyed.

She looked at the dresser again, and the thought of going through all her father's things made a weight settle on her chest. Olive was right, she needed to take this slowly. She would take a few things today, and come back for more later. Maybe bring Jason and the girls with her.

And next time, she would talk to Leland about Dad's baby quilt.

Sarah unlocked her front door and got to the phone before it switched to the answering machine. "Hello?"

"Hi Sarah, it's Roseanna Walsh. I'm sorry I didn't get your message yesterday. We were in Concord all day and came back rather late. You said you wanted to come by to chat?"

"Is now a good time?"

"Now's perfect. I just finished doing laundry and dusting the attic."

Sarah bit back a smile at the priorities in Roseanna's life. Sarah was a good housekeeper, but not on the scale of Roseanna's standards. "I'll be over in a few minutes."

She approached the house with a slight tremble in her stomach. Why had Roseanna covered the names? And what had Roseanna thought when she saw the names? After all, Liam was going to be the father-in-law to her only son.

Sarah rang the doorbell and immediately saw Roseanna's figure through the glass panels in the door. Roseanna opened it with a "Come in, come in. Be sure to wipe your feet on the mat."

Sarah gave Roseanna her coat to put away before following her hostess into the living room, which had been restored to its stately elegance after the chaos of the bridal shower. She seated herself in a rather thinly cushioned Regency chair while Roseanna sat across from her in a brocade love seat. "Tea?" she offered, indicating the polished silver tea set on the coffee table between them.

"Thank you." Sarah tried to dive right in while Roseanna was preparing the tea. "I came to ask you about—"

"Sugar? Milk? Lemon?"

"Milk and sugar would be great." Roseanna apparently had her own particular sequence of events for a morning visit.

When she had handed Sarah her cup and prepared her own, Roseanna took a sip, then said, "You needed to talk about something?"

"Caitlin came to me yesterday in a panic because the quilt had fallen into a mud puddle."

"Oh, no!" Roseanna set down her cup with a click in the saucer. "Is it all right?"

"The water was making the silk patch you embroidered shrink a little."

"But that silk was prewashed. It shouldn't have shrunk." Roseanna frowned at Sarah.

"I'm not sure why it shrank, although the puddle was very cold and maybe the temperature change..."

Roseanna pursed her lips together. "I suppose so. Did you bring the quilt? I can clean it and repair the patch."

"Actually, I wanted to soak the patch before the mud set in, so I took it off the quilt."

Roseanna's face didn't change expression at all.

Sarah continued, "Under the patch, I saw the names Liam Connolly and Fiona Hamill."

Roseanna blinked at her. "I don't know what you're talking about."

"You didn't see those names on the quilt when Liam gave it to you?"

"The quilt was filthy and dusty when I got it from him. I had happened to be at his house when he was bringing it out, and so I offered to clean it for him and embroider the patch. I didn't see any names on it." Her eyes flickered away from Sarah's direct gaze for only a moment, then returned with a guileless expression.

There was no way Roseanna couldn't have seen the names, not when she laid the patch directly over them. "Roseanna, the names were right there."

"I didn't see any names," she insisted, her brow wrinkling in confusion. "I don't know what you're talking about."

A thought occurred to Sarah. "Did you know Fiona Hamill?"

"Who?" she said calmly. "I haven't the faintest idea."

"Liam's name is written in pen, and Fiona's is embroidered beneath it. You placed the patch directly over them."

"Sarah, you must be mistaken. There was nothing there when I sewed the patch on."

"The names are on the quilt now."

"Maybe someone's playing a practical joke on you," Roseanna said.

Was it possible? Caitlin had come directly to Sarah. Sarah couldn't believe that Caitlin would risk destroying that lovely embroidered patch and the quilt just for a joke.

Roseanna sat sipping her tea and watching Sarah, who grew uncomfortable under the watchful gaze. She realized there wasn't much else she could say if Roseanna was insisting she didn't see the names.

"Uh ... thank you for seeing me today." Sarah rose to her feet slowly, her mind whirling with her own confusion at what was going on.

"I'm sorry I couldn't help you."

At the door, after Roseanna collected her coat from the hallway closet, she bade Roseanna a quiet good-bye.

"Good-bye, Sarah."

Sarah stepped out of the house and the door closed with a soft *whoosh* and a firm click behind her.

She walked back to her car, feeling a little numb. What a strange interview that had been. She had hoped for some answers, but she was coming away with more questions.

There was one thing she knew for certain: Roseanna was obviously hiding something and Sarah was sure that something had to do with Fiona Hamill.

"I can't believe it," Martha said as they walked through the doorway of The Spotted Dog Café.

Sarah immediately looked at the counter, and it was strange not to see Liam there. But his Corgi, Murphy, trotted up and greeted them. As usual, he sat on Sarah's feet as if to prevent her from moving on and therefore stopping her scratching of his ears.

Karen Bancroft came up. "Hello, ladies. Here for lunch?" She led them to a table near the window. "Can I start you off with some drinks?"

"Hot chocolate for me," Martha said.

"And I'll have—"

"Let me guess," Karen interrupted with a grin. "Chai latte, extra whipped cream?"

Sarah laughed. "There's something a bit depressing about being so predictable, but I can't seem to get myself to order something different."

"What's your special today, Karen?" Martha asked.

"Spinach, ham, and cheese quiche."

"Oh, I'll have that," Sarah and Martha both said at the same time, and then laughed.

"Coming right up." Karen whisked away.

"Why would Roseanna Walsh lie to your face like that?" Martha asked, continuing their conversation.

"I have no idea. She was so calm about it too. I began to doubt I'd even seen those names. I went straight home and looked at the quilt again to make sure I wasn't crazy."

"Well, you're not crazy, because I saw those names too. She's definitely hiding something."

"It all has to do with Fiona Hamill," Sarah said, "which is why I'm going to the library after I have lunch with you today. I want to see if her disappearance was reported in the *Maple Hill Monitor*."

"Do you know the date she disappeared?"

"Well, I have a general idea ... "

Martha raised her eyebrows at her. "As in, you know within a few months?"

"Or a few years."

"The *Monitor* came out every day. That's 365 editions every year. And you know the date within a few years? You'll be in the library until Christmas."

Sarah was afraid her friend might be right. "Well, we know it was the years I was in Concord."

"So, that's only seven hundred or so newspaper editions to go through," Martha said. "Lucky you."

"Oh you." Sarah gave her a playful swat to the arm.

"Did you try looking for Fiona Hamill on the Internet?"

"I did, but I didn't find anything from 1968 to 1970, just a few present-day Fiona Hamills. Too young to be the one we're talking about."

"Do you think the Hamills still live in Maple Hill?" Martha said.

"Hmm. Maybe they do. I can look it up at the library."

When their quiches arrived, they each took bites of the hot, savory pie. "Mmm," Martha said.

Then something occurred to Sarah. "I wonder if the reason Roseanna lied about the patch was because she didn't embroider it."

Martha sat up straight in her chair. "That would explain it. She's always so proud of the state fair ribbons she wins for her embroidery. If she didn't make the patch herself—for whatever reason—then she wouldn't know anything about the names on the quilt."

"But wouldn't the person who did the embroidery tell her before sewing the patch over the names?"

Martha's shoulders sagged. "That's true."

"So we're back at square one."

"Not quite at square one."

"What do you mean?"

Martha gave her a sly look. "Why, you've got seven hundred or so editions of the *Maple Hill Monitor* to look through."

Entering the library, Sarah went straight to the librarian Spencer Hewitt, who sat at the front desk processing some returned books.

"Hi, Sarah." His handsome face lit up at seeing her. After seeing Karen so lately at The Spotted Dog, Sarah once again thought that the two of them would make such a nice couple.

"I was just going to call you," Spencer said. "That mystery novel you requested from Springfield library just arrived." He reached under the desk and rooted around for a few seconds before pulling out a hardcover book.

"Thanks, Spencer," Sarah said, "but I also need your help with something else."

"Oh?" Spencer's eyebrows rose. "What do you need?"

"I'd like to find out if the Hamill family lives in Maple Hill, or maybe the surrounding area. The library has telephone books for the entire county, right?" She remembered trying to find Alice Ward in a Concord directory a few months ago.

"In the reference section." He led her upstairs to the reference room to a bookshelf of telephone directories in the back. The room was long but narrow and crammed with steel bookshelves laden with heavy reference books. "Do you know which town?"

"I think Maple Hill, but it might be in one of the outlying towns."

"Well, our area is this shelf and half of the one below it." Spencer pointed out the shelf on a steel bookcase near the door. "If you want to go outside of a hundred mile radius of Maple Hill, you'll have to go by county name or city, and they're arranged alphabetically from here." He pointed to a shelf.

"That sounds easy enough. Thanks, Spencer."

"If you need help, just grab me. I'm only catching up on returned books today."

Sarah took the Maple Hill book and sat at a small table just outside the reference room.

The Maple Hill directory had no Hamills listed. Well, it was a long shot. Sarah returned the directory to the shelf and picked out several books for adjoining towns.

Twenty minutes later, she had checked all the towns around Maple Hill and had even checked several towns a little farther afield, but there were no Hamills listed. She found several Hamills in Concord and Boston, but since they were large cities, she couldn't be sure those Hamills were the same ones who had lived in Maple Hill. She hesitated to call the entire list of Hamills and bother them all. Still, she wrote them all down in her notebook. She headed downstairs to see Spencer.

"Any luck?" he asked.

She shook her head. "I'd like to look at the *Maple Hill Monitors* in the archive room, if that's all right."

"Sure." He took the key from the metal box behind the circulation desk and headed upstairs again with her to unlock the door to the archive room. The smell of dust and old newspaper made her nose twitch as they entered.

"You know where they are." Spencer gestured toward the shelves holding the newspaper bound in large green leather binders. "What are you looking for?"

She hesitated. She didn't want to tell Spencer about the quilt—it just seemed better to keep that secret. "I'm researching a young woman from Maple Hill who disappeared, but I don't know the exact date."

"It happened here?"

"Yes, so I don't think it would have made the news outside of Maple Hill."

"I think you're right." Spencer sighed. "What date?"

"I think between 1968 and 1970."

"Too recent to be filed away at the historical society."

"Yes, Irene likes people best when they've been dead at least a hundred years."

Spencer chuckled. "I saw her having lunch with General Bradford the other day." He meant the statue of the general in the center of Patriot Park.

"Can you think of any other way I can search for Fiona?" Sarah asked. She wasn't looking forward to paging through so many editions of the *Maple Hill Monitor*.

He shook his head. "If it was a small event that happened in Maple Hill, your best bet would be to ask people who were around then."

"I was getting my master's degree in Concord at the time."

"What's your master's degree in?" Spencer asked.

"Teaching. After I got my master's, I taught history at Maple Hill High School for four years, then Jason was born."

Spencer grinned. "I would have guessed history." He headed toward the door. "Well, good luck. Let me know when you're done."

"Thanks." Sarah headed toward the bookshelves and scanned the spines of the volumes, which were shelved chronologically. She found the set of volumes for 1968 and pulled them out, placing them on a table set up in the middle of the room.

Several hours later, she looked up at the sound of Spencer's knock on the door. "I'm getting ready to close up," he said.

Sarah groaned.

"Going that well, huh?" Spencer gave her a rueful smile.

Sarah stretched the crick in her neck. Her shoulder blades felt like someone had glued them together. She closed the binder in front of her, which was from January 1969. "It took me so long just to go through 1968. There has to be a better way."

"Eventually these papers should be scanned into a searchable digital format, but until we have the money and the manpower ..." Spencer shrugged.

Sarah collected her things and restored the newspaper binders to the shelf, then followed Spencer downstairs.

As she drove home, she wondered who she could ask who might remember Fiona Hamill. She had struck out with her top contender, Roseanna.

But Roseanna had a cousin, Angela Miller.

Her heart took a flying leap. She could ask Angela. If Roseanna had known Fiona, there was a good chance Angela had too.

The answers to her questions might be closer than she had first thought.

CHAPTER FOUR

The next morning, Sarah knocked on Angela's front door with a firm knock. Angela opened it immediately, wearing a smart business suit in a vibrant red that made her light hair look strawberry blonde.

"Hi, Sarah." Angela stepped aside so she could come in. "Sorry I wasn't home last night when you called. I've been trying to sell a house and I got a last-minute couple who wanted to see it last night." Angela and her husband had worked together until he died a few years ago, when she took over their real estate business.

"I hope I'm not keeping you from your work," Sarah said.

"Oh, no. I just came back from showing a house and I don't have another appointment until this afternoon, so I told my secretary I was going to work from home this morning."

Angela led the way through the living room, where a huge embroidery hoop was set up before the television, into the dining room. Angela gestured to the oak dining table.

"Have a seat. I'll get tea." Sarah could hear a kettle just starting to whistle, coming from the open door to the kitchen.

Sarah sat at a smooth table with rounded edges and a streamlined design that looked Scandinavian. The chairs were also square and Scandinavian in design, with the seats soft and covered with a tweedy woven material.

Angela returned with a tray laden with cups steaming with hot water and a basket of tea bags. "Here you go. I've got a bunch of different teas to choose from."

She certainly did. Sarah chose a strong English breakfast tea and dunked the bag in her mug of hot water.

"Want honey or milk with that?" Angela asked. She was dripping golden honey into her Irish breakfast tea.

"Both would be nice."

Angela slid the honey pot and creamer jug toward her, and Sarah couldn't help but compare her to her cousin, who had handled all aspects of the tea tray herself.

"I didn't know you embroidered too." Sarah gestured to the embroidery hoop she could see through the doorway into the living room.

"I'm not as good as Roseanna," Angela said, "and definitely not as good as Aunt Imogene. But Aunt Imogene taught both of us to embroider when we were little girls."

"I saw that lovely patch Roseanna made for Caitlin's quilt."

"Wasn't that something? What did you think of the bridal shower?" Angela asked as Sarah stirred honey into her fragrant tea.

"I thought it went well. Roseanna's a very good organizer."

"She is that. She used to organize our tea parties as girls." Angela dimpled. "I'd deliberately annoy her by sitting in the wrong spot or not following directions."

Sarah could see Angela, impish and playful, clashing with Roseanna's calm sense of order. "Have you and Roseanna always been close?"

"Since we were both little babies. We're only a few months apart in age."

"Do you know if she was friends with a woman named Fiona Hamill?"

"Fiona!" Angela's brown eyes lit up, turning golden. "I haven't thought of her in years."

Sarah could barely suppress her excitement. "You knew Fiona Hamill?"

"Gosh, yes. Do you remember Mr. Olsteen who used to run that photography studio a little outside of town?"

"Of course. I had my high school senior pictures taken there."

"Roseanna and I both got part-time jobs working for Mr. Olsteen. Roseanna would help him with taking the photographs—if there's one thing that woman has, it's an incredible eye for detail—and I'd work at his retail counter. He sold photography equipment and supplies too, and Fiona would come in for film, developing fluid, and photo paper."

"She was a photographer?"

"Amateur, but from what I saw, boy, she was good. She did a lot of nature and wildlife shots, but she took great candid shots of people too."

"What was she like?"

"Quiet, but she wasn't a mouse—it was like there was a steel core in her, you know? She never said much, but when she did speak, she always had a good point. I don't think she made friends easily, but I was outgoing enough to pull her out of her shell right quick. Roseanna and I just really liked her. At times..." Angela paused. "At times, it felt like we were taking an injured bird under our wings. I don't really know how to explain it."

Sarah could imagine the vivacious Angela and generous Roseanna befriending a shy young woman.

Angela continued, "Fiona was a few years younger than Roseanna and me, maybe your grade in school?"

"I don't remember her."

"Oh, you wouldn't have. She went to boarding school in Boston. Her parents owned Hamill Shipping, a company in Boston, and they were a very wealthy set of folks. They wouldn't send their only daughter to public school. She spent more time in Boston than Maple Hill, but she came home during the summer and that's when we met her."

"She and her family lived here in Maple Hill?"

"Do you know, we hung around with Fiona after we got off work, but we never actually went to her house. We'd go to the diner or maybe catch a movie in Pittsfield. I think her parents must have owned some large estate just outside of town, but I couldn't tell you where it is."

If they were wealthy, they may have paid extra to have their name, phone number, and address not listed in the telephone directory for Maple Hill, leaving Sarah unable to find a listing for them. "What happened to her?" Sarah asked.

Angela gave a heavy sigh and sipped her tea. "She went to Thompson University in Boston and majored in business and international relations, because she was set to work for her dad when she graduated. After she graduated, though, she went abroad to Ireland—apparently the Hamills still have family there. She wrote to me."

"Ireland?" Sarah leaned forward. Had Fiona met Liam there? "Do you still have her letters?" Reading Fiona's own words would help Sarah understand who she was.

"By golly, I do." Angela rose and bustled toward the back of the house while Sarah sat and fidgeted.

Angela returned with only one envelope in her hand. "I'm sorry, I don't know where the other ones are. When Roger and I moved into this new house, it was such a hurried thing. I just threw everything from my desk into boxes. When we were moving in, I shoved my boxes wherever I could find space. Then Roger died a couple of months after the move, and I never got around to fully unpacking everything. Fiona's other letters are probably in one of those boxes somewhere." She handed the envelope to Sarah.

The Irish stamp was colorful, faded only slightly with time, and the letter had been written on unusually thin, international letter paper.

October 6

Dear Angela,

It's been raining today, but Aunt Mabina has a fire going in the fireplace and the house is toasty. Everything outside looks green and gray, but inside the house is orange and gold (from the fire) and purple—yes, purple. Aunt Mabina has taken out her fabrics and is separating all the purple prints and solids. She's threatening to make a skirt for me with the scraps left over. Can you imagine me in purple? I didn't think so.

I'm going to my first rugby game this weekend. Uncle Ailfrid is taking me with a few of my cousins. Do you know what Aunt Mabina said when I agreed to go with them? "Good luck."

To be honest, I'm more excited about the trip to Lough Neagh in a couple of weeks. It's the largest lake in Ireland. We're staying with yet more Hamill cousins I haven't met yet. Uncle Ailfrid promised to take me to Cookstown to try to find a good photography shop so I can buy more film. While Pomeroy is a beautiful village, it's definitely a far cry from Boston.

Aunt Mabina is after me to practice my sewing stitches. At this rate, by the end of the next twelve months I might give you and Roseanna a run for your money!

I'll write more in a few days. Give my love to Roseanna.

Miss you,

Fiona

Fiona's dry humor flowed from the pages as if she were in the room speaking to Sarah. "She sounds fun," Sarah said.

"Roseanna and I knew her for only about three years, but we had so much fun together." Angela gave a heavy sigh. "When she got back from Ireland, she was a different person."

"Different, how?"

"Livelier. As if someone had fired up her engine. She laughed more, she seemed almost wild. And yet, she also seemed more stressed. She had lost weight and she had bags under her eyes. She told us she wasn't sleeping well."

"What was wrong?"

"She never told us. We kept asking her, but she said she was fine. Actually, one time she answered, 'Nothing is different.' And she said it in a strained, hard voice that I hadn't ever heard from her before."

"'Nothing is different'? That's an odd phrase to use."

"That's what I thought, but then she made up some excuse about driving to see someone and she had to leave. We didn't see much of her during the months right after she came back from Ireland. Roseanna had just gotten married, and I was working for Les McLean at his jewelry shop downtown."

"And I suppose Fiona had started working for her father?"

"No, she kept putting him off, promising she'd start in a few months. I don't think he was too upset—at least, Fiona said he wasn't because the fall and winter were the busiest times for him and he didn't want to have to bother training her while he was so stressed."

"What did she do?"

"She took a lot of pictures, that's for sure. She was always driving around, from early morning until early evening. She got some of her best photos at dusk, she said." Angela stared unseeing at her cold teacup. "I don't know where she went, or if she was alone or with some other friend. I should have asked. I should have pushed more to find out what was going on with her." Angela's normally cheerful face had become drawn and grave.

"What happened to her?" Sarah asked.

"It must have been early December. Yes, I think it was. It was about two months after she'd returned from Ireland. I was about to go to work one morning when I got a telephone call from Mrs. Hamill, Fiona's mother."

"Her mother?"

"You have to understand, I had met Mrs. Hamill only once, briefly, when Fiona and I bumped into her in downtown Maple Hill. Mrs. Hamill wanted to know if I'd seen Fiona, and I hadn't since Sunday. She was really upset, and she hung up. I found out a few hours later that Fiona had gone missing in the night."

"Someone took her?"

"No, her bed hadn't been slept in, but she also hadn't packed any clothes or taken anything from her room. Her purse was still there. She'd come home that night and gone to her room, but the next morning, she was gone. No evidence of foul play."

Sarah was astonished. "The police never found her?"

Angela shook her head. "Mr. Hamill even hired a private detective—several, I think—but no one found a trace of her."

Sarah remembered what Angela had said about Fiona's photographs. "She didn't take her camera?"

"She had several cameras, actually, but her parents said that all of them were still in her room."

How strange. "It's as though she vanished into thin air," Sarah said.

Angela sipped her cold tea. "I miss her. Every so often, I wonder what happened to her."

Sarah tried to figure out how to find out about Fiona's connection to Liam without actually mentioning him. "So she went to Ireland for a year, and then two months after coming home, she disappeared. Do you think maybe it had anything to do with her time in Ireland?"

Angela looked thoughtful. "I honestly don't know."

"Did she mention any friends in Ireland?"

"She met oodles of cousins. Every letter was about some new cousin she met. But actually, now that you mention it, two people came to Maple Hill from Ireland with her."

"Who?"

"One guy was here for a little while—he was a real cutie— but he left soon after she disappeared. I don't remember his name, but I think he had a crush on her. She met him through one of her cousins. And the other person was Liam Connolly."

Sarah nearly choked on her tea. "Liam?"

"Oh yes. At the time, I didn't know him at all, because he hung out with Fiona mostly. Plus..." Angela tilted her head. "It was a little strange, but then again, Fiona was acting a bit strange those months after coming back from Ireland."

"What was strange?"

"Naturally Roseanna and I asked Fiona about Liam and that other guy. To be honest, she hung out more with that cute guy, and she didn't say much about Liam. But I got the feeling there was some reason he had left Ireland, and not just to get a better job in America."

"Like what?"

"Maybe I'm just being fanciful about the fact Fiona didn't want to talk about Liam very much. A few years later, when he married Jeannie, I got to know him better because I knew Jeannie from high school. I know he's a pretty private person, so maybe she didn't talk about him because she didn't know much. Or maybe he asked her not to say anything."

"When did all this happen?"

"The year? Gosh, I don't remember. In the seventies, I think. Oh, I know how we can tell." She picked up the envelope and glanced at the postmark. "This was written in October 1969. She had just arrived in Ireland. That means she came home in October of 1970, and disappeared in December."

1970? But Liam had said he had arrived in Maple Hill in 1975.

This time when Spencer let Sarah into the archive room, she moved unerringly toward the binders for 1970, and picked up the one that included December. "Thanks, Spencer," she said as he moved toward the door.

"If you need to make a copy, you know where the copier is," he replied.

"No need." She patted her purse. "I brought my digital camera with me. It's easier to read when I can blow up the picture on my computer screen."

"That's a smart idea," he said as he left.

Sarah sat down at the table and opened the binder to December first. She found the article she was looking for on December seventh.

Local Heiress Missing
by Charles Blodgett
Fiona Hamill, 24, disappeared from her home four nights ago and police have not been able to locate her. Her mother, Clarissa Hamill, first discovered her bedroom was empty around eight o'clock in the morning. There was no sign of a struggle, but sources say that nothing had been taken from Fiona's bedroom, which some believe proves she did not run away from home.

Groundskeepers for the Hamill's home denied any disturbances the night before Fiona Hamill was discovered missing.

Her parents, Robert and Clarissa, were at a Christmas party in Boston, returning home only a few hours before discovering their daughter's bed unslept in.

Robert Hamill owns Hamill Shipping in Boston, an international shipping enterprise that has been in business for twenty years. Clarissa Hamill, nee Woltherstorf, is a native of Maple Hill.

If anyone has any information about the whereabouts of Fiona Hamill, please contact the Maple Hill Police Department.

Next to the short piece was a picture of Fiona, professionally done. She had clear eyes—perhaps blue? It was impossible to tell in black and white. She wore a calm, quiet expression, but something about her eyes lent a hint of strength to her character. There was also something about her face that made Sarah look again. It struck a chord with her in a way she didn't understand. She touched the delicate girl's high cheekbones, tracing her face down to the pointed chin. Her eyes were strong, but her mouth, while smiling, seemed a bit sad.

"You poor girl," Sarah said aloud. "I wonder what happened to you."

Under Fiona's picture was a candid shot of her parents, clinging to each other as they spoke to a police officer. Robert Hamill looked distressed, with lines of frustration around his eyes and mouth. He looked like he might have had the same coloring as his daughter, with clear eyes and dark hair.

His wife, however, had light hair and dark eyes, and her features reminded Sarah strongly of Genie Woltherstorf Collins, whom she had met before. Clarissa must have been one of Genie's cousins, because Sarah knew Genie didn't have any siblings. The Woltherstorfs were a wealthy local family, full of successful businessmen with interests in nearby cities as well as Boston.

What had happened to the Hamills? Did they still live in Maple Hill? What had happened with the investigation?

Sarah took pictures of the article and the photos and continued looking through the newspapers for any other articles about Fiona's disappearance, but she found nothing in the month of December. She checked January, February, and March of 1971, but again found nothing—just stories about Apollo 14 and the Super Bowl game between the Baltimore Colts and the Dallas Cowboys.

Sarah considered continuing her search through 1971, but realized that she could be searching for days. There had to be a better way to find the information she needed.

And she knew exactly where to go.

As Sarah was leaving the library, she got a call from Martha on her cell phone. "Hello?"

"Are you free for lunch? We just got back from a neurologist appointment and Ernie's tired, so he's going to nap."

"I'm downtown."

"Perfect. I'll meet you at Liam's?"

"See you there."

Sarah entered The Spotted Dog and was immediately hailed by Murphy, who came up to her with his backside wiggling and promptly sat on her feet. "What a wonderful foot warmer," she said to him. "I suppose I have to pet you."

Murphy panted.

Karen Bancroft came up to her and laughed. "Murphy's attacking everyone today, but he always saves his most hearty welcome for you."

"It's always nice to be loved." Sarah scratched his ears.

"Do you want to sit at the counter, or do you have a to-go order?"

"I'm meeting Martha here. Is there a table free?"

"Right this way." Karen led her to a small table near the back of the café. "I'll be right back with your drink."

Sarah sat, anticipating her steaming chai and the mound of whipped cream Karen always heaped on top.

Martha arrived a few minutes later and spotted Sarah. When Karen came to take her order, Martha asked, "Could you make me one of those mocha double-chocolate things?"

"A mocha double-chocolate almond latte?" Karen asked with a grin. "You haven't had one of those in a while."

"I'm in a sweet mood today," Martha said.

"Coming right up."

Martha took out her crochet project from her bag, this time a pretty pink yarn she was making into a baby cap. Her crochet hook flashed as she said, "So tell me all about what you found out about Fiona Hamill. Did you check the old newspapers?"

Sarah told her about her first futile search, and then about speaking to Angela and discovering the date of Fiona's disappearance.

"You hit the jackpot," Martha said in amazement. "That must make up for how unhelpful Roseanna was when you spoke to her."

Sarah showed Martha the pictures of the newspaper article on her camera.

Martha squinted at the camera screen. "Robert Hamill looks frantic, and maybe a little angry, too."

"Maybe because the police hadn't found anything. The article was written four days after it happened."

"Well, isn't it police procedure that they can't investigate a missing person until they've been gone for forty-eight hours? Maybe that's what happened."

"That would upset me too," Sarah said. "Poor man."

"When did this happen?"

"December 1970."

"I was pregnant with Ruth," Martha said. "I had quit my job with Doc McLean. I remember Duncan was a little over a year old and getting into everything. It was especially hard because it was a really difficult pregnancy."

"Do you remember anything about this?"

Martha shook her head. "I didn't know who Fiona or the Hamills were, so I probably didn't really pay much attention. Plus I was so tired from taking care of Duncan and being pregnant, I don't know if I even read the newspapers much."

"Now that I look at it, I vaguely remember my parents mentioning it when I came home on a weekend," Sarah said, "but I was like you—I didn't know who she was, so I didn't pay much attention to it."

"Your parents probably paid attention to the story because Fiona was about your age, and they would have worried about you."

"You're right."

Karen came up with Martha's mocha and a breathless, "Sorry that took so long. One of the other waitresses called in sick today so we're shorthanded with Liam gone. What can I get you?"

Sarah ordered a turkey club sandwich while Martha ordered the special, baked potato soup and a salad.

"So where are you going to look now?" Martha asked when Karen had left to get their order.

"The article was written by Charles Blodgett."

"You know him?"

"I first met him a few months ago—he lives at Bradford Manor." The name of the place made her suddenly feel cold, but she tried to shake it off. She gave Martha a bright smile. "Chuck can hear a little, but he pretends to be completely deaf because then the other residents tell him all kinds of juicy gossip, thinking he can't hear them. He played a good joke on Olive Cavanaugh once when she read him her laundry list, pretending it was a letter."

Martha chortled. "That sounds like Olive. She's such a rascal, even at her age."

"Mr. Blodgett got back at her because he managed to find twelve pairs of purple socks and left them all around her room. He told her that her 'letter' mentioned she loved purple socks."

The two friends laughed.

"When I saw him a few weeks ago—It had been just before Dad died." Her voice faltered, but she pushed on ahead. "Chuck told me that he and Olive are having a 'sock war.' He hides a certain pair of hideous purple socks somewhere for her to find, and then she hides them somewhere for him to find."

"Like a laundry scavenger hunt," Martha said.

"Anyway, he was the reporter who wrote the article, and he mentioned 'sources,' so I'm thinking he talked to people about the disappearance and might know more than what was published." Sarah looked down at her chai tea, suddenly feeling tired. "I have to go back to pack up more of Dad's things, so I can talk to him then."

"Oh Sarah." Martha reached over to touch her hand. "Maybe you shouldn't talk to Chuck."

"No, it'll be something to help distract me. Going through Dad's things is so hard, just like when I had to go through Gerry's things."

Martha's eyes shone with sympathy. "I would offer to come help you, but I need to check on Ernie."

"Thanks for the offer, but I wouldn't want you to come." She gave a slightly watery smile. "I think the two of us would end up bawling all over each other."

Martha squeezed her hand. "Let me know if you need me to do anything."

"You know I will."

CHAPTER FIVE

A s Sarah was leaving the café to head to Bradford Manor, she got a call from her daughter-in-law Maggie. "Hello?"

"Sarah, I'm sorry to ask this at the last minute, but do you think you could pick up the girls from school today?"

"Of course." A part of her was relieved to cancel the visit to collect her dad's things, but another part of her regretted that she would need to put off the visit to Chuck Blodgett.

"I'm sorry to impose on you, but a large shipment of furniture that was supposed to arrive tomorrow just drove up to my front door. Jason had planned to take tomorrow off so he could pick up the twins, but he can't today, and I need to stay here to supervise unloading these pieces."

"I'll take them for the entire afternoon if you'd like."

"Oh, would you? Thanks so much."

Sarah picked the girls up from school and explained what had happened.

"We love spending time with you, Grandma," Amy said. "And with your chocolate chip cookies," she added with a grin.

Audrey's brow wrinkled. "You weren't busy today, Grandma?"

"Don't you worry, it's nothing that can't wait."

Amy looked concerned now too. "What were you going to do?"

"It wasn't anything important. I was going to Bradford Manor to pack up a few things."

Both the twins grew silent.

"We can help you, Grandma," Audrey said softly.

Her words made Sarah's heart overflow. She regarded them tenderly. "Are you sure?"

Amy nodded solemnly. "We *want* to help you."

Rain started to fall as they parked the car in front of the nursing home, and the three of them raced to the door and into the front room.

The first person she saw was Leland, sitting in a chair set apart from everyone else. He didn't seem to be doing anything besides staring at a point on the wall.

"Hello, Leland," she said to him in a pleasant voice, although inside she wondered how he would respond to her today. Maybe she would be able to convince him to return Dad's quilt.

Leland glanced up at her almost carelessly, not responding to her before looking away. But then he did a double take and stared a moment at the twins, one on either side of her.

His eyes seemed to warm to amber for a second or two, but they faded back to brown and he turned his head.

Amy crowded closer to Sarah. However, Audrey whispered, "Didn't he hear you, Grandma? Why didn't he say hello?"

Sarah didn't feel like trying to make excuses for Leland's rudeness, but she also knew kindness would be a better tack if she wanted to get her dad's quilt back. So she put a protective arm around each of the girls and drew closer to him, speaking in a clear voice.

"Leland, these are my granddaughters, Amy and Audrey. Girls, this is Mr. Mercer, one of Grandpa's friends."

"H-hello." Audrey straightened her shoulders and faced Leland. After standing there, holding her breath, she belatedly held out her hand.

The seconds ticked by, and for a moment Sarah wondered if he would leave her darling girl's hand suspended in midair. Protective instinct began to build in her.

But then Leland slowly raised his own hand and shook Audrey's. His gaze focused on her.

Audrey's eyes grew wide, but she didn't flinch.

Leland released her hand as if it burned him and looked away.

Amy remained stiff at Sarah's side, pressed hard against her. Naturally a little shy, Amy was even more intimidated by Leland's flipping back and forth between indifference and intensity.

Sarah deliberately sat in a chair near Leland. "How are you doing today?" she said to him, in a slightly louder voice than normal.

He seemed startled when she sat down, and a frown briefly pulled down his mouth.

But then Amy and Audrey, taking their cues from Sarah, pulled chairs close to her and sat down. True, they were stiff backed and perched on the edges of their seats, but they had identical polite expressions on their faces.

The edges of his mouth softened a fraction. "Er...I'm fine."

Leland acting unsure was much better than Leland being morose and bitter, as he had been a few days ago.

"I don't see your walker," Sarah said. "Does that mean you're feeling stronger today?"

He settled deeper in his chair. "Not really."

"Who's your physical therapist?"

He looked like he didn't want to respond to her, but then he reluctantly said, "Katherine."

"Oh, she's wonderful." Sarah knew that Katherine typically did rehab for stroke victims, so she guessed Leland was recovering from a stroke.

Was that why he was slow to answer her questions? Because a stroke had made it difficult for him to speak?

But a stroke wasn't responsible for the indifferent lift of his shoulder in response to her comments and the way his eyes skittered away from hers. She had initially wondered if he was lonely, but if he was, wouldn't he be motivated to respond to her?

"Uh, Mr. Mercer?" Audrey said. "What did ... um ... what did you and Grandpa William talk about?"

Leland seemed a bit startled by her question. He blinked a few times, then said, "Baseball." Another pause. "We both liked baseball."

"Amy plays baseball," Audrey said.

"Softball," her sister corrected in a low voice. She darted glances at Leland during the awkward silence that followed.

Sarah was about to say something when Leland asked, "Like the Red Sox?"

Amy's eyes flew up. "Yeah."

"Go to any games with your grandpa?"

Amy and Audrey both shook their heads. Dad had often talked to the girls about going to a game one day, but realistically Sarah's father hadn't been able to go anywhere. Amy pressed her lips together and Sarah wondered if she was thinking of the many things she hadn't been able to do with her great-grandfather.

"He told me once about the home run he caught at a Red Sox game," Leland said.

Amy nodded, a bit vigorously. "He showed me the base-ball."

Leland looked at her, but Sarah thought he might be seeing a distant memory instead of Amy as he said, "I was with him when he caught it."

"You were?" Amy asked.

He was? Sarah leaned forward in her seat.

"We both reached for it at the same time," Leland said. "But at the last minute, I pulled back so he could catch it."

"That was nice of you," Audrey said.

Her voice seemed to bring him back from where his mind's eye had wandered. Leland focused his gaze back on them, and then his expression cooled. He sniffed and shifted his head slightly away from them as he said, "I already had a home run baseball I'd caught a year earlier. And the old fool kept whining about how he wanted one too." He pulled his mouth shut firmly.

Sarah stood. "It was nice chatting with you, Leland. We have to go pack up my father's things."

The twins got to their feet quickly.

"It'll only take a couple more trips to finish packing Dad's stuff," Sarah continued. "I hope you'll give me Dad's quilt back before our last visit."

Leland's jaw tightened, but he didn't look up or respond.

"Goodbye, Mr. Mercer," Audrey said in a small voice. Amy murmured something even lower that Sarah couldn't make out.

Sarah moved away, her granddaughters beside her. They all seemed to breathe easier as they left the front area and headed toward her father's room.

"He's grouchy," Audrey said.

"He's scary," Amy whispered.

"He's just lonely," Sarah said, trying to sound confident. Why was Leland so distant, even to the point of rudeness? Why wouldn't he give her dad's quilt back?

As they entered her father's room, Sarah wondered if Leland really had it. Maybe it was hidden somewhere among Dad's things, and they would find it eventually. Sarah hoped so. She didn't want to have to deal with Leland again.

"I hope we don't have to talk to him again," Amy said at the same time Sarah thought it.

Her fervent words made Sarah check her own aversion to Leland. Didn't God ask her to love everyone, regardless of how they treated her? Wasn't it her responsibility to model Christ to her granddaughters, no matter how hard it was sometimes?

"He probably really likes the company," Sarah said to her. "We should try to be loving toward him."

"Even when he says mean things about Grandpa William?" Audrey said, a touch sharply.

"Maybe he didn't intend for it to come out that way," Sarah said, although privately she didn't really believe her own words.

But the few short minutes with Leland had been enlightening, although awkward. Leland had apparently known her father when they were younger. Yet Dad had never mentioned him. Had they been good friends who just lost touch? Had there been a falling out? Despite her exasperation at Leland's manner, she was curious.

She looked around Dad's room. "I emptied a few drawers from the dresser last time," she said to the girls. "Let's clear the rest of the drawers."

The girls seemed eager to be doing something, and they tackled the task with more enthusiasm than when they had to help clean their own house.

Sarah glanced out the open doorway just as a nurse wheeled Mr. Blodgett past.

"There's someone I need to speak to," Sarah said. "Will you two be okay in here for a few minutes?"

"We'll try not to throw a wild and crazy party while you're gone, Grandma." Amy's spirits seemed to have recovered, and she sounded almost normal.

Sarah smiled and headed out the door. She scanned the front room, where she had seen the nurse taking Mr. Blodgett, and saw she had parked him next to Mrs. Russo, who was knitting in an easy chair. The woman was chatting with Mr. Blodgett, who sat and nodded at her with a rather vacuous look on his face.

Sarah wandered around the other side of the room toward him.

Tiffany Henderson came up to her. "Hi, Mrs. Hart. Is there something I can do for you?"

"Actually, I need to speak to Mr. Blodgett, but it looks like Mrs. Russo has him by the ear. Do you think you could help me?"

Tiffany glanced in their direction and gave a rueful smile. "He likes listening to Mrs. Russo because she doesn't realize he can hear, and she likes to ramble on about her Russian mafia relations. I have to take Mrs. Russo's vitals soon, anyway, so I'll whisk her away for you."

"Thank you so much, Tiffany. I feel a little devious asking you to do this."

The young nurse laughed. "Intrigue at Bradford Manor. I could be a CIA agent."

Tiffany spoke to Mrs. Russo and then led her away, and Sarah immediately sat down next to Chuck Blodgett. "Hello, Mr. Blodgett."

"Sarah." He spoke in a voice slightly louder than it should be. "Guess where Olive hid those purple socks yesterday? In the plant in my room!" He chuckled to himself. "I had soaked it with water before I realized it was there."

Sarah smiled. "Where did you hide it for Olive?"

"Well, I'm drying it first. But I have a good idea, never you fear."

Sarah leaned forward. "I have a question to ask you about an article you wrote for the *Maple Hill Monitor* back in 1970."

His gray eyebrows rose. "Nineteen seventy? That was just before I got a job with the *Concord Times* and moved out of Maple Hill."

Sarah hoped he had been in Maple Hill long enough to know what had happened to Fiona. "It was about the disappearance of Fiona Hamill."

Mr. Blodgett's mouth settled in a tight line. "That was a bad business. It was also one of the more exciting things that happened during my stint at the *Monitor*. Poor girl."

"I read your article, but is there anything you can tell me that you couldn't publish in your story at the time?"

Mr. Blodgett nodded slowly. "I didn't know the Hamills, but I was friends with one of the maids, Charlotte, and she told me what she told the police. But some of it was information that was only hearsay, not solid evidence, and I couldn't publish it."

"What kind of information?"

"The Hamills actually didn't know that much about Fiona's photography. They just didn't pay attention to it. I got the feeling her father thought it was only a frivolous hobby. So when the police asked if all her cameras were still there, they said yes. But Charlotte said she thought one of the cameras was missing."

"It was stolen?"

"Could be. It was an expensive camera. But Charlotte also said it was the one Fiona used the most."

"Do you think Fiona took it with her?"

"If she did, she apparently didn't take anything else. That's what Charlotte said. And that's kind of odd, don't you think?"

A missing camera, but nothing else. Had Fiona taken a picture of something that got her in trouble? "Was Charlotte close to Fiona?"

"As close as a servant could get to a girl in that family. Robert Hamill ruled that house with an iron fist. The servants knew their place. But Charlotte was only a little older than Fiona, and the two women got along well. Charlotte cleaned Fiona's room, so she was familiar with Fiona's things."

"The Hamills were away from home that night?"

"Yes. They were at a Christmas party in Boston that night, and although Mr. Hamill insisted his driver take them home rather than stay overnight in Boston, the only person who can vouch for the Hamills after they got home is each other. None of the servants saw or heard anything in the house, and there wasn't a peep from the guard dogs."

"Did Fiona have any other, um…male friends?"

Mr. Blodgett's face was blank. "No, I don't think so."

No mention of Liam or the other handsome man. Strange. The picture from the paper flashed through her mind. "What were the Hamills like?"

Mr. Blodgett shook his head slowly. "Now remember, this is just what Charlotte told me, but she said Robert Hamill was selfish to the bone and was always criticizing his daughter and his wife. Charlotte said it was hard to see Fiona treated the way she was. It didn't seem as if he loved her, or his wife."

"Was he like that with the servants too?"

"He treated the servants like servants—invisible, beneath his notice."

"Do you think Robert Hamill had anything to do with his daughter's disappearance?"

"Well, the police said there was little chance of foul play on Mr. Hamill's part. I have a hard time believing that, but then again, I'm not a cop. But I always suspected maybe Mrs. Hamill knew something she wasn't telling anyone."

"What makes you say that?" Sarah asked.

"She and Fiona were very close, maybe because they were both contending with Robert's personality. He put up a good front, pretending to be distraught, but I think he liked the publicity it gave him, being in the paper. But Mrs. Hamill just didn't seem as concerned as her husband at the time. I couldn't put my finger on it, but that was the impression I got."

"You don't think she did something to Fiona, do you?"

"Not that she did something to Fiona, but she might have done something for Fiona."

"You think she *helped* Fiona disappear?"

Mr. Blodgett gave her a hard look. "There is one thing I know for sure about this entire business. Even though the disappearance was so mysterious, Fiona Hamill had very good reason to want to get out of that house."

CHAPTER SIX

D o you think Fiona ran away?" Martha asked on Sunday morning.

"I'm not sure what to think," Sarah said as she gathered her purse from the pew. The two friends had stayed in the sanctuary talking after the service, and now there was only a scattered handful of people left in the building. "She didn't take anything with her except *maybe* a camera. That just seems so strange."

"What happened to the Hamills?" Martha asked. "Do they still live in Maple Hill?"

"Mr. Blodgett said that he moved to Concord a few months later, and he doesn't know. When he moved away, the case still hadn't been solved."

"Is Hamill Shipping still around?"

"I don't think so. I searched on the Internet, but didn't find anything about it. There are a few Hamills in Boston, but I don't know if any of them are the Hamills or completely unconnected. I may have to just cold-call them and see, but there are quite a number of people on the list."

Martha shrugged as she followed Sarah out of the pew and up the aisle of the church. "Well, if it's your only lead..."

"Actually, I want to talk to the servant Mr. Blodgett was friends with, Charlotte Carter, but I forgot to ask him if she was still in Maple Hill. She's not in the phone book."

"Maybe that's her maiden name."

"If that's the case, I don't know how to find her."

Martha looked around the empty sanctuary. "I was wondering if Pastor John knew the Hamills. He seems to know everyone."

"Angela mentioned that Fiona didn't have many friends in Maple Hill—her friends were mostly in Boston. Plus, he'd have been ten or twelve years old when Fiona disappeared."

"Oh." Martha laughed. "I should have thought of that. We were in our early twenties, after all."

"I keep thinking about what Ernie said," Sarah said. "About his co-worker who was dating a maid at the Hamill estate. Do you think it would be too much of a long shot to hope it was Charlotte Carter?"

"Well, how many full-time maids would a large house need to hire? Two? Three?"

"So maybe he *did* date Charlotte. I think his last name was Bitty. We could look up Charlotte Bitty in the phone book."

"Wait a minute. Mrs. Bitty?"

Sarah stopped and looked at Martha. "You know her?"

"I don't think she goes to this church, but last week I heard Pastor John say that Mrs. Bitty told him about a light being out on the church sign. She must live nearby."

Pastor John was speaking to Mavis Hoyt—or rather, Mavis was speaking to him. As they drew near, they heard her retelling her frog-in-the-church-chili-contest story to Pastor John, and he had a slightly glazed look in his eyes.

"Excuse me, Mavis," Martha said, cutting into the part where the kids were looking for their pet frog. "I'm so sorry to interrupt, but I was wondering if Pastor John could help us with something."

"That's all right, Pastor," Mavis said. "I'll tell you the rest later. I was just getting to the good part too."

"Ahem," Pastor John said. "Now that I've heard some of it, I think you've told me this story already."

"Oh." Mavis blinked. "Well, did I tell you about—"

"I'm sorry to interrupt again, Mavis, but we really do need Pastor John's help." Martha gave her a bland smile.

"Oh certainly. I'll see you both later." Mavis smiled and turned, spotted Julie Lessman and Sandra Pohlman, and headed their way.

"What can I help you ladies with?" Pastor John asked, his green eyes alight with curiosity.

"We're looking for Mrs. Charlotte Bitty," Sarah said. "Did she come to church today?"

"No, she's home with a sore back. She walks around the neighborhood daily and yesterday, she slipped in a puddle and fell."

"Is she okay?" Martha asked.

"I visited her this morning before the service. Physically she's a little stiff, but mentally she's bored silly."

Sarah smiled. "I probably would be too. Could you tell us where she lives? Maybe we could visit her this afternoon."

"I think she'd like that." Pastor John wrote her address down on a piece of paper and gave it to Sarah and Martha. "What did you want to speak to her about?"

"We found out she used to work for the Hamills, and we wanted to ask her about them."

Pastor John's black eyebrows rose. "The Hamills? I don't think I know them."

"They lived in Maple Hill about forty years ago," said Sarah. "I don't know what's happened to them since then. I'm hoping Mrs. Bitty will tell us."

"If I know Mrs. Bitty, she'll be glad for the company," he said.

Sarah had lunch with Jason and his family and stopped at home to pick up some blueberry muffins she had baked. Martha went home with Ernie to get his lunch and set him up in his ratty old recliner to nap for an hour or so. Then the two friends met back at the church and headed to Mrs. Bitty's house, which was only a short five-minute walk down Bridge Street.

She had a small bungalow-style home that had recently been repainted white with gray trim. Sarah and Martha climbed the short flight of steps to the tiny front porch and knocked on the door.

"Who is it?" called a voice inside.

"It's Sarah Hart and Martha Maplethorpe from Bridge Street Church," Sarah called. "Mrs. Bitty, Pastor John said you injured your back yesterday so we came to see how you were doing. May we come in?"

"Yes, door's open."

The front door opened directly into the living room, where it looked like the overstuffed sofa was drowning a tiny woman with snow-white hair. She lay lengthwise on the sofa, surrounded by pillows and covered with a knitted blanket in waves of bright jewel tones. Her brown eyes were bright and eager as they came inside.

"I never thought it would be possible to die of boredom, but by golly, I was close to it. So I told Jesus, 'Lord, if you want to take me now, go for it, but if you don't, please send me someone to save me.' And here you are!"

Sarah couldn't hold back her smile. "I'm Sarah, and this is Martha," she said as they removed their coats.

"Pleased to meet you," Martha said.

"The coat closet is to your left, behind the door," Mrs. Bitty said.

The closet was crammed with coats in a rainbow of bright colors, purples and greens being dominant. They managed to squeeze theirs in between a sapphire blue rain jacket and a sunshine yellow parka.

"I brought some blueberry muffins," Sarah said. "Would you like some now?"

"I will if you'll go into the kitchen and put the kettle on to boil."

"I'll be happy to do that," Martha said, and exited the open doorway to the left where the kitchen could be seen.

Sarah sat in a chair opposite the sofa. "How's your back?"

"It feels like there's a gigantic stiletto heel grinding into the base of my spine," Mrs. Bitty said, rolling her eyes like a teenager. "I need a pill to keep me from getting old."

Despite her words and her injury, Mrs. Bitty struck Sarah as a firecracker who wouldn't act her age even when she was a hundred. "Pastor John said to tell you hello."

Mrs. Bitty grinned. "Is that all he said? I gave him an earful the other day because there were two lights out on the church sign."

"Well...I'm sure he appreciates your telling him about that."

Mrs. Bitty waved her words away. "He probably thinks I'm a busybody, but I just notice things like that. Always have. Don't want the church to look shabby."

"I know for a fact Pastor John wouldn't want that either."

"How was his sermon today?"

Sarah told her while Martha made tea and brought it out to the living room. She had also toasted the muffins in Mrs. Bitty's toaster oven and she set them out in a basket with a cloth napkin.

Mrs. Bitty took a large bite. "Mmm, I don't have these so often anymore. I'm too busy to bake like I used to."

"Did you bake a lot?" Martha asked.

"I learned how to bake the best maple pecan pie from a cook at a house where I used to work."

A house? Sarah leaned forward. "Was that at the Hamills?"

Mrs. Bitty gave her a pointed look. "Is that why you came over today? To ask about them?"

Sarah's cheeks pinkened slightly. "We were happy to come over when we heard you were hurt, but yes, we were hoping to visit you today regardless."

"Well, it's a good thing my back is giving me problems today, because normally I'm not home on Sunday afternoons. I usually go for a long walk through the woods if the weather's good."

"I'm glad we caught you then," Sarah said.

"And we're glad to keep you company since you can't go for your walk," Martha added.

"So what did you want to know about the Hamills?" Mrs. Bitty asked.

"You worked there as a maid?" Sarah asked.

"That was my first job out of high school—I didn't go to college, learning wasn't my thing—and it was a good position. I was with them, oh, fifteen years or so. Later I married my husband. By then, I was an upstairs maid."

"You knew Fiona?"

Mrs. Bitty's chocolate eyes warmed. "Dear Fiona. She and I were friends. I was only about five years older than she was, and she needed a friend in that house."

"I spoke to Mr. Blodgett. He said you told him a bit about what Mr. Hamill was like."

"That man believed life revolved around him. If anything happened, it had to do with Mr. Hamill in some way, whether real or imagined. When he was with his family, he always steered conversations back to himself. Everything his wife and daughter did had to benefit him somehow or else he wouldn't tolerate it."

Sarah was shocked. "But he was a successful business-man. Surely people wouldn't do business with him if he was like that all the time."

"He was charm itself with business associates, but in his family circle, he was a very different man." Mrs. Bitty said. "I noticed that Mrs. Hamill and Fiona got his approval only when they complimented him in some way. But then he would put down their feelings and interests—like Fiona's love for photography. If they ever dared to disagree with him, he'd become colder than an icicle until they apologized and he got his way."

"It sounds like an unhappy home." Sarah couldn't imag-ine what it would have been like for Fiona, having her spirit beaten down every day like that.

"I was glad when she left. Glad," Mrs. Bitty said with a lift of her chin.

"She left? She ran away?"

Mrs. Bitty looked away. "No, of course not. I guess I want to believe she left. I don't want to think something happened to her. She was such a beautiful person. She could see beauty where all you saw was a thistle, and then she'd take a picture and you saw the beauty she saw. She was amazing. Hey, that reminds me ... " Mrs. Bitty suddenly straightened, then winced as her back protested. "Do you want to see some of her photos?"

"We'd love to," Sarah said quickly.

"In my bedroom. Through that door." She pointed to a door in the wall behind the sofa. "There's a blue box on the top shelf in my closet. If you could please bring that to me?"

Sarah entered the bedroom, which had lavender walls and spring flower prints in frames. The blue box was in fact bright robin's egg blue, but not heavy. She set it in Mrs. Bitty's lap.

The woman opened the top and pawed through the mounds of photos inside. "Fiona had her own darkroom at the house, in the back. She and I were close enough that she would show me her pictures, and she made copies for me of the ones I liked." She squinted at the photos in her hand. "My eyesight has never been good. Where are Fiona's pictures? I kept thinking I should organize all these other pictures but I never did." Sarah stared at the piles of loose pictures and wondered if she would ever find Fiona's photographs.

"Here they are." Mrs. Bitty pulled several larger photographs out of the box, all eight by eleven inches. She smiled fondly at the top one. "That's the tree that was in the Hamill estate's backyard." She passed it to Sarah and Martha.

It was a gnarled oak tree, twisted every which way. There was an elaborately carved swing dangling from a strong branch, but the way the photo had been taken, it was as if the child playing on the swing had left only moments before.

"Here's Mount Greylock." She passed Sarah a photo, and at first Sarah thought Mrs. Bitty must be mistaken. It didn't look like Mount Greylock, more like a painting of a majestic mountain with swirling clouds, straight out of *The Hobbit*. Then she realized it *was* Mount Greylock, but the photographer had somehow captured a whimsical aura caused by autumn clouds.

Photo after photo followed of nature shots: a close-up of a bee with wings so delicate Sarah could almost hear it buzzing; a photo of the Collinses' maple grove from some high vantage point, with the colors of the leaves rich and lush; a black-and-white photo of a rosebud just opening, with the morning sun gilding its edges.

Mrs. Bitty snorted at the next picture. "Frank. What a loser."

Martha bit back a surprised guffaw.

Mrs. Bitty passed her a picture of people, this time Fiona with a young man, perhaps in his early twenties. He had a handsome, rugged face and a stubborn jaw, but there was something in his eyes that seemed wild and reckless and daring.

"I took that picture," Mrs. Bitty said. "Fiona was trying to teach me, so she had me take a picture of her and Frank, and she gave me the photo I took. Otherwise I wouldn't want a picture of that man."

"Frank?" Sarah asked.

"Frank Shields," Mrs. Bitty said. "He was obsessed with Fiona. She dated him for a while, but then broke it off with him. Good riddance. He did almost everything illegal that he could do in Maple Hill—drugs, theft, assault. Not murder. I don't think."

"Was he involved in Fiona's disappearance?"

"No, he left town the summer before she went to Ireland. He hasn't been seen since. I heard a rumor he went to jail, but I don't know that for a fact."

Sarah looked again at Frank's broad shoulders, thrust back in arrogance, and the challenge in his eyes. Yes, she could see how a girl could fall for a bad boy like this. "How long did they date?" she asked.

"Quite a while, actually, because he could see her only when she came home from college on weekends, so it took her awhile to realize what a bottom-feeder he was. Maybe a year or two? When they broke up, he left town. Here's another photo of her. This was taken only a month before she disappeared."

Sarah looked at the photo and noticed a lovely, although old-fashioned, necklace around Fiona's neck. She had also been wearing the necklace in the photo with Frank. "Did Frank give her that necklace?" she asked Mrs. Bitty, pointing to the picture.

"Probably not. Fiona liked buying jewelry. She was always wearing some new piece."

Sarah made a mental note to stop in at McLean Jewelers to see if Les remembered Fiona. If she bought jewelry often, maybe Les knew her and could shed more light on her disappearance.

"She was such a pretty girl. Fiona didn't have any other men in her life?" Sarah asked.

Mrs. Bitty thought a moment. "Not before Frank. Fiona kept to herself a lot until she met Angela. That girl was like a tonic for Fiona—pulled her out of her shell, kept her from being beaten down by her father. But Fiona kept her relationship with Frank secret from Angela and Roseanna. She told me about it because once I caught her climbing back in her bedroom window in the early morning hours. After that, she confided in me, I guess, because she couldn't confide in her girlfriends. She knew they'd disapprove, and I did, too, but..."

Mrs. Bitty took another bite of muffin and washed it down with some tea. "But after she came back from that year in Ireland, she had a slew of men. Or at least, it seemed like it. There was a reporter in town, Peter Bickham, who was pursuing her pretty hard. She'd met him in Ireland."

That must have been the man whose name Angela couldn't remember. "Did she like him too?" Sarah asked.

"I'm not sure. Sometimes she seemed to fancy him, but there were a few times I saw her with Peter and she just didn't look at him the way a girl looks at a lover, you know?"

Sarah remembered the way Gerry would look at her, and the thrill it sent through her. Yes, she could understand what Mrs. Bitty was saying.

"But Peter was doomed from the start. She was engaged by then."

"Engaged?" Sarah fumbled with her teacup.

"The week she came back from Ireland, her father called her into his office and she came out crying. He'd apparently gotten her engaged to Roger Marstadt, son of the owner of a rival shipping company in Boston."

"How archaic," Martha said.

"She was crying, so I'm not sure I heard correctly, but I think she said it was some kind of arranged marriage," Mrs. Bitty said.

"So she was engaged to Roger Marstadt the week she returned from Ireland, but then Peter Bickham started pursuing her?" Sarah asked.

"Peter was in Maple Hill for some story he was doing for the newspaper he worked for," Mrs. Bitty said. "I don't exactly remember what. Truth be told, I probably didn't pay much attention. My, that boy was handsome." The old woman smiled. "If he'd given me the least encouragement... ah well. He didn't have eyes for anyone but Fiona, and I got the sense he was more her class of people too."

"Her class of people?"

"He didn't dress it or act snobby, but he smelled like family money. Well-groomed, neat in appearance, very athletic.

Thick, wavy brown hair and blue eyes and dimples a foot deep. Such a cutie."

Mrs. Bitty then sobered a little. "There was another man too, but I don't know who he was. Or rather, I don't remember—it's been so long. Tall, lean, with reddish hair. She met him in Ireland and he came to Maple Hill with her."

Liam? Sarah shifted in her chair, her shoulders tight.

"I saw him only a few times," Mrs. Bitty said. "He didn't hang out with Fiona as much as Peter did. He was...a little mysterious. And what Roger said about him didn't help."

"You knew Roger? What did he say?" Sarah asked.

"After the engagement, he came here from Boston once in a while, so I saw him at the Hamills' home. One time I heard him talking to Fiona, and he mentioned how that man—I can't remember his name—was a murderer. That he'd killed a man back in Ireland."

Sarah's heart stopped. Liam accused of murder? She couldn't believe it. "He wasn't talking about Peter?"

"No. But I wouldn't pay any heed to what Roger said," Mrs. Bitty replied. "I didn't like him. He didn't love Fiona, so why get engaged to her?"

"Was the redheaded man in love with her too?" Sarah asked quietly.

"I don't really know. He didn't hang out as much with Fiona as Peter did."

That seemed odd. Why would Liam's and Fiona's names have been on a wedding quilt if they weren't even spending much time together? What was going on between them?

"Though I did see Fiona arguing with him in the library a couple of weeks before she went missing," Mrs. Bitty said.

"What were they arguing about?" Martha asked.

"I couldn't hear, but Fiona was pretty upset. I asked her about it later, but she didn't want to tell me."

Roger Marstadt, Peter Bickham, and this redheaded stranger, who might be Liam. Did any of them have anything to do with Fiona's disappearance?

"By any chance did Fiona or any of the Hamills sew quilts?"

Mrs. Bitty scoffed. "Ha. They couldn't even sew a button on to save their lives."

Well, that answered the question about whether Fiona had made Caitlin's quilt. "What happened to those men when Fiona disappeared?"

"I'm not sure. Peter and Roger both seemed upset that she was gone, but they didn't stay in Maple Hill long after Fiona went missing. I'm assuming Roger went back to Boston, and maybe Peter went back to Ireland."

"What happened to the Hamills?" Martha asked. "Are they still around?"

"No, a few years later, they died in a train wreck, one of those big ones that are on the TV. All the servants were let go, so the house was probably sold. Mr. Bitty got a position as an office manager in a company in Pittsfield, so we got married and moved there until he retired."

Sarah handed her the photos, but Mrs. Bitty asked, "Would you like to keep them for a while?"

"You don't mind? I'd love to, thank you." Sarah slipped the photos into her purse. "Mr. Blodgett mentioned Fiona's camera. That it was missing?"

"I remember the camera, because it was one of Fiona's favorites. It was missing from her room when I went snooping around in it after the police had gone."

"Are you sure?" Sarah asked.

Mrs. Bitty frowned. "I'm not a photographer so I couldn't tell you the make or model, but I think I remember how it looked. Mr. and Mrs. Hamill didn't know anything about Fiona's photography, so even though they said all her cameras were in her room, they wouldn't have noticed if one was missing."

How odd that nothing was taken except that camera. Had there been something on it? That might explain why Fiona disappeared. Maybe she had taken a photo of something she shouldn't have.

Sarah rose and took the photo box from Mrs. Bitty. "I'll put that away for you."

"Thank you."

A knock at the door sounded simultaneously as it swung open. "Hi, Aunt Charlotte." A woman with gray-streaked brown hair in a cute bob poked her head into the living room as she wiped her feet on the mat outside the door. "Oh, I see you have company."

Sarah recognized the woman—Jane Carter, the historian for the county fair. She had given a few talks at the Bridge Street Church women's group, and she was good friends with Irene Stuart, the historian at the Maple Hill Historical Society. "Hi, Jane," she said.

"Hi, Sarah, Martha." Jane smiled. "I didn't know you knew my aunt."

"They took pity on me," Mrs. Bitty said, "because I was ready to expire from nonactivity."

Jane laughed. "Aunt Charlotte, you should have been on the stage. I told you I'd be here to help you with supper. Did you forget?"

"Pain does that to me," she replied in a dramatic voice of long suffering. "Next I'll forget to brush my teeth in the morning."

"We should go," Sarah said. "Thank you so much for talking to us."

"Anytime. If you have any other questions, just give me a ring."

As they walked back to the church to get their cars, Martha said, "It feels like we got a fire hose of information."

"You can say that again. I'm not sure where to begin."

"What's easiest?"

Sarah thought about the names she had been given. Frank Shields—but he had left Maple Hill even before Fiona disappeared. Roger Marstadt—she had forgotten to ask Mrs. Bitty if she knew the name of Roger's family's shipping business. Peter Bickham—roving reporter.

And the mysterious redheaded stranger. Liam. Who might have killed a man in Ireland.

She couldn't believe that. She wouldn't.

Except he must have had something to do with this. His name and Fiona's were on that quilt.

Well, until he called her, surely there was no harm in finding out more about Fiona, Roger, and Peter.

"If Peter was a newspaper reporter in town, he might have checked in with the *Maple Hill Monitor* offices, don't you think?" Sarah asked.

Martha nodded. "I would guess. But who would still be around from when Fiona disappeared?"

"I don't think I have to talk to anyone at the *Maple Hill Monitor* offices."

"You don't?"

"I can just go back to the library to find out who was editor in chief of the paper when Chuck Blodgett wrote that story."

CHAPTER SEVEN

S arah couldn't believe her luck. The editor in chief of the *Maple Hill Monitor* in 1970 had been Ivan Hillman.

She and Martha both peered at the newspaper in front of them. They had gone to the library archives to look at the article about Fiona's disappearance, and the edition had listed the head newspaper staff members at the time.

"Ivan?" Martha straightened in her chair. "No wonder he was such an avid photographer. He probably took pictures for the paper."

Sarah and Martha had met him earlier that year. He had taken some pictures of the choir at Congregational Church back in the sixties that they had wanted to see, to try to find out more about Debby Neely.

"Want to see if we can visit him today?" Sarah asked.

"You bet. Ivan's quite a character."

Sarah called Ivan's number with her cell phone while Martha put away the newspaper. Ivan's daughter Alana Marquez answered the phone. "Hello?"

"Hi, Alana, this is Sarah Hart."

"Hi, Sarah."

"Would it be all right if I come over to speak to your father?"

"If you do, come now, because he has to take his nap in a couple of hours."

"I do not need a nap!" groused a voice in the background. "Who are you talking to?"

"Sarah Hart."

"Sarah! Give me the phone." There was a soft scuffling noise, and then Ivan Hillman's deep voice boomed over the telephone. "How are you, Sarah? Need more photos?"

"No, thank you. Did you finally get your photos organized?"

"Yup. I would have done it sooner if *someone* wouldn't make me nap at noon. Who naps at noon, tell me that."

In the background, Alana's voice called, "Ninety-year-old people who insist on getting up at four in the morning."

"I'm eight-five. Don't you know your own father's age?"

"Last week you told Mrs. Johnson you were eighty," Alana retorted. "Make up your mind."

Sarah bit back a laugh. "Actually, Ivan, I wanted to talk to you about something that happened in Maple Hill in 1970, when you were editor in chief of the *Monitor*."

"Nineteen seventy, nineteen seventy…I think I even know what event you're talking about," he said triumphantly. "Not much else happened that year. Well, except for Apollo 13."

"Could I come over with Martha right now to chat with you?"

"Sure, bring the whole gang. It'll keep *someone* from making me take a nap."

They drove to Ivan's house, which was in an older part of Maple Hill. The bricks of his two-story house were in muted, autumnal shades, and basement windows peeked out of the front toward the street.

Alana smiled when she opened the door to them, tucking a lock of ash brown hair behind her ear. "Come on in. Dad's in the living room."

"I'm in the living room!" he called from the back of the house.

Ivan sat in his usual overstuffed recliner, looking more like a skeleton than a spry old man. He met Sarah and Martha with his wide, toothy grin and a large outstretched hand. "Good to see you two again, good to see you. Have a seat. Sorry I can't get up, my bum knee's bothering me today."

Sarah and Martha sat on the sofa opposite his recliner, while Alana sank into a plush chair. Both the chair and the sofa were new since Sarah had last been there, but Ivan's recliner looked as ratty as ever. It reminded her of Ernie Maplethorpe's decrepit recliner, which he kept repairing with duct tape. Luckily, Ivan hadn't yet had to resort to that for his chair.

Ivan rubbed his hands together. "You want to know about Fiona Hamill's disappearance, don't you?"

Sarah was duly impressed. "How did you know?"

"It's like I said, nothing else happened that year in Maple Hill. You need to talk to Chuck Blodgett, he's the reporter who covered that." He added dryly, "Actually, he was the only reporter we had back then."

"I did, and he gave me some information that wasn't in the article he wrote."

"He and I both interviewed a lot of people from Maple Hill. I made Alana dig out my old notepad from the case. Most of what we learned was a lot of gossip, and we don't print gossip. But where there's smoke, there's usually fire."

"What kind of smoke?"

Ivan flipped through an old spiral notepad, about the size of his hand, and just as narrow. "Roger Marstadt, for one. After Chuck left to take an editor in chief position in Concord, I took over the story whenever I had free time, and I found out a few things about Fiona and Roger."

Sarah leaned forward in her seat.

"Roger was heir to M&S Shipping," Ivan continued, "up in Boston. But he came to Maple Hill all the way from Boston almost every weekend in the two months before Fiona disappeared. Rumor had it he was engaged to Fiona."

"And you think he had something to do with her disappearance?"

"What I discovered was that it was mighty convenient that Fiona disappeared when she did," Ivan said slowly. "It wasn't just an engagement—one of my sources mentioned that there was a betrothal contract."

Sarah was confused. "A legal contract?"

Ivan nodded. "A legally binding betrothal contract."

Martha's mouth dropped open. "They still have those?"

"They did back then."

"That seems a bit extreme," Sarah said.

Ivan put a finger to the side of his nose. "I heard a rumor about a merger between Hamill Shipping and M&S Shipping."

"But weren't they competitors?" Sarah asked.

"Sure were. But maybe they thought they'd be more powerful together than apart."

"How did you find all this out? And how do you know it's true?" Martha asked.

"I, ahem . . . got to be friends with a guy who worked in a particular law firm in Boston."

"Dad!" Alana protested. "What happened to lawyer-client privilege?"

"He wasn't a lawyer," Ivan insisted. "He was a source."

Alana rolled her eyes but said nothing more.

"What made you suspect Roger Marstadt?" Sarah asked.

"I saw his wedding announcement, that's what," Ivan said. "Chuck had found out that Fiona had been engaged to Roger, but I saw the announcement of his wedding to some other woman barely two months after Fiona disappeared.

Two months after he had spent all that time in Maple Hill pretending to be in love with her. That looked suspicious to me, so I looked further into him and M&S Shipping. Actually, when I investigated the merger, people speculated that the Marstadts weren't too keen on it because the Hamills had more to gain. But the Marstadts reluctantly agreed with the plan because it was in their best interest."

"So you're saying that the betrothal contract was connected to this merger?" Sarah asked.

"To give Roger credit, when he came to Maple Hill, he seemed devoted to Fiona," Ivan said. "It wasn't like he was announcing it was going to be a business marriage—not that anyone here knew about the engagement. They probably intended to announce it at the shareholders' meeting the following quarter, at least, that's what my source thought. Nobody knows the terms of the betrothal contract, but if it was tied to the merger plans, neither Fiona nor Roger could back out of it. At least, that's how my source explained it to me. If Roger backed out, the Hamills could have sued him for breach of promise or something like that."

Sarah digested this information. "And he married only two months after Fiona went missing. So if he had fallen in love with someone else after he signed the betrothal contract, he couldn't have broken his engagement."

Ivan slowly nodded. "It gives him an excellent motive for making Fiona disappear."

"Ivan, you said Roger acted devoted to Fiona," Sarah said. "What about Peter Bickham? I heard he was pursuing

Fiona during that same two-month period before she disappeared."

Ivan's eyes widened. "Peter! I haven't thought about him in a while. Yup, he and Roger were a bit like two dogs with a bone. He was pretty upset when Fiona went missing."

"Did he ever accuse Roger of being involved?" Sarah asked. It was a bit of a stretch, but she figured it didn't hurt to ask.

Ivan frowned as he thought. "I don't think so. The first time I suspected Roger was when I saw the wedding announcement. I never heard Peter say anything about Roger after Fiona disappeared."

"What was Peter like?"

"Oh, he was friendly and outgoing and the ladies in town loved him. Very personable—it's probably what made him a good reporter."

"What story was he doing?" Martha asked.

"He was doing a series of stories on small historic towns," Ivan said. "He'd done some research in Ireland—that's where he met Fiona. And probably because of her, he decided his next stop was Maple Hill. Although ..." He hesitated.

"Although ...?" Sarah prompted gently.

"That series on small historic towns seemed a rather tame topic for a man like him."

"What do you mean?"

Ivan paused to choose his words. "Don't get me wrong, he was a very friendly guy. But as a reporter, he reminded me of a big-game hunter. He walked softly, he planned carefully and far in advance, he set his trap, and then he captured his prey—or, the story. He reminded me of those hard-core investigative reporters I knew who pursued the big stories— murder, conspiracy, those sorts of things." Ivan shrugged. "But he was young when I met him. Maybe his stories on small historic towns was a stepping-stone for him. I'm sure he went far. He had to have been good to have landed a job at *New England Sunrises*."

Martha blinked. "That's a Boston magazine, not a newspaper."

"Sure enough."

"I thought Peter was a newspaper reporter."

"Oh no. He was doing a piece on small historical towns in Massachusetts for *Sunrises.* He came to talk to me as a professional courtesy when he first arrived in town, but he wasn't working for the *Monitor* or anything like that."

"Was Peter close to anyone in town?" Sarah asked. Maybe she could speak to someone who had known him well.

"I wasn't keeping tabs on him, but I didn't see him with anyone besides Fiona. And Roger, but I don't think they were friends." He chuckled.

"Anyone else?" She thought it strange that Chuck hadn't mentioned Liam, and so far Ivan hadn't either. Yet Angela and Mrs. Bitty had known about his being friends with Fiona. And if Liam knew Fiona, of course he knew Peter, who had come to Maple Hill from Ireland with them, and there was a chance he knew Roger as well.

Ivan leaned his head back for a minute. "Actually, now that I think about it, Liam Connolly was friends with Peter."

Sarah's body stilled. "Was he?"

"I saw them together a couple of times, especially in the week after Fiona disappeared."

Sarah supposed that Ivan would naturally note who spoke to Peter, since he knew Peter as a fellow journalist. "Did Liam pursue Fiona too?"

"I don't know. No, I don't think so."

This was getting more and more curious. What was Liam's connection to Fiona? Friends? More than friends? Was it possible he had married her at some point?

Liam should be leaving his retreat today sometime. She would have to call him this afternoon.

From her chair on the other side of her dad's recliner, Alana was giving Sarah significant looks. She probably wanted to get him to go down for his n-a-p.

"We should get going," Sarah said. "I have errands to run this afternoon. Thank you so much for talking to us, Ivan."

"Is that all you need?" His shoulders sagged and his eyes pleaded with her.

"If I need to know more, I'll be sure to call you," Sarah assured him. "Thank you so much."

"Anytime."

As Martha drove them away in her minivan, Sarah said, "I wonder how we can look up Peter at *New England Sunrises*."

"You know, last week I was chatting with Irene Stuart about a new war journal she'd just come across by Colonel Briggs, who supposedly served with General Bradford. She mentioned she'd had a phone conference with *Massachusetts Living* magazine."

"You're thinking she has contacts at *New England Sunrises* magazine?" Sarah asked.

"She probably has to give lots of magazine interviews. She's one of the foremost experts on General Bradford, and of course she worked at the John F. Kennedy Presidential Library in Boston before coming to Maple Hill."

"I'll give her a call."

Sarah took out her cell phone and dialed the Maple Hill Historical Society. She knew she would be able to trust Irene's discretion if she told her she was looking into Fiona Hamill's disappearance.

"Maple Hill Historical Society," Irene answered the phone, although her voice sounded a bit muffled.

"Hi, Irene, it's Sarah."

"Hi, Sarah." There was an audible crunching sound on the line.

"I'm sorry, am I catching you at a bad time? I didn't interrupt your lunch, did I?"

"Not at all. I'm just snacking with Colonel Briggs."

"Is he very chatty?" Sarah teased. Irene's tendency to talk about her beloved historical figures as if they were still alive always made her smile.

"Yes, but he's terribly boring. He seems to only want to talk about how much his horse ate or how many shirts he has left."

Sarah laughed.

"What can I help you with?" Irene asked.

"This is a more unusual request. I'm looking for a man named Peter Bickham who worked at *New England Sunrises* magazine about forty years ago."

"Only forty years? If you'd said one hundred and forty years ago, that might have been really fascinating." Sarah could hear Irene's smile in her voice.

"Does that mean you can't help me?"

"Oh of course I can help you. *New England Sunrises* calls me all the time if they need historical verification or a quote for a story. I'll call an editor I know in their office and get back to you."

"Thanks so much, Irene."

"I'm the woman with connections," Irene said with a laugh, and hung up.

"That's great," Martha said. "Now all you need to do is find Roger Marstadt. I wonder if he really did have something to do with Fiona's disappearance."

"He certainly had motive."

Martha turned the car into Sarah's driveway. "I'm sure the police investigated both Peter and Roger forty years ago, but they're unlikely to tell us what they found."

"I wonder if Dale Wexler would speak to us about this. He retired as chief of police awhile ago, but he would have been an officer on the force when Fiona disappeared."

"If you want me to come with you, just let me know." After dropping Sarah off, Martha waved good-bye and headed home.

Sarah fixed herself a chicken sandwich and a cup of homemade vegetable soup, and thought about what she knew about Liam.

He was an intensely private person. He had mentioned to her once that his father had worked for the British Secret Service and liked to get his son to solve puzzles, but she knew almost nothing else about Liam's childhood.

Was this quilt, this connection to Fiona Hamill, another part of his past that he wanted to keep private? But if so, why had he given the quilt to Roseanna Walsh to embroider the patch and then give to Caitlin?

Sarah shook her head. That was assuming Liam had known about the names and had even had a connection with Fiona Hamill. What if he hadn't, and he truly had no idea that their names were on the quilt? What if this was some practical joke gone wrong?

She glanced at the clock. It was close to twelve thirty. According to what Liam had told her, the retreat had ended the night before, and the men would all be heading out from the retreat center this morning.

She was about to dial Liam's cell phone number when her home telephone rang. "Hello?"

"Hi, Sarah, it's Caitlin. I know this is a bit last minute, but do you have time this afternoon?"

"Of course. What do you have in mind?"

"I was going to my last dress fitting this afternoon with Roseanna, but she had to cancel because her dishwasher broke this morning and she has to wait for the repair guy. I had wanted to spend some time with you, and I thought it might be fun if you came with me."

"I'd love to." She would love to get to know Caitlin better, especially since her relationship with Liam had shifted and changed in the past few months.

"Great! I can come by to pick you up in about fifteen minutes. Is that okay?"

"Perfect."

In the car, Caitlin asked, "Did you manage to clean the quilt?"

"Yes," Sarah replied. "All I need to do now is sew the patch back on." Except she had no intention of doing so until she could figure out why Liam's name was on the quilt. "You said your great-aunt made the quilt? From which side of your family—your mother's side or your father's?"

"Oh, from Mom's side. Mom's Great-Aunt Louise made fantastic quilts."

Jeannie's great-aunt made a quilt with Liam's and Fiona Hamill's names on it? This was getting stranger and stranger.

"I remember that quilt being on my parents' bed in their first house," Caitlin said. "The family moved to our current house when I was five, and that's when I think the quilt went into storage."

Their current home? "I never knew your dad's house wasn't your family's first house."

"Yeah, we used to live in a smaller house on the south side of Maple Hill, near Grandma and Grandpa Crofter," Caitlin said. "Mom got a job at the bank, and Dad was helping Grandpa Crofter with their dairy farm."

"I remember his mentioning that once. He didn't like working on the farm, but your grandfather didn't have anyone else who could help him at the time, and he was getting too old to do it all by himself."

"Grandpa Crofter was *very* stubborn," Caitlin said. "Dad told him to sell the farm, but he wouldn't, even though he knew my parents didn't want to take over for him. Mom and Dad opened the bookstore in December 1980, and it forced Grandpa to hire help, but that only cut into his profits, and he was barely making even. When my grandparents died, Dad sold the farm."

It was fascinating to hear about Liam's past. Although Sarah had been in Maple Hill at the time, she hadn't known him at all.

She reminded herself to find out more about the quilt. "You said your mother's great-aunt made the quilt? Such a shame to put it in storage. It's beautiful."

"Great-Aunt Louise didn't make many quilts, and I think Mom put it in storage to prevent jealousy from some of her cousins who might see the quilt and think they ought to get one of Great-Aunt Louise's quilts rather than Mom. We don't get along with some of Mom's cousins—they drive Dad crazy."

"How many quilts did your great-aunt make?"

"I think only six. She died back in the fifties, and she had four siblings. Now there are twenty-seven cousins."

"Gracious." But Sarah's mind was whirling. If Jeannie's great-aunt had died in the fifties, there was no way she could have made the quilt. The polyester batting hadn't been manufactured until the sixties.

So who could have made the quilt? Considering the names on the quilt, it would make more sense if the quilt maker was someone from Liam's family, not Jeannie's.

Sarah asked Caitlin about wedding plans, and the young woman chatted about cakes and flowers while she drove them to a cute clothing boutique, which also did alterations, that sat just off the main street in downtown Maple Hill.

"Hello, Miss Connolly," said the shopkeeper/seamstress. "I have your gown ready."

Sarah sat in an overstuffed chair just outside the fitting room while Caitlin got into her dress. When she walked out, Sarah caught her breath.

The creamy white gown draped over her slender frame perfectly. Pale green beads sparkled in embroidery across the bodice, and gentle folds decorated the sides of the skirt to create a subtle movement like water.

"You look beautiful," Sarah said.

Caitlin colored a little, but her smile was bright as she turned in front of the large mirrors. "I look so different. Especially since I'm normally in nurse's scrubs."

"You *should* look different. It's your wedding day. You want to look so amazing that your husband will remember it forever."

Sarah couldn't help thinking that she would like to look a little amazing too, so that Liam would remember. She still had to find her own dress for the wedding.

"The green embroidery goes perfectly with your colors," Sarah said. "Your bridesmaids are in green too?"

Caitlin nodded. "And Dad has a sage green vest."

"He'll look so handsome walking you down the aisle."

Suddenly, Caitlin's eyes in the mirror dimmed. "I wish Mom could be here."

Sarah hesitated, then stood and tentatively placed an arm around Caitlin's shoulders. "She's with you. I'm sure she's very proud of you." She smiled at Caitlin's reflection. "I'm so amazed. You have your father's hair and green eyes, but you look exactly like Jeannie."

"That's what Dad always says."

"Do you have a lot of relatives coming to the wedding?" Sarah felt faintly guilty about pumping Caitlin for information, but she wouldn't press for anything Caitlin didn't want to tell her.

"A lot of Mom's relatives are still in the area, so it'll be mostly the Crofters," Caitlin said. "Dad said his relatives are all still in Ireland and can't make the trip."

"Have you met any of them?"

"I met a couple of cousins when they came here to visit, but I was only about ten at the time."

"You've never gone to Ireland?"

Caitlin shook her head. "I'm not sure why. Dad's entire family is there, so you'd think we'd go back to visit at some point. But we never have."

How strange. "Maybe he's too busy with the bookstore and café. After all, he's missed his church's men's retreat every year because of that, even though he's really wanted to go."

"But we'd go on other trips. Once we went on a three-week driving trip down the East Coast."

Sarah wasn't sure what to say in response to that.

"When I was young, I'd ask him about Ireland," Caitlin said. "He always put me off—you know the way he does that with a smile?"

Sarah nodded. She certainly understood that.

"But one time, he said something strange. He said he *couldn't* go back to Ireland."

"What did he mean by that?"

"I asked him, but he only backtracked and made it into a joke, something like his mug was too ugly for them to let him on the plane."

That sounded like Liam—shying away from something too deeply personal. "Do you think there's something in Ireland he's trying to escape?" *Like a murder charge?*

Caitlin shrugged. "I don't know."

"Maybe he's running from a crazy ex-girlfriend," Sarah said, trying to lighten the mood.

Caitlin laughed. "I could totally see Dad boycotting the entire country of Ireland just to avoid seeing an old flame."

"When did your father come to America?" Sarah asked.

"Nineteen seventy-five," Caitlin said. "He married Mom the next year."

The seamstress came in, pincushion in hand, and the rest of the fitting went smoothly and quickly, with Caitlin chattering about the bridesmaid dresses, about patients at the hospital where she worked, about Travis's stellar qualities. Caitlin's exuberant conversation distracted Sarah from the one thing bothering her the most.

Liam had lied to both Sarah and his daughter about what year he had come to Maple Hill.

CHAPTER EIGHT

Sarah looked at the caller ID on her cell phone. She took a deep breath, then answered it. "Hi, Liam."

"Hello, Sarah," he answered. His deep voice, with that playful brogue, made warmth blossom in her chest.

A voice squawked in the background. "Sorry," he said. "I'm at my gate waiting for my flight to board."

That's right, he was going to an invitation-only booksellers event in Nashville. He was probably at Albany International Airport.

Sarah settled into the rocking chair in her living room. "Did you have a good time at the retreat?"

"It was wonderful, Sarah. Although I did miss you."

"I missed you too."

"I'll be gone another two weeks."

"I know."

"Try not to solve any mysteries while I'm away, eh?" he joked.

But his words made a hard knot form in her stomach. She tried to laugh, but it sounded false to her ears.

"How did Caitlin's shower go?" Liam asked. "I know you were looking forward to it."

"Oh, it went wonderfully. That quilt you gave to Roseanna to give to Caitlin..."

"How did the patch turn out? I didn't see it before I had to go."

The ease with which he said this implied he didn't know anything at all about the names under the patch. It gave Sarah the courage to say, "Caitlin brought the quilt to me the day after the shower because it had fallen in some mud. She asked me to save the patch, so I removed it."

"If anyone can clean a ruined quilt, it's you, Sarah."

"Liam..." She swallowed, then continued, "I found names written on the back of the quilt, hidden under the patch."

"Names?" He sounded genuinely confused.

"It said Liam Connolly married Fiona Hamill."

There was silence on the line.

Sarah resisted the urge to babble, because she wanted to hear Liam's response. Except he didn't say anything for the longest time.

When he finally answered, his voice seemed strangely unemotional. "It says I married Fiona Hamill?"

"Yes. Liam, why would it say that?"

"I don't know, Sarah. I didn't marry her."

The confirmation made the knot of tension release in her stomach. "You knew her though, didn't you?"

There was another odd pause, then he said, "Yes."

She waited a moment, but he didn't elaborate. "Do you know what happened to her?"

"No," he answered quickly. "How did you find out about Fiona?" His tone was almost accusatory.

"Martha remembered her disappearance," Sarah said. "How did you get the quilt?"

"I got it as a gift."

Again, he didn't elaborate, and the silence dragged on between them. It made Sarah shift in her seat. "Who gave it to—"

"A friend," he interrupted her. "No one you know."

His curt answers stung. Considering how their relationship had grown over the past few months, she would have thought it would be understandable for her to be curious about the names and the quilt, but he seemed irritated by her questions.

She also couldn't shake the feeling that he wasn't being truthful in his answers to her. Liam had always been truthful to her before. Why did she think he was lying now?

It made her heart twist like a wrung-out dishcloth.

"You didn't see the names on the quilt when you got it?" she asked.

"I didn't really look at the back side."

Another awkward pause. There were so many questions she wanted to ask him, but she wasn't sure how he would respond.

"Did you tell Caitlin?" he asked her.

"No, of course not," she said. She thought she heard him blow out a long breath.

"I'd be guessing you've been investigating, eh, Sarah?" He tried to say it in a teasing voice, but Sarah could hear the strain in his tone.

"You know I wouldn't investigate you behind your back like that, Liam." Except wasn't she doing just that, in investigating Fiona?

"I know, I know."

"Can you tell me about Fiona?" she asked gently, hoping he would be willing to talk to her.

"I don't want you to tell Caitlin. I'll tell her, in my own way. You're a parent, you understand these things."

"Yes, I do. I promise I won't tell her."

"Thank you, Sarah." He gave a long, drawn out sigh. "I met Fiona in Ireland."

"During her year abroad after college?" She was glad he seemed open to talking about Fiona, even though he hadn't wanted to talk about the quilt.

"That's it. The Hamills came from Tyrone County, which is next to Monaghan County, where my family is from. I never met any of them before I was introduced to Fiona. She was staying with her uncle and visiting cousins in the county, but there weren't many young people in her uncle's village, so we all gravitated toward each other."

He had said "we all." That was curious. "How did you meet Fiona?" Sarah asked.

"We were introduced by Peter Bickham."

"You were friends with him in Ireland?"

"Found out about him, did you? You're a smart one, Sarah m'girl."

She wasn't about to be distracted by his blarney. "How did you know Peter?"

"Who in the village didn't know Peter? The man never met a stranger. He was renting a room in a house down the street."

"He was good friends with Fiona?"

"She said they'd met only a few months earlier. I don't know how he met her, because her uncle's village was a good thirty or forty minutes away by bicycle. But I had a car"—his voice had taken on a strange, hard note as he said the word—"and so we went to catch a show or out to dinner, and we hiked around Lough Neagh."

"Why was Peter in Ireland?"

"Writing a story, he said, for his magazine."

"*New England Sunrises?*" Sarah asked.

"That's the one. He said he loved his job. Strange, though, I wouldn't have picked him for a journalist. He seemed more like the sort to be a detective in Boston or someone who had climbed Mount Everest."

"What was his story about?"

"Small historical towns in Monaghan. He said he was doing an entire series. He found out Fiona was from Maple Hill and decided to return to the states with her when it was time for her to leave."

That must have been when he arrived in Maple Hill—at the same time Fiona did. That reminded her—"Liam, when did you come to Maple Hill?"

There was a pause, then he said, "I came to Maple Hill with Fiona and Peter in October 1970."

"You've told me before that it was 1975."

Another pause. "I was in Maple Hill for a few months in 1970, but I left soon after Fiona disappeared. I was a wild kid back then. I'm not proud of some of the things I did during those months—that's why I didn't want to admit I was in town. But then I fell in love with Jeannie and I wanted to prove to her parents I was trustworthy, so I left Maple Hill and took two jobs in Boston to save up some money. I worked full-time at a bookstore and part-time at a coffee shop." He chuckled. "Jeannie and I corresponded for four years, bless her heart, and I came back to Maple Hill in early 1975 to court and marry her."

That made sense to Sarah. He didn't really come to stay in Maple Hill until his marriage, so he might be excused for saying he had come to Maple Hill in 1975 rather than in 1970.

"So you knew both Peter and Roger Marstadt," Sarah said.

"Roger," Liam said in a low, growling voice, "was a snake. He always had a smile on his face, but you could never trust him. He acted the part of a man in love with Fiona, but sometimes I think he did it just to needle Peter. Peter was head over heels for Fiona, that much was obvious."

"I wouldn't expect him and Roger to get along."

"From things they said, I think they knew each other even before they both pursued Fiona."

"How?"

"I'm not sure, but my guess would be in school. Maybe grade school or high school. Just from things they mentioned, like 'old times.'"

That was an interesting angle. It hadn't occurred to Sarah that Peter and Roger might have known each other before they met in Maple Hill. How curious—and a little too coincidental, perhaps?

"Did Fiona love Peter? Or Roger?"

Liam again hesitated. "I don't think she loved either of them."

"Really?"

"She liked the attention, certainly, although she never led them on. Especially Peter—she was friends with him, but she never deliberately made him believe she felt more for him. Poor man."

Sarah, too, sympathized with Peter's unrequited love. It would have made Fiona's disappearance that much harder for him.

A thought occurred to her. "Did Jeannie know Fiona? Or—"

"No," Liam said, "Jeannie didn't know Fiona at all."

"You never introduced them?"

"Jeannie was working her way through school at the time and didn't have much time for hanging out with anyone. She was waitressing at the Miss Maple and taking night classes in business and accounting in Pittsfield. Any free time Jeannie had she usually spent with me. She didn't know Peter or Roger, either."

Again, Sarah had that nagging feeling that he wasn't being entirely open with her. But why in the world would he lie to her? And what exactly was he not telling her?

It was that hurt that made her say, "I had a nice time chatting with Caitlin today, getting to know her better. She mentioned that you've never taken her to Ireland. Why not?"

There was a different sort of silence over the phone now, something that seemed much more tense than before. Sarah realized she might have pushed too hard. She and Liam had grown closer, yes, but her question seemed to have crossed some invisible line.

Sarah was the first to break the silence. "I'm ... I'm sorry, Liam. I shouldn't have pushed."

"Maple Hill is my home now," Liam said. But rather than comforting, the words seemed to grate.

The sound of a voice over a loudspeaker could be heard in the background. "I've got to go, Sarah," Liam said. "They're boarding my row."

"Have a safe trip, Liam."

After she hung up the phone, Sarah paused to get her bearings. The conversation had been so uncomfortable, she didn't know what to make of it.

The suspicion Liam had lied to her about how he had gotten the quilt made her wonder what else he might have lied to her about, and it all gave her a horrible feeling of dread.

Why couldn't he be open with her about this?

Maybe he had a good reason to be evasive. Maybe it was a misunderstanding.

But it still bothered her and hurt her.

Sarah put her energy into dusting furniture and vacuuming floors, and the mindless work allowed her to reflect on what she had learned today. With luck Irene would find out something about Peter. In the meantime, she could search for Roger Marstadt, especially now that she knew his family's company name. She hoped there was something on the Internet about them, but if not, perhaps she could visit the Chamber of Commerce in Boston.

The telephone rang just as she shut off the vacuum, and she raced to answer it. "Hello?"

"Sarah, it's Irene."

"That was quick. Did you find out about Peter?"

"Yes and no."

"Oh?"

"I talked to several people at *New England Sunrises*. They were very helpful even though they didn't have to be—after all, I'm only a historian and I was asking about a writer from 1970. But I finally spoke to a woman in human resources who looked up old employee records."

Irene sighed mightily. "Sarah, *New England Sunrises* has never had a journalist named Peter Bickham."

Sarah awoke early the next morning to the light of dawn just streaming over the trees. It was too cold to drink her coffee outside on the back porch, but she stood at her kitchen window with a steaming cup cradled in her hands, watching the glorious rays extend out like welcoming arms to the day. *Lord, your creation is so beautiful.*

She sat at her kitchen table with her Bible and turned to Psalm 68. "A father to the fatherless, a defender of widows, is God in his holy dwelling."

As she read, a clear picture of Leland Mercer's face suddenly came into her mind. She remembered the closed look on his face when she first met him.

Lord, why would you bring him up? He was such an unpleasant man and he wouldn't give me Dad's quilt back.

But the verse she had read pricked at her, even though her heart felt sore at Leland's rudeness. Despite what she had virtuously told her granddaughters, she didn't really *want* to think about him as lonely, or someone the Lord wanted her to befriend.

Reluctantly, she prayed, *Lord, please guide me in what you want me to do for Leland. You bring everyone into our lives for a reason. Please help me to fulfill your purpose for me. Amen.*

Leland's crankiness had seemed to soften toward her granddaughters for at least a moment or two. Maybe things would improve the next time she saw him. Jason had volunteered to help her pack up and carry some of Dad's books on Thursday, and Maggie had volunteered her daughters again to help Sarah finish packing up Dad's things next Tuesday. Maybe by then Leland would have had a change of heart.

But this morning, she was going to find Roger Marstadt.

After a fortifying breakfast of oatmeal with grated apple and a sprinkling of cinnamon, she took a second cup of coffee with her to her sewing room and fired up her computer. She did a Google search for *Roger Marstadt Boston*.

The top search results were for Roger Marstadt, CEO of M&S Shipping. Bingo.

She began to pore through all the Web site articles. Most of them were about M&S Shipping, which was apparently doing quite well. Their stock was up and they had just received several business awards.

Sarah looked up the company on a business history Web site that did stories on the history of companies like Apple, Paramount, etc. She found an entry for M&S Shipping.

Founded in 1907 by Frederick Marstadt, M&S Shipping transported goods between Europe and Boston. They built their own ships in privately owned shipyards in the Boston area.

Frederick Marstadt was the son of a wealthy Dutch businessman. His mother was related to Austrian royalty, and the M&S in his company name stands for Marstadt and Stohl, his mother's maiden name.

Marstadt immigrated to the United States in 1905 for the sole purpose of setting up his shipping company, which was to complement his father's transport company in Holland. However, a fire in the Holland offices caused Frederick's father to move to the United States to help his son continue to build M&S Shipping. Under his father's guidance and with the investments of his father's contacts and his mother's family, Frederick Marstadt quickly built a small but stable shipping company that had a firm foothold in the Boston area.

The 1920s brought M&S Shipping to its knees, but Marstadt rallied and kept the company alive with the support of his overseas family members. His persistence paid off with international mail carrier contracts from the U.S. Post Office that carried the company through the leaner years.

World War II brought tough times for M&S Shipping, and profits dwindled. After the war, the company started to steadily gain ground, but it remained a small, reputable company until after the Vietnam War.

CEO Albert Marstadt made risky investments in equipment and strong marketing pushes that paid off in international shipping contracts with powerhouses of the era like General Motors, Procter and Gamble, and DuPont.

Since then, the company has continued to grow. Under Albeert Marstadt's leadership, it was among the first shipping businesses to purchase its own cargo planes, and today it owns a fleet of 234 cargo planes, as well as 112 ships. M&S Shipping is headquartered in Boston but has offices in Chicago, Dallas, San Francisco, and Los Angeles, as well as satellite offices in Tokyo, Hong Kong, London, Sydney, Paris, Rome, and Athens.

Sarah couldn't help but be impressed at how Albert Marstadt had helped his family's business not only to survive but to thrive tremendously. From what she had read, Albert was Roger's father. Roger was now CEO of M&S Shipping.

Sarah didn't know how in the world to approach Roger Marstadt. She could imagine the phone call: "Hello, this is Sarah Hart, and I'd like to speak to Mr. Marstadt about a girl who conveniently disappeared forty years ago thus allowing him to marry his wife without being sued by his company's rival, Hamill Shipping." The company operator would hang up on her faster than if she were a telemarketer. They would probably think she was a crank caller.

She decided to look up *Hamill Shipping* on the company histories Web site.

Founded in 1952 by American-born Donovan Hamill, Hamill Shipping began as the American arm of British shipping company Stockwood Fleet. Hamill Shipping quickly gained international shipping contracts with Ford and various textile companies, forming trade routes to Europe and Asia.

Hamill Shipping was a strong player in trade with Hong Kong and Australia, but in the early 1970s, the company fell into rapid decline. Missed delivery dates and missing shipments, unreliable planes, and poor customer service caused Hamill Shipping's reputation to suffer, and the company declared bankruptcy in January 1980. Tragically, Hamill's CEO, Robert Hamill, and his wife died in the Mountain Pearl Train Company accident just outside of Boston in March of that year. Hamill Shipping was dissolved by December of 1980.

Sarah read the article again. It seemed that after Fiona disappeared in 1970, her father's company declined, but

Roger Marstadt's company grew and became increasingly profitable.

Ivan Hillman had mentioned that the Marstadts had reluctantly agreed to the proposed merger, and she could now see why. At the time, Hamill Shipping had been larger and more successful than M&S Shipping, which would have lost some control in combining with a stronger partner. But after Fiona disappeared, the merger didn't occur, and Hamill Shipping spiraled downward while M&S grew exponentially.

However strange it might seem, the truth was that Roger Marstadt ended up gaining the most after Fiona went missing. Would someone really kidnap—and possibly murder—a girl in hopes it would cause the failure of her father's company? She supposed some crimes were committed with even flimsier motives. Yet Hamill Shipping *had* declined, and Sarah was willing to believe that its demise had at least partially been caused by Fiona's disappearance in 1970. No matter how horrible a father Robert Hamill might have been, he must have had some love for his daughter, some worry over what had happened to her, and that worry may have distracted him from running his business well.

Sarah next concentrated on Web sites that said something about Roger Marstadt himself, and not his business. Being a CEO, he had quite a few bios posted across the Web.

He had been born in 1949 in Boston. He had graduated with honors from Regency Academy and had gone on to attend Boston University. He graduated summa cum laude and got his MBA at Harvard.

Sarah looked at the impressive résumé, accompanied by pictures of Roger. His face had a serious, stern look to it, with a wide forehead, square jaw, and flat black hair. He seemed the type of person who could make hard decisions.

"But in between that summa cum laude and that MBA, you came to Maple Hill," she said to her computer screen. "Why did you sign that betrothal contract? Did you regret it after you did it? Did you love Fiona Hamill, or was the betrothal just a business transaction for you?"

The Web site was unhelpfully silent.

Roger worked at M&S Shipping with his father until his father retired, becoming CEO about fifteen years ago. He was married in February 1971 to Margaret Fieldhahn, daughter of Mel Fieldhahn, owner of the Fieldhahn Hotel in Boston.

Sarah blinked. The Fieldhahn Hotel was a nice hotel, certainly, but it wasn't as large or impressive as other hotels. Margaret Fieldhahn wouldn't have been an heiress. Perhaps Roger had indeed loved Margaret, but he had been pressured to become engaged to Fiona Hamill to secure his future in business.

Sarah remembered what Liam had said about Peter and Roger knowing each other, and it suddenly occurred to her that since she knew where Roger had gone to school, she might be able to locate Peter.

Sarah was inclined to think Peter had used his real name in Maple Hill, since Roger hadn't called him out on using a false name. She couldn't imagine Roger letting that go when Peter was making such a nuisance of himself in the midst of Roger's engagement.

She could start with Roger's high school, Regency Academy. A quick search on the Web showed that it was a private boarding school in Boston.

Sarah had used class yearbooks before—why not again? And she knew the perfect person to help.

She looked up the telephone number of Laura Baird, research librarian at the Concord Free Public Library. Laura had helped Sarah awhile ago in looking up students at Concord High School, but would she be able to help her with students from Regency Academy in Boston?

"Hello, this is Laura Baird," she said as she picked up the call.

"Hello, Laura, this is Sarah Hart. You helped me awhile ago, though I'm not sure—"

"Yes, I remember! Concord High School yearbooks, right?"

"You have a good memory."

"What can I help you with today?"

"I'm looking up students at a different school, Regency Academy in Boston. It's a private boarding school, so I'm not sure if their yearbooks are available to anyone outside the school."

"These days, people are putting up yearbook information on the Web, especially at subscription sites," Laura said. "Since our library is so large, we have a subscription to a yearbook site. Let me look it up for you and see if anyone from Regency Academy put their yearbook information up. What year were you looking at?"

Sarah did some rapid mental calculations. What she had read about Roger didn't specify when he had graduated from high school, but she could make a guess. "I'm not entirely sure, but perhaps 1962 to 1965. I want to know if Roger Marstadt and Peter Bickham went to Regency Academy together." Sarah spelled the names.

"That should be easy to find." There was the sound of tapping on a keyboard and clicking with a mouse for a few minutes. Then Laura said, "I don't see any Regency Academy yearbooks for 1962, 1964, and 1965, but someone submitted a yearbook from Regency Academy for 1963, and it shows...Roger Marstadt was a sophomore that year. Let's see if Peter Bickham was there..."

Sarah waited silently, her pen poised over a notebook.

"There!" Laura said triumphantly. "Peter Bickham was a junior."

For a moment, Sarah couldn't speak. She had found the mysterious Peter Bickham, before he had showed up in Maple Hill and lied about why he was there. She took a few deep breaths, then said, "Thank you so much, Laura. Was there any other information about either of them?"

"Let me check." More sounds of a clicking mouse. "Peter was on the varsity basketball team. He was also on the debate team. Oh, Roger was on the junior varsity basketball team, so they probably practiced together."

Had their rivalry started there? Had they been good teammates or had there been friction between them even then?

"It looks like Regency Academy was a very small school in those days," Laura said. "Even if they hadn't been on the basketball team together, they would definitely have known each other. They were probably housed in the same dormitory."

It would make sense, then, that Peter would remember Roger. They would have had three years together—Roger's freshman, sophomore, and junior years, Peter's sophomore, junior, and senior years. Boyhood impressions sometimes ran deeper and stronger than adult memories. Sarah wondered what their relationship had been during those three years.

"That's it," Laura said. "The yearbook doesn't mention anything else about those two. Anyone else you want me to look up?"

"No, just them."

"If you'll give me your e-mail address, I'll send pictures of the two boys and their extracurricular clubs."

"That would be wonderful." Sarah gave her the address. "Thank you so much."

"No problem!"

Sarah hung up and received the photos only a few minutes later, thanks to Laura's efficiency.

Peter Bickham had a wide, confident smile that made him look older than sixteen or seventeen. A lock of his thick, wavy hair spilled over his broad forehead in a tantalizing curl. He was handsome, but his eyes weren't reckless or daring. She remembered what Ivan Hillman had said about him—a hunter. Yes, he looked calm, collected. His gaze was intense and purposeful—if he had a mission, he would get it done.

Sarah laughed to herself. She was getting a little carried away. She turned to Roger Marstadt.

He looked much like his current Web site pictures, except his face was more slender, and his thin, dark, straight hair covered his entire head. He already had that serious look in his eyes, but as a high school sophomore, there was also a bit of insecurity there. Natural in a young teenaged boy.

She looked at the basketball team pictures. In the varsity team photo, Peter stood tall and athletic. Roger, on the other hand, slouched a bit in the junior varsity team photo, making him look even skinnier. His hands and feet looked large and he seemed a bit awkward, still growing into his body.

The debate team photo arrested her attention. Peter had a more serious expression on his face, and she could see the determined look in his eyes more clearly. Yes, he wouldn't stop until he had accomplished what he had set out to do. He would plan patiently in order to execute flawlessly.

"A story on small historic towns, huh?" she asked the picture. "If I'd seen your photo first, I would have had my doubts."

Sarah printed out the two young men's photos and lay them side by side on her desk. She stared at Roger's dark, serious eyes and Peter's friendly, intense ones, but neither of them told her what exactly had happened to Fiona Hamill, and why her name ended up on a quilt with Liam Connolly's.

CHAPTER NINE

After making a broccoli and cheese omelet for herself with a slice of whole wheat toast for lunch, and fortified with a strong cup of tea, Sarah called Regency Academy, using the number listed on the school's Web site.

"Regency Academy, how may I direct your call?" asked a smooth, pleasant woman's voice.

"Hello, my name is Sarah Hart. I'm interested in finding a student who went to your school in 1963."

"Are you with a school board?"

"Uh ... no."

"Then I'm sure you understand we cannot give out student information," the woman replied.

"Is there any way I can write a letter to him and send it to you, and you can forward it to his family's address?"

"He attended school in what year, did you say?"

"Nineten sixty-three."

"I'm afraid that all school records from that long ago are in boxes in archival storage." The woman's tone didn't change at all, but Sarah got the impression she thought Sarah was a loony. "Even if you had authorization to contact an old student, it would take weeks before we'd be able to unearth his contact information. Is there anything else I can do for you?" Her tone seemed to imply that she didn't think there was, and she wanted to get off the phone.

"No. Thank you."

"Thank you for calling Regency Academy." *Click.*

Sarah scanned through the Regency Academy Web site again. How could she get Peter Bickham's family's address? She couldn't even be sure they still lived in the area, but there was a chance they did. Or perhaps if she found their old address, she could also find a forwarding address, or she could speak to the Bickhams' old neighbors.

Then she saw a tiny link at the top of a Web page: "Alumni members, click here to log in."

The alumni association, of course. They might even have the Bickhams' current address. She clicked on the link, which took her to a log-in page.

There were fields for alumni to enter a username and password to enter the secure, alumni-only section of the Web site, but beneath those fields was a link to e-mail the alumni coordinator about getting access. Sarah clicked the link and it took her to another page with fields to fill out.

She filled out her name and e-mail address, but skipped the field asking for year of graduation, and in the large "Comments" field, she typed:

To whom it may concern,

I am hoping to contact a Regency Academy alumnus, Peter Bickham, who attended this academy in 1963. He was a junior at the time, and he was on the debate team and the varsity basketball team.

If you are unable to give me his contact information, could you please forward my message to him? I am from Maple Hill and want to ask him about Fiona Hamill.

Thank you,

Sarah Hart

She clicked "submit," and that was that.

She hoped the alumni coordinator would at least e-mail her to let her know if she couldn't receive Peter's contact information or if her message couldn't be forwarded to him. It would be better than waiting and not knowing.

The next day, Sarah spent the entire morning poring over the quilt and the patch, then poring over Fiona's photos.

Having fresh eyes look at the quilt might help, so after a quick lunch of a ham and cheese sandwich, she carefully folded the quilt up, put it in a sturdy plastic storage box, and put it in her car. She headed into downtown Maple Hill to visit Vanessa at Wild Goose Chase.

Sarah entered the store, greeted by the flock of Canada geese painted along the walls, but then realized her mistake. The store was full of people, and the last thing she wanted was for someone to see the names on the back of the quilt.

She waited for Vanessa to finish with a customer, then beckoned her closer.

"You're being secretive," Vanessa said. "What's up?"

"I have a quilt that I want to show you, but I don't want anyone else to see it."

"Hmm, then the fabric cutting table is out. We could try my office, though my desk is rather small."

"I think it'll be fine. Lead the way."

Vanessa gave some instructions to her assistant, then led Sarah to the back of the store and to a tiny office. The desk was relatively clear except for a few papers which Vanessa swept into a drawer.

When Sarah opened up the quilt, Vanessa caught her breath. "That's magnificent," she breathed. She leaned in to look closely at the quilting. "Those stitches! The piecing! The color scheme!"

Sarah smiled at her excitement.

Vanessa noticed the amateur stitching in the quilted arcs in the melons immediately. "Done by at least one other person," she murmured.

When Vanessa had had her fill of the front, Sarah flipped it over and braced herself for Vanessa's gasp of shock at seeing Liam's name. Sarah explained everything she had learned about Fiona and Liam.

Vanessa peered at the names with her dark brows knit. "I'm completely clueless about this, Sarah. I have to admit I haven't worked with many vintage wedding quilts, though. That's your area of expertise. The quilts I work with tend to be newly made."

Sarah sighed. "I was hoping you might see something I missed."

Vanessa laughed. "Unlikely. You have a fantastic eye for detail."

Vanessa couldn't take too much time looking over the quilt since she had customers in the store, but it was with reluctance that she allowed Sarah to fold it up again and stow it away. "If you find out anything more about the quilt, let me know," she said to Sarah before heading back to the main area of the store to help some customers.

On the way back home, Sarah impulsively pulled into a parking spot in front of Magpie's Antiques.

The bell over the door jangled as she entered, and her eye fell on a new—or rather, very old—antique mirror, a new item Maggie must have just set out.

From the register, Maggie looked up and smiled. "Hi, Sarah."

"I just came by to say hello. I'm on my way back from Wild Goose Chase."

"Grandma!" The twins came running into the front area of the store from Maggie's office in the back.

"Hey, did you finish your homework?" Maggie asked.

"We'll finish it," Amy promised, "but Grandma doesn't come into the store all the time."

"And we want to spend time with Grandma," Audrey said.

Maggie tried to give them a stern look, but it was marred by the smile twitching at her mouth.

"Anything interesting happen at school today?" Sarah asked them, and the twins immediately launched into a long-winded tale involving Pam, who was passing a note to Brita, who was trying to pass a note to Pru, who was *not* passing notes, but who got caught when Brita threw the note onto her desk.

"And, of course, you two weren't passing notes?" Sarah asked them.

"Of course not," Audrey said.

Maggie said in an aside to Sarah, "They've been extra good since they got their phones confiscated for texting in class."

"Mom, that was last year," Amy said.

"That was in May," Maggie said.

"It was last *school* year," Audrey said. "We don't do stuff like that anymore."

"Oh. Of course," Maggie replied.

Sarah's cell phone rang and she set her bag on the counter to rummage for it. The phone had fallen to the bottom of the bag, and she took out her wallet, a packet of tissues, and Fiona's photos before finally finding it. It was Martha. "Hello?"

"I got a call from Mrs. Bitty. She's feeling better and wants to know if we can come over for coffee sometime next week. How about Tuesday?"

"Next Tuesday, I'm picking up the twins from school and taking them to Bradford Manor," Sarah said with a sidelong look at them.

"Do we have to?" Amy asked.

"Hey," Maggie said, "we agreed it was important for us all to help Grandma with this."

Amy bit her bottom lip. "I know. It's just that Mr. Mercer is kinda mean."

Audrey nodded solemnly.

Sarah knew it was hard on them, dealing with Leland and also going through their great-grandfather's things, which made them miss him even more. "Well..."

"No, Sarah," Maggie said. "They'll go with you on Tuesday."

"Tuesday's out," Sarah told Martha.

"How about Wednesday, then?" Martha asked.

"That sounds good."

"I'll pick you up at ten."

"I'll make cranberry orange bread to take to her," Sarah said.

"Mmm, perfect. See you then."

Amy started idly flipping through the photos Sarah had put on the counter.

"Amy, you should ask Grandma before you look through those," Maggie said.

"Oh, sorry. Is it okay, Grandma?"

"Of course. They're from the late sixties."

"Wow, they're ancient," Audrey said as she looked through them.

Maggie pursed her lips to keep from laughing as Sarah gave the twins an exasperated look they didn't see.

"I think I know this swing." Amy pointed to the photo of the large oak tree with the elaborately carved swing. "The tree looks a little different, but the swing is the same."

"Are you sure?" Sarah asked. "Mrs. Bitty said that swing was on the Hamill estate."

"Amy, were you trespassing on private property?" Maggie asked.

"He let us in," Amy protested. "That's not trespassing."

"Who?"

"The gardener."

"At first we were just on the other side of the fence looking at it," Audrey said. "Then this guy in overalls came by and asked us if we wanted to play on it. He unlocked the gate for us so we could go in."

"Who's 'we'?" Maggie asked at the same time Sarah had her own question.

"He unlocked it?" Sarah asked. "Then he must be part of the estate staff, if he had a key."

"So we weren't trespassing, if he said it was okay," Amy said.

"We were with Pru and Lexie and Trina," Audrey answered her mother. "Near Pru's house."

"Colin and Mandy's house?"

Amy and Audrey nodded. "The fence is a little ways down the road from them," Amy said.

"And we only played on the swing, we didn't go beyond the woods or see the house."

"When was this?" Sarah asked.

"This past summer."

Prudence's parents, Colin and Mandy Maplethorpe, lived in a large, ranch-style home on the edge of Maple Hill, with lots of land for Mandy's horses. She trained horses and gave riding lessons, although she'd had to go on hiatus for a few months when she was pregnant, but after the baby was born this spring, she had taken up the reins again, so to speak.

The Maplethorpes' house was on a lonely stretch of road. It shouldn't be difficult to find a large estate on that road if Sarah could look at a map of Maple Hill.

"Well, you should get back to your homework," Sarah told the twins. "I'm going to do some homework too. I'm going to the library."

"Your homework is probably more interesting than ours," Audrey said.

Sarah thought back to the pages and pages of newspapers she had searched through. "Not always," she said.

The library was only a few blocks away from Maggie's store, so Sarah walked. The wind was a bit gusty, but not as strong as it had been yesterday, and there was a bit more sunlight filtering through the clouds today. Still, she was glad for the shelter of the library building.

Spencer Hewitt was helping Evie Gibbons, a little girl who went to Sarah's church. "I just got a new crocodile book," Spencer told Evie. "Do you want to see it?"

Evie rolled her eyes. "Crocodiles are so last year." The teenage words coming from her seven-year-old mouth made Sarah's lips twitch into a smile. "Now I'm into wolves."

"Well, I have just the book for you." Spencer winked at Sarah over Evie's head and led the way to the juvenile section. He returned a few minutes later alone. "She is happily captivated by *Lon Po Po*," he said. "How can I help you, Sarah?"

"I'd like to look at a map of Maple Hill," she said. "I think I know where the Hamill estate is."

"Wasn't that the name you looked up in the phone books?" Spencer led her upstairs to the reference room again. "Are you looking for something on the estate?"

"No, I just want to see where they lived."

Spencer found a scroll in the corner of the reference room and unfurled it on the large desk outside the room. It showed a full-color map of Maple Hill.

Sarah pored over the map until she saw Colin and Mandy's plot of land on the north side of town. She ran her finger down their road and saw a large plot of land, which could be the Hamills' estate.

However, while other plots of land weren't named— Colin and Mandy's wasn't, although it was about half as large—this particular plot was labeled "Stifflemire Hall."

Sarah pointed to the plot of land. "Why is this plot labeled when the others aren't?"

Spencer squinted at the name, then started scanning the rest of the map. "Hmm. The only plots that are labeled like that are either historical landmarks, geographical land-marks, or ... no, wait. The Draper house is labeled."

"Well, that's a historical landmark," Sarah said. "Ben Draper founded Maple Hill."

"Here too," Spencer said, pointing. "Peters's Maple Grove."

"That's strange. It belongs to the Collins family now. They bought it in the thirties," Sarah said. "Is this map recent?"

"It was made in 2005," Spencer replied.

Sarah looked at the map closely. "Is it referring to the *original* Peters's maple grove?" Sarah guessed. "Maybe as a historical landmark? After all, the Peters family helped found Maple Hill."

"Here are a few others." Spencer pointed to another large plot of land on the west edge of Maple Hill. "Woltherstorf Estate."

"I know that the Woltherstorfs are an old Maple Hill fam-ily," Sarah said. "They were one of the first families to set-tle here after the Drapers and Peters families. Maybe the Stifflemires did the same, and the map is simply pointing out original estates."

"In that case," Spencer said, "you can find out more about Stifflemire Hall at the historical society."

"You're right," Sarah said, and headed down the street to the Maple Hill Historical Society.

The sign hanging from one of the front porch columns, *Maple Hill, Incorporated 1786,* was swinging in the wind.

Sarah stepped around the old-fashioned hitching post out front and hurried up to the porch.

The "Closed" sign was in the window, but Sarah could see Irene Stuart, the historian, standing behind the counter, paging through a book. Sarah knocked on the door, and when Irene saw who it was, she smiled and came to let Sarah inside.

"Only for you, Sarah Hart, and only because you look like you need to find some information urgently."

The pine plank floor squeaked as she stepped inside. "I'm sorry to pull you away from your book."

"I'm just spending a little time with General Custer," Irene said, nodding at the open pages. "I'm sorry my contact at *New England Sunrises* didn't work out."

"That's not your fault. In fact, it was very intriguing because he was supposed to have worked there. But now I have another fact-finding hunt for you."

"Oh goody. It's got to be easier than trying to explain to the third graders who were here today why they can't make Indian arrowheads for themselves." Irene laughed.

"I hope so. I'm looking for information about Stifflemire Hall."

Irene's brown eyes gleamed. "Haven't thought about that place for a while. The Stifflemires were one of the first families in Maple Hill."

"Does the historical society have anything about the estate?" Sarah asked. "I'd like to know if the Stifflemires still live there or if someone else bought the house." Like the Hamills. Although Mrs. Bitty had said all the servants were laid off after Fiona disappeared, indicating the estate had probably been sold. It might be another dead end.

Irene twirled her charm bracelet as she stopped to think. "If memory serves me right, it was sold to someone, but I can't recall to whom or when. Let's check." Coming out from behind the counter, she skirted a display table filled with old homestead cooking utensils and headed toward the back area of the building. She zeroed in on a filing cabinet and pulled out a drawer. "Stifflemire..." she murmured to herself as she fingered through the files. "Ah ha!" She pulled out a manila folder and handed it to Sarah.

Inside was a photocopy of a plat map, showing the Stifflemire land. There was also an old photograph of the original hall, which had been built in the Edwardian style. On the back, the photo was dated "1940."

"The Hall was built before that," Irene said, "probably in the early 1920s."

A newspaper article had been clipped and slipped into the folder.

Stifflemire Hall Sold
Maurice Stifflemire held a press conference today to announce that he had sold his ancestral home to Robert Hamill, owner of Hamill Shipping.

"Much as we love Maple Hill, the Stifflemire estate simply cannot continue the upkeep of the house and grounds,"

Stifflemire said. "Since the majority of our investments are in New Hampshire, and as the bulk of the family lives there, the heads of the family decided to sell the estate here in Massachusetts so that another owner can enjoy its beauty and give it the care and love it deserves."

Robert Hamill is CEO of Hamill Shipping, a successful shipping company in Boston. Mr. Hamill indicated that while he will be splitting his time between Boston and Maple Hill, his family will be enjoying the town's hospitality, and he hopes Maple Hill will welcome them with open arms.

Stifflemire Hall and its extensive grounds encompass fifty acres on the north side of town, just outside of Maple Hill. Stifflemire Hall was built in 1927 by Agnus Stifflemire for his bride Laura, who was a cousin of Ben Draper, the founder of Maple Hill. The Stifflemires raised sheep for many years, but the declining market forced them to invest in other businesses, namely, industries in New Hampshire. They sold the last of their sheep in 1956 and moved to New Hampshire, and Stifflemire Hall has stood empty for the past seven years.

So the estate near Colin and Mandy Maplethorpe had indeed been owned by the Hamills. But there was nothing else in the folder, and no information about who owned the Hamills' home now that they were gone. Speaking of which...

Sarah interrupted Irene's perusal of the newspaper article to ask, "Irene, would you have the obituaries for Robert and Clarissa Hamill?"

Irene put the article back in the folder. "Do you know the dates they died?"

"They both died in that Mountain Pearl Train crash." She tried to remember the date she had read in the Internet articles. "Nineteen eighty, I think."

Irene went to a shelf that held several leather-bound volumes. She had continued the practice of previous Maple Hill historians of cutting obituaries from the newspaper and consolidating them in books, but she had added the precaution of storing them in special archival-quality volumes.

"These aren't indexed yet," Irene said. "Chris said he's working on a program that would let us scan obituaries with a digital scanner that would automatically download information onto a database, but it's got a few bugs." Irene's husband Chris loved history as much as Irene, but he was also very tech-savvy.

She pulled out a volume and flipped through the pages, finally stopping at the obituary she was looking for.

Hamill, Robert and Clarissa
Tragically killed in the Mountain Pearl Train Company accident on Oberon Pass near Linx, Massachusetts. Robert Hamill was CEO of Hamill Shipping, headquartered in Boston. Clarissa Woltherstorf Hamill was the great-granddaughter of Ignatius Woltherstorf, patriarch of one of Maple Hill's first families, and cousin to Eugenia Woltherstorf Collins. Survived by

daughter, Fiona Hamill, who went missing in 1970. No memorial service.

"What an uninspiring obituary," Irene remarked, reading over Sarah's shoulder.

"Well, if there wasn't any family left to write it, I suppose the newspaper editor had to do it," Sarah said. She handed the book back to Irene. "Thanks."

"Do you need anything else?"

"Is that all you have on the Stifflemire estate? I wonder who owns the Hamills' home now."

"No, everything on the estate would be in that folder." Irene nodded at the folder in Sarah's hands. "I'm afraid you'll have to visit the courthouse for that information."

"You wouldn't by any chance have anything else on the Hamills?"

Irene shook her head. "You know me, I'm not really up to speed on anything in this town after 1950. If the Hamills came in the sixties, I doubt we'd have a file on them. I know I didn't make one."

Sarah handed the Stifflemire Hall folder back to her. "That's okay. I got the information I wanted, anyway. I wonder if I could go see the estate. Since it's a historical landmark, maybe the owners will let me take a tour."

"I haven't heard of any tours of the house," Irene said. "Shame, really."

As Sarah left, she found herself absorbed in thought. She might not be able to get a tour of the house, but could she, like her granddaughters, be let into the grounds by a kind gardener?

Time to find out.

The visit might not unearth any clues about Fiona's disappearance, but Sarah was eager to see even a little of the estate and imagine what it was like for her to grow up there. It would bring Sarah just a little bit closer to Fiona.

CHAPTER TEN

Sarah felt a bit like a thirteen-year-old herself as she followed her granddaughters down the country lane toward the Hamill estate. The point where the Maplethorpes' land ended and the Stifflemire land started was obvious. The Maplethorpes' acres were bordered by a horse fence, but the Stifflemire grounds had an ancient hedge border that separated it from the lane and from the other property.

The twins left the lane and raced along the Maplethorpe-Stifflemire hedge toward the back of the estate grounds. The hedge seemed to go on forever, but then there was a break where a fence had been built. It was padlocked shut.

Sarah stood at the gate and peered into the estate grounds. Trees dotted the lawn, and where they stood at the gate, the clusters of oak trees opened into a large clearing.

Fiona's gnarled oak tree with the elaborately carved swing lay fifty yards ahead of them, but because of the other trees, they couldn't see the house.

"If you go around this way," Audrey said, leading them farther down the hedge, "you can see a little bit of the house."

Through a thinner portion of the hedge, Sarah could see a stately chimney and two steepled rooflines, but nothing else. They wandered back to the gate.

"I guess there's no one here today," Amy said. "Last time the gardener was mowing the grass right here."

"He probably doesn't mow very often in the fall, if at all," Sarah said.

The twins knew better than to ask if they could climb over the gate, and they headed back toward the lane.

As they reached the lane, a truck came rumbling down from the direction of the Stifflemire front gates.

Audrey's face lit up and she waved to the driver. "That's the gardener we met. That's Justin."

The truck slowed to a stop and the driver climbed out. He was several years younger than Sarah, with midnight-black hair peppered with white and warm brown eyes. "Back again, are ya? Let me see if I remember your names. Amy and Audrey, right?"

The twins grinned. "This is our grandma," Audrey said politely.

"Sarah Hart." She extended a hand to him, and he shook it. "I hope you'll forgive us. I wanted to see the Stifflemire estate."

"Would you like to see the house and grounds? I have my wife's keys."

"Would that be okay?"

"Sure. My wife takes care of the house and I take care of the grounds, but no one lives here now."

"Thanks. I'd love to."

Justin walked with them to the gate in the hedge and unlocked the padlock. He led the way through the trees to the lawn in front of the house.

The lawn was smooth and well manicured, so the twins were able to run around with abandon.

"Who owns the house now?" Sarah asked Justin.

"The Hamills."

She paused in her step. "They never sold the house? Who runs the estate?"

"The Hamill estate pays for me and my wife to take care of the house and grounds. My Aunt Jessie said that the house was for sale for several months after the Hamills died, but then the house was taken off the market."

"Maybe because they couldn't sell it?" Sarah guessed. "This must be one of the largest and most expensive houses in the area. But if the Hamills died, and their daughter is missing, who exactly owns the property now?"

"I think an executor handles a trust fund for the daughter," Justin said. "She was never declared dead."

Sarah was surprised no one had come forward to contest the trust and declare Fiona dead so he could claim the property. The house must be a terrific drain on the trust. It had to pay for a housekeeper and groundskeeper, but no one lived here.

Justin let Sarah and the girls into the house to look around, and so the girls could have a drink of water. While Edwardian in style on the outside, the house had been redecorated and remodeled on the inside to a state of pretentious modern extravagance. Sarah didn't care for the decorating. She had been expecting antique furniture and quiet elegance, not the garish colors of the modern art that the Hamills had chosen for their walls, or the sleek design of the black ebony dining room table, or the remodeled living room fireplace with glass insets in bright red marble.

Sarah didn't disturb many of the Holland covers, mostly because the furniture she could already see didn't appeal to her. The layout of the house was lovely and airy, and she wished she could have seen it when it had first been built, filled with Laura Stifflemire's furniture. She would hazard a guess that it fit with the house's Edwardian style much better than these modern pieces.

Audrey and Amy were getting bored, so Sarah let them go explore the grounds outside. Justin led her upstairs and she was able to look into Fiona's bedroom.

It had only been tidied up, for although the pale blue carpet was immaculately clean and clear of personal possessions, Sarah could see that the clothes were carelessly hung in the closet, and objects were haphazardly piled on the shelves above. When she idly opened a drawer at the vanity table, she saw spilled facial powder dusting the bottom and various bottles and jars and brushes. A typical room for a young woman in her early twenties, just out of her teen years.

A second closet was deeper and better organized, obviously Fiona's photography closet. The cameras were carefully laid out on one shelf, lenses on another. Various development papers and supplies were neatly put away in drawers and other smaller shelves against the walls, and photographs were stored in archive boxes with the subjects written on the outside in a quick hand: Ireland, Mount Greylock, Lake Como, Maui, Boston friends, etc. The boxes were stacked high on top of each other.

If Fiona had taken anything from the room, it was hard to tell. There weren't any obvious empty spots on the camera shelf, and there were so many boxes of photos, she could have taken ten boxes and it would be difficult to notice the missing ones.

"So sad," Justin said, shaking his grizzled head. "Everyone said the young lady was very nice."

"Do you remember when she disappeared?"

"I don't remember much. I was still in high school and up to lots of no good at the time. I didn't care much for anything besides what I was doing. I remember the adults saying it didn't look like she ran away, and after looking at this room, I tend to agree. It looks like my granddaughter's room after her mother has cleaned up after her," he joked.

Returning to the first floor, Sarah and Justin stood at the front door and looked out at the gardens. They were depressingly sparse. "I try to plant what I can, and I culti-vate the bulbs that are left," Justin said. "But I work here only one day a week, so sometimes I'm limited by how much time I've got left after taking care of the rest of the grounds."

"It's fifty acres, isn't it?" Sarah asked.

"I don't need to tend to all fifty," he said with a smile. "There're some fine woods taking up most of that space."

They found the twins playing near the oak tree and the swing. They'd apparently tired of the swing and were now climbing the sturdy branches.

"Be careful," Sarah warned them.

"We'll be fine, Grandm—" Audrey's foot slipped a little, but she caught herself by grabbing the trunk. She smiled back at Sarah sheepishly.

Amy had climbed higher than her sister, and she sud-denly called out, "Grandma!"

Sarah's heart kicked into high gear. "What is it? Are you all right?"

"Oh, I'm fine." Amy poked her head out from around the trunk. "Grandma, *I found something.*"

Intrigued by Amy's melodramatic tone, Sarah walked forward to see what it was.

Amy held out an old tin lunch box, pockmarked with rust. "It was hidden in this hole in the tree."

Sarah's heart beat fast again, this time with anticipation. "I wonder if it belonged to Fiona."

"I'll bring it down." Amy started climbing back down. Audrey got down ahead of her and took the lunch box while Amy got her feet back on terra firma.

They tried opening the lunch box, but it was so rusted that the lid wouldn't budge.

"I've got a screwdriver in the gardening shed," Justin said. "We should be able to pry it open with that."

They followed him to the shed and he wiggled the end of the flathead screwdriver under the edge of the lid. He levered it up and down a few times, and the lid finally popped open.

The rust sealing the box had perhaps protected the contents, for the inside surfaces were still relatively shiny. There was a large white handkerchief inside, wrapped around something the size of a postcard. Sarah took it out and unwrapped a photograph.

A young man stood next to Fiona, both of them smiling into the camera. Fiona's eyes were brilliant and her smile ecstatic—she looked young and carefree. Gone was the calm, quiet, and somewhat sad young woman Sarah had seen in the photo that had accompanied the *Maple Hill Monitor* article.

The couple stood to one side of a signpost that said "Lough Neagh." Ireland, Sarah thought. Wasn't that the lake Fiona had mentioned in her letter to Angela?

The young man looked terribly familiar, but she couldn't quite place him...

Then she realized it was *Liam*.

He had a light moustache and beard, which had made it hard for her to place him since he was clean shaven now, and his hair in the photo was a brighter red. He was more slender, his shoulders wide and bony, but he wore the same smile, charming and warm.

He had said he had met Fiona in Ireland during her year there. But why was this photo of them tucked away here in this box rather than in Fiona's box of Ireland photos in her room? Sarah turned the photo over.

"Fiona and Liam" was written on the back, and a heart had been drawn around the two names.

The air solidified in Sarah's lungs and she couldn't breathe for a moment. Then she let out a long, unsteady breath. The heart, the secret hiding place—

Had Liam and Fiona been in love? If so, why would he not admit it to her? Did his feelings for her have something to do with why she disappeared?

There was the rumor of a murder in Ireland...

Sarah pressed her lips together. She had to stop coming up with these wild scenarios.

But she knew that something about Fiona's disappearance had made Liam not answer her truthfully the last time they had spoken. What could it be?

Maybe they had been engaged and someone had put their names on the quilt after they announced the engagement. Then they could have broken their engagement, which might explain why Fiona's name was embroidered but Liam's wasn't. The quilter started embroidering the names, but stopped when the engagement was called off.

Mrs. Bitty had mentioned that she had seen Liam arguing with Fiona in the library only a few days before she disappeared. Had that been a lover's quarrel?

Sarah couldn't lie—the photo made her suspect Liam was somehow involved in Fiona's disappearance. But if he had loved her, why would he make her disappear?

Sarah realized she might never know the answer to that. And for Caitlin's sake, and her own, did she really *want* to know?

"I'm sorry to come by so early," Irene said, standing at Sarah's front door early the next morning, "but after you left yesterday, I found something that I think you might want to read."

At that intriguing statement, Sarah led the way into the kitchen. "You know you're welcome anytime, Irene. Can I get you coffee? Blueberry muffin?"

"Yes to both," Irene said.

Sarah poured her a cup and gestured to the basket of toasted muffins on the small breakfast table. "Help yourself."

Irene sat and asked, "Do you remember crazy Daisy Anderson?"

"Excuse me?"

"You know, everyone's favorite unofficial Maple Hill historian?"

The name sounded familiar to Sarah. "It was last year, wasn't it? Did Tim Wexler work on that project?"

"Yes. Daisy had boxes of notes she had taken on Maple Hill people and places, interviews she had done, and some newspaper articles she had cut out and filed away. When she died, her family donated her files to us. Tim finally organized all her files last fall and integrated them with our official historical society files."

Irene held up a manila file folder. "The newspaper article on Stifflemire Hall had sloppily cut edges, which is typical of Daisy's cutting style. It made me wonder if she might also have had a file on the Hamills."

"Was Daisy still around in the seventies?" Sarah asked.

"She died in the eighties, and she was still taking historical notes on the town. The only problem is that sometimes she had details on things that weren't very important, and then other more important events she ignored completely. As you'll see." Irene pushed the folder across the table at Sarah.

There was only one thing in the folder, a newspaper article with sloppily cut edges. It was a very tiny article, possibly from the Lifestyle section in the *Monitor*.

Hamills' Historical Artifacts Donated to Museum.
Robert Hamill, CEO of Hamill Shipping in Boston and owner of Stifflemire Hall, announced today that he had found

some historical artifacts in an old family trunk. The trunk had a false panel in the lid and inside were letters written to the Hamills from relatives in Ireland, circa 1899. Mr. Hamill has donated the items to the Irish Historical Museum in Boston.

"I know it isn't much. I had hoped Daisy might have some notes on Fiona's disappearance. Maybe handwritten notes of interviews she conducted with people. But this was it."

"It's still intriguing, even though it doesn't have anything to do with Fiona. If I could go see the letters, I would in a heartbeat." Sarah gave the folder back to Irene.

"I can actually help you out there," Irene said.

"Really?"

"I'll be in Boston for half of next week to do a consultation with a history professor at Boston College. I can stop by the Irish Historical Museum and see if they'll let me take pictures of the letters. That way you can read them if you want."

"I'd love that. If only to see what the Hamills' family was like. Thanks, Irene."

"It's no skin off my nose. You know I love looking at things like that." Irene finished off her muffin before asking Sarah if she had found anything new.

Sarah took a sip of coffee before answering, but she knew she could trust Irene's discretion. "You know I've been looking into Fiona Hamill's disappearance. She was rumored to be engaged to Roger Marstadt, heir to M&S Shipping in Boston. I looked Roger up on the Internet and called a research librarian in Concord to find one of his school yearbooks. He was on the junior varsity basketball team in his sophomore year."

Irene nodded and sipped her coffee.

"Guess who I saw in the varsity basketball team photo?" Sarah said.

Irene's eyes lit up. "Let me guess. Peter Bickham?"

Sarah nodded. "The reason I asked you to look up Peter is because he had been pursuing Fiona in the months before she disappeared."

Irene crumpled her napkin between her fingers as she thought through what Sarah had told her. "So Roger and Peter knew each other before they were rivals over Fiona."

Sarah nodded. "I spent some time trying to see if I could find a way to get the Bickhams' old address. I e-mailed the Alumni Coordinator, but I haven't heard back yet, and it's been almost two days."

"I have an idea." Irene said. "Want to come down to the historical society with me?"

"What do you have in mind?"

"I'll tell you on the way."

She actually didn't tell Sarah on the drive over, because extra strong gusts of wind caused Irene to concentrate on driving safely. They avoided a few downed tree branches and crept along carefully with the other drivers on the road.

They rushed inside the historical society building to avoid the cutting wind, but once indoors, Irene said, "I've personally dealt with several alumni associations. They're easier to deal with than the school administration, and they love it when I tell them I'm doing an article. If I need to contact someone, whether to interview them or to let them know something I've found about one of their ancestors, I've been able to chat up an alumni coordinator to get a person's contact information."

"You have? And they just give it to you?"

Irene grinned. "It's amazing what doors can open to you when you're a historian doing a paper. Schools like the publicity of being mentioned in an article—well, if the person being written about did something cool or interesting or important. If the person was a criminal..." She shrugged. "Not so much."

She moved behind the desk. "I wanted to use my phone here because if the school operator or the alumni coordinator has caller ID, the historical society name shows up."

That made sense. Sarah leaned against the counter.

Irene went to her computer and found the Regency Academy Web site, and she called the main number, putting her phone on speaker phone.

"Regency Academy, how may I direct your call?" It was the same smooth-voiced woman who had spoken to Sarah before, but somehow her voice seemed a little crisper, more respectful. Perhaps the academy *did* have caller ID and the identification "Maple Hill Historical Society" was according Irene a bit more respect than an ordinary person would get.

"This is Irene Stuart from the Maple Hill Historical Society." Irene's voice was also crisp and professionally polite. "Could you please put me through to your alumni coordinator?"

"May I ask what you're calling in regard to?" The question was asked a little more warily.

"Certainly. I'm working on a research paper and I've discovered that some Regency Academy alumni might have made significant contributions to historical research in Maple Hill."

"Oh. Regency Academy is thrilled you will be honoring our graduates," the operator cooed. "I'm afraid I can't put you through to the alumni coordinator, but I can give you her telephone number."

"That would be wonderful," Irene said in a honey-sweet voice. She got the telephone number and the name and hung up in triumph.

"Irene, you sly thing," Sarah said.

"I didn't lie to her. I would like to add these events to the file on the Stifflemire estate, and it'll make a nice paper someday."

Sarah couldn't help worrying that a paper on the events of 1970 would bring up Liam's connection to Fiona. She hoped not.

Irene called the alumni coordinator, who quickly gave her the number for the reunion organizers for the graduating year of 1964, Peter's year, and 1965, Roger's year. Irene never even had to mention Peter's and Roger's names.

They first called Shelley Gray, the organizer for Peter's graduating class. "Hello?" answered a friendly woman's voice.

"Hello, Mrs. Gray. My name is Irene Stuart, and I'm the historian at the Maple Hill Historical Society. I'm doing a paper on an alumnus from your graduating year and was hoping you could answer a few questions about the graduating class."

"Oh, certainly. Anything you need to know."

"Were you familiar with the varsity basketball team?"

"I was a cheerleader, so I went to every game."

Irene gave Sarah a silent thumbs-up. "How did they do that year?"

Mrs. Gray continued, "They worked so hard, but those poor boys just couldn't pull it together in the last quarter. They always seemed to run out of steam."

"Any notable players I should write about?"

"Well, they were all such nice boys—and some of them were so cute! That Peter Bickham was just to die for."

"Who was Peter Bickham?" Irene asked quickly. "What was he like?"

"Tall, with the most luscious wavy brown hair. Confident, killer smile and dark eyes. All the cheerleaders were swooning after him. He was a point guard, I think, in his senior year. We made up a special cheer for every time he made a basket. I think it was, 'Click the Bick! Points that stick!'"

With a confused expression, Irene mouthed to Sarah, *What does that mean?*

Sarah shrugged.

"After the games, he would always whip his towel at the cheerleaders. I have to admit, we didn't usually mind when he got us," Mrs. Gray tittered.

"Did he get along with all his teammates?" Irene asked.

"Oh, yes. Well..." Mrs. Gray hesitated. "He and Roger Marstadt were kind of stiff with each other, but after what happened between them, you really couldn't blame them."

Irene leaned closer to the phone. "What happened?"

Mrs. Gray's voice got lower as she said, "Well, I probably shouldn't tell you this, but in our senior year, Peter and Roger—he was a junior—both went after this girl from Queen's Academy. It's a girls' boarding school a mile away. She was such a flirt. She was encouraging both of them, although I think she favored Roger because he was from a wealthier family. She should have just cut Peter loose rather than stringing him along like that."

"So they were rivals in love?" Irene raised her eyebrows at Sarah.

"You could say that. But then a few weeks later, police came to the school and they pulled both Peter and Roger out of their classes—I know because I was in Peter's trig class when two officers came in and talked to the teacher and walked him out of the room, and one of my friends was in Roger's French class when they got him."

"Why did the police need to speak to them?"

"It was the strangest thing. That girl they'd both been pursuing? Elysa Quinton? She had disappeared."

CHAPTER ELEVEN

isappeared?" Martha paused as she flipped
through dresses on a clothing rack. "Just like
Fiona?"

"Well, perhaps not just like Fiona," Sarah said. "We don't
know what happened yet." She stopped to look at a dark blue
dress that might be good for the wedding, but the color was
a little too electric for her taste. She put it back on the rack.

"There wasn't anything in the newspaper about it?"
Martha pulled out a beige colored dress, held it out toward
Sarah, then shook her head and put it back on the rack.

"Irene's using her contacts to see if there was an article
in one of the Boston newspapers at the time," Sarah said.
"And I've been searching on the Internet and I also went to
the library, but no luck. Boston's such a large city that the
disappearance might not have been newsworthy enough to
have been written about."

"What a coincidence," Martha said. "Do you think the
two disappearances are related?"

"I don't know."

"Well, I'll tell you what I think. Two girls, both pursued by the same two men, both disappearing—I think it's some crazy woman who's in love with both Peter and Roger, and she gets rid of anyone they like."

Sarah laughed. "But what about Roger's wife? She's still alive."

"Are you sure?" Martha asked mysteriously.

Sarah laughed.

"Well, you have to admit, it's an interesting theory." Martha said.

"You may not necessarily be wrong," Sarah said. "It could be a woman obsessed with Peter, who gets rid of anyone he likes. Roger's being engaged to Fiona might have been just a coincidence. Peter was also pursuing her."

"That would be a good mystery novel." Martha smiled. "Did you get Peter's address like you hoped?"

"No, Mrs. Gray said that after the first couple of years, the alumni association mailings came back with 'return to sender, no longer at this address' on the envelope."

"That's too bad. What're you going to do next?"

"Mrs. Bitty said Fiona liked buying jewelry, so I thought I'd talk to Les McLean to see if he knew anything interesting about Fiona. I don't really have any other leads."

"Well, that sounds like a good idea. Mrs. Bitty seemed to know a lot about her, and she was just a maid in the house." Martha held up a dark green dress. "How about this?"

The dress was in the simple style Sarah preferred, but something about it just didn't excite her. "It's okay."

"Just okay?"

"It's nice, but…" Sarah gave a shrug. "I was hoping to find something that really stands out. I'd like Liam to perk up and take notice when he sees me."

Sarah had told Martha about her uncomfortable telephone conversation with Liam and also about the photo of Liam and Fiona with the heart drawn around their names.

"Have you talked to Liam recently?" Martha asked gently. She understood how Sarah felt conflicted, wanting to dress up for Liam, but still suspecting he had lied.

"I thought about calling him, but something made me hold back." She had also not answered a call he had made to her a few days ago. "I just want to find out more about this before I talk to him again. I feel like I need to understand the situation before I try to get him to open up."

"He might have legitimate reasons for not being forthcoming about this," Martha said.

"I'm starting to realize that. It must be something very painful for him to feel that he can't confide in me. That's why I want to understand everything better so that I can tread lightly when I speak to him next."

"That seems wise." Martha studied Sarah's face, then said, "Is that what's bothering you? I can tell you're down today."

Sarah sighed. "It's just…I woke up this morning really missing Dad, but I had already arranged with Jason to go to

Bradford Manor today to pick up more of Dad's things. He rearranged his schedule so he could help me, so I can't really back out of it."

"Oh, Sarah." Martha reached over and hugged her.

"Going there is so hard. I see Tiffany Henderson, and I immediately think she's going to tell my dad I'm there."

"It'll get better. You know that."

"I do know that, but today, could you pray for me?"

"I'd be honored to."

They both bowed their heads right then and there.

"Lord," Martha prayed, "please put your comforting arms around my dear sister in Christ, Sarah. She's missing her father today and we thank you for the love she has for him, and the love William had for her. Help her now to rely on her Heavenly Father and be comforted by the fact that her earthly one is safe in your arms. Please give her strength as she goes to Bradford Manor today with her son. Oh, and Lord," Martha added with a sharper tone, "will you please get that Leland man to give Sarah her father's quilt back? It's so rude of him to keep it like that."

Sarah had to bite back a smile at Martha's exasperation.

"Well," Martha continued, "I suppose you love him too. All these things we pray in Jesus's name. Amen."

"Amen," Sarah said. "Thanks, Martha."

"You can thank me when you get that quilt back," Martha said. "If you want, I can go there and wrest it away from him for you."

Sarah smiled. "I don't think you'll need to get violent."

"You never know," Martha said darkly. "Some of those old men can get kind of feisty."

As Sarah and Jason entered Bradford Manor, she couldn't help glancing around to see if Leland was there. Luckily, he wasn't in sight as they passed through the front common room.

"You look like you're trying to avoid someone, Mom." Jason had a teasing glint in his eye.

They headed down the hall toward her father's room. "Oh, no, I'm not—" Sarah began to say, but then suddenly a door they had just passed was flung open. Sarah saw only a blur before a man grabbed at Jason's arm.

"Douglas?"

Jason stiffened in surprise and turned toward the man. It was at that moment that Sarah saw it was Leland.

His face wasn't openly emotional, but somehow he seemed vulnerable. As Leland got a good look at Jason, his cheeks drained of color and he snatched his hand from Jason's arm. "Of course you're not Douglas." His voice was gruff and vibrated down the echoing hallway. "I don't know what I was thinking."

"Was Douglas your son?" Jason asked before Sarah could make an excuse and lead him away.

Leland didn't answer right away, his expression closed once more, and Sarah held her breath. But there was a haunted edge to his eyes, and he slowly nodded. "Yes."

"I'm Jason." He extended his hand.

Leland wasn't outright rude, but he was slow to shake Jason's hand. "Leland. I heard your voice and thought..." He turned his face away. "I'm just getting old, I suppose." He turned to head back into his room, but he stumbled. Sarah realized Leland had rushed out of his room without his walker.

"Here, let me help you." Jason took a firm hold of Leland's arm and helped him walk back into his room.

Sarah followed, feeling like she was on pins and needles because she hadn't told Jason about how Leland had acted with her and the twins on their last visit. Had the girls told their father about Leland? Jason tended to be friendly and helpful with everyone, but did he know Leland was likely to tell him to get out of his room rather than thank him?

Leland's bedroom was jam-packed with things. Jason helped him maneuver around a large old-fashioned sea chest and a stack of books on the floor until Leland could ease into a chair by the window.

"Thanks," Leland mumbled, his mouth pulled into a slight frown.

Jason nodded and pivoted to exit the room when his eye fell on a fishing rod propped up against the window sill. "Nice rod. Daiwa?"

Leland blinked at Jason's comment, and his gaze fell on the sleek rod. Then he said, "Yes. Graphite, titanium-frame SiC guides, machined-aluminum fore-nut..." He went on listing things Sarah was completely clueless about, but Jason nodded appreciatively.

"That's a premium rod," Jason said. "You must be pretty good."

The compliment made Leland turn his stare out the window, but he replied, "I'm serious about fishing. Whether I'm good or not depends on the catch of the day."

"My dad used to take me and my sister camping every summer, usually to Mount Greylock. We'd always take at least one day and drive out to this one mountain lake to go fishing. Mom, do you remember it?"

Jason's question startled her a little, and she had to clear her throat before she replied. "Yes, Lake Questor. It's the same lake your Grandpa William took me and my brother to go fishing." She could picture the glassy surface, the ring of trees all around the edges, shutting out the rest of the world.

"Questor." Leland's voice was suddenly gruff. "William and I went there all the time for fishing."

Sarah stared at him. "You did?"

He glanced up at her, then looked away. He hesitated. He finally said, "It was always so cold I thought my toes would freeze off."

Jason laughed. "I'd forgotten about the cold. I'd move around to keep warm, and Dad would tell me I was scaring away all the fish. Jenna always did catch more than me."

"Drayton women are just good fishers," Sarah said. "I caught a largemouth bass at Lake Questor, and my brother was completely jealous."

A rusty laugh erupted from Leland's throat. At first, Sarah didn't know where the sound was coming from—then she realized Leland's face had softened into a smile.

"William always had a hard time catching largemouth bass at that lake," Leland said. "It drove him crazy. Good for you."

Sarah thought back to that day. "Now that explains why Dad looked so dumbfounded when I landed it. It was a good six or seven pounds."

Jason gave a gleeful chuckle. "Did you take your son fishing?" he asked Leland.

The old man abruptly clammed up—his eyes narrowed, his mouth closed, even his nostrils tightened. There was a stiff silence, then he said in a taut voice, "Sometimes. Thank you for helping me to my room, but don't let me keep you."

Jason took his sudden mood swing in stride. "Nice to meet you, Leland. I need to hurry off, anyway. Have a good day."

Leland nodded in his direction but didn't quite meet his eyes.

Sarah thought about bringing up her dad's quilt again, but considering Leland was in a nice enough frame of mind to be polite to Jason, she didn't want to spoil the moment. "Goodbye, Leland." She headed out the door and Jason closed it behind him.

When they got to William's old room, Jason remarked, "He's a little odd."

"He was more open today."

"He reminds me of someone, but I can't figure out who."

Sarah looked at him with raised eyebrows. "Have you met Leland before?"

"No, I'm positive I haven't. Something about his manner just reminds me of someone I talked to recently. Maybe a client." He shrugged. "I guess it'll come to me."

"Is that client distant, rude, and prickly?" The words were tart, and Sarah regretted them as soon as they were out of her mouth. "I'm sorry, that was rude of me."

Light dawned on Jason's face. "Is he the one the twins were talking about?"

"Yes."

"Hmm. He seems nicer than the girls made him out to be."

"Maybe because he thought at first you were his son." The look on Leland's face when he had first grabbed at Jason's arm passed in front of Sarah's eyes, and the memory gave her a slight pang.

Leland made her uncomfortable. And she didn't want to be uncomfortable because her father's death already made her feel unsteady. She wanted to get past this feeling of grief and find a safe, happier place. She didn't want to deal with Leland's remembrances of her father tempered by the occasional cold shoulder that threw her off balance.

"You didn't ask him about the quilt," Jason said as he knelt in front of her father's bookshelf. He started taking books out and stacking them.

"I'll do it next time," Sarah said.

She would get her father's quilt back, and then she wouldn't have to interact with Leland again.

The next day, Sarah drove into downtown Maple Hill and parked outside of McLean Jewelers. Aiden McLean was with a customer, a young woman looking at men's watches, and he gave Sarah a friendly nod and said, "I'll be right with you."

"I'm in no hurry," she told him, and browsed around the shop, looking at the lovely pieces in the glass cases.

The décor remained the same as it had been since Les McLean had first opened the store several decades before. Gleaming wood-paneled walls, a colorful marble tile floor, and the glass top cases boasting smooth oak edges rather than steel. While one case had some traditional pieces of jewelry, the others showed pieces with a more modern flair from new European designers. Sarah saw a bracelet with a retro design, the colorful enamel links shaped like scrolls in a paisley pattern. Maggie loved paisley—she took special care of her blue paisley Vera Bradley bag—and Sarah wondered if she would like this bracelet. She had forgotten to suggest to Jason that he visit McLean Jewelers for Maggie's Christmas gift. She made a mental note to remember to do so later.

The woman finally chose the watch she wanted, and Aiden rang it up and boxed the watch for her. She smiled in a friendly way to Sarah as she walked out of the store, apparently well satisfied with her purchase.

"How can I help you?" Aiden asked her.

"I have a rather unusual request," Sarah said. "I'd like to speak to your grandfather Les McLean."

Aiden's brow wrinkled. "Are you dissatisfied with anything he sold to you, or do you have a question about something from the shop?"

"Oh no, nothing like that," Sarah hastened to assure him. She pulled the photo out of her purse. "I'm wondering if he might possibly remember selling this piece of jewelry to this girl." She pointed to the delicate necklace. "If he did, then I wanted to ask him if he knew anything about her, or maybe if he remembered any town gossip about her disappearance forty years ago."

"Oh, I see," Aiden said. He looked a bit relieved that Sarah hadn't come to complain about a piece of jewelry. "You're in luck. Grandpa's at the store today. I'll get him." He entered a door at the back of the store and returned a minute later with Les McLean.

Sarah remembered coming in with Gerry to look at wedding bands after he had proposed to her. Les had been patient, helpful, and had seemed genuinely happy for them. He had remembered Gerry because he had come in earlier to pick out Sarah's engagement ring.

The years had been kind to Les—his hair was whiter and wispier now, and there was a lot less of it, but he still had the kind blue eyes that had welcomed Sarah to his store.

Les's tastes ran to old-fashioned settings, so his store had seen a gradual decline over the past several years. Maple Hill had slowly become a popular place for young families to settle, and the younger generation favored the more modern jewelry they could find in Concord and Pittsfield.

But Sarah hoped that Fiona's necklace, which was definitely an old-fashioned piece, would help him remember her disappearance. Right now, it was the only lead she really had.

"I remember you," Les said to Sarah with a smile. He reached out to grasp her left hand and studied her wedding band. She had stopped wearing her engagement ring a few years ago but hadn't yet been able to leave her wedding band off.

"Yes, you and your fiancé came in to buy wedding bands, I remember. Such a lovely couple, you were. How is he?"

Sarah returned his gentle smile. "He passed away six years ago, I'm afraid."

"I'm so sorry to hear that. He spent so long picking out just the right engagement ring for you. I suggested the design he chose, the oval-cut diamond with the little bagettes on the two ends."

What an amazing memory. He had described her engagement ring exactly. And what a wonderful little thing to know about Gerry. "Thank you for suggesting it. I love my ring."

"Aiden says you wanted to ask me something about an old necklace?"

She showed him the picture of Fiona and Frank, since the necklace was clearer in this photo. "Do you remember selling this piece to this girl?"

Les shook his head. "I didn't sell that necklace to this girl. I sold it to the fella." He pointed to Frank Shields.

"It must have been very expensive." From what Mrs. Bitty had said about Frank, she was surprised he could afford a piece of jewelry like that.

"It was," Les said grimly, "and at the time, I almost didn't sell it to him, because I didn't know where he'd gotten the money for it. Paid in cash. But he seemed pretty eager and in love. I'm a sucker for couples in love. But he came back a few days later, angry because the necklace was too long. So I sent him to Wayne Lessman."

"I know his wife Julie," Sarah said. "They go to my church."

"Wayne used to do metalwork, before his rheumatoid arthritis set in. I contracted him to do a lot of our resizing orders. I was tired of dealing with this guy"—Les nodded at Frank's photo—"so I sent him to Wayne directly."

"Do you happen to remember when you sold it to him?"

"Oh, a year or two before this girl disappeared." He pointed to Fiona.

"I heard she was fond of jewelry. Did you know her well?"

"Pretty girl. A bit quiet, but nice and polite. Back then, it was getting harder to find a nice, polite young lady."

Certainly the late sixties, early seventies had been a time of transition—the rise and fall of the hippie era, the growth of feminism, the panic of the 1973 oil crisis, the lengthening Vietnam War. Sarah remembered her own sense of wonderment at the time at how the social, economic, and political atmosphere had been changing.

"What do you remember about when she disappeared?" Sarah asked.

Les hesitated, as if he had intended to say something, but then changed his mind. "It was a real tragedy," he said. "Pretty mysterious too. No signs anyone broke into her room, but she hadn't taken anything with her, either, so it didn't look like she'd run away."

"What were people saying about it?"

Les laughed. "Lots of speculation." He waved his hand. "Most of it nonsense."

"Do you happen to remember what the police did to try to find her?"

A spasm of emotion crossed his face. "Not enough," he finally said slowly.

"What do you mean?"

He hesitated again, as if weighing his words. Then he leaned closer to her, resting his weight on the glass case. "There was a fella she was hanging out with. Peter something, I don't remember his last name anymore."

"Peter Bickham," Sarah said.

"That's it. He was in town a few months, I think. Well, one day about a week before she went missing, Peter came into my shop and bought an engagement ring."

Sarah gasped. "Are you sure it was him?"

"As sure as I remember your husband picking out yours. He was…" Les sighed, "he was so in love."

"With Fiona," Sarah breathed. "I can't believe it. He proposed to her."

"But she wouldn't have him," Les said.

"What?"

"He came back a few days later, asked if I'd buy the ring back. It had been quite a stunner, a marquise-cut diamond, three baguettes on each side." Les scratched the back of his neck. "I bought it back from him."

"Grandpa," Aiden protested. "You just lectured me on not doing that."

"I couldn't help it, I just felt so sorry for the guy. He looked like someone had run over his puppy." He added to his grandson, "And I did buy it back at a lower price than I sold it to him. I also knew I could sell it to old Mrs. Woltherstorf because she had just come in the day before looking for something to match her necklace with the marquise-cut diamonds, and while she was one of the wealthiest women in the county, she was also a skinflint. When I offered it at a sale price, she snatched it up faster than a pickpocket."

"Are you certain it was Fiona that Peter proposed to?" Sarah asked.

Les nodded. "Everyone knew how he was dangling after her. It was more obvious than the nose on your face. And then she disappeared," he added in a dark voice.

"What do you mean?"

"I told the police about the engagement ring. I actually closed up shop and went down to the police department and demanded to see someone about that girl's disappearance. And I told the detective about this Peter fella and the ring. The detective took down my statement, but in a kind of careless way, as if he didn't believe me." Les glowered. "So I went back a different day and got in to see the police chief, and I told him. The bugger didn't even bother to take notes. Just brushed me off with promises to look into it."

He stared intently at Sarah. "But I knew the B and B where Peter was staying—I was friends with the owner. And she said that the police never came to the B and B after that girl went missing." He shook his head. "I'm telling you, the police had every reason to question this guy about this girl, but they never did."

CHAPTER TWELVE

Sarah decided it was time to give former Police Chief Dale Wexler a ring.

"Hello, Sarah," he greeted her when he answered his phone. "Nice to hear from you. What've you been up to? Find any more missing women?"

He said it jokingly since she had found his old friend Debby Neely a few months ago, but the question made her hesitate because of the *other* missing woman most recently in her thoughts.

"Sarah?" Dale asked when she didn't respond. "Are you saying you're looking for another missing girl?"

"Uh...sort of. Do you have time to meet me for coffee this afternoon?"

"Now I'm intrigued," Dale said with good humor, "as long as I'm not someone on your suspect list."

"No, of course not. The Spotted Dog?"

"I'll meet you there in half an hour."

Since Sarah was already in downtown Maple Hill, she whiled away the time at a table near the window. The lunch crowd had dispersed and the only people there were Sarah, a few young mothers with their strollers, gabbing over their lattes and cappuccinos, and a college-age student in the back working furiously on his laptop computer.

Dale arrived a little early, his tall figure still erect and solid from his years as a police officer and then the Maple Hill chief of police. Chief Webber had taken over for him a few years before when Dale retired.

"Hello, Sarah." He greeted her with a buss on the cheek.

"What can I get you?" asked Karen Bancroft. When she had taken Sarah's order earlier, Sarah had noticed she looked distinctly more harried than she had the last time Sarah had been in the café. The longer hours and extra stress during Liam's absence seemed to be catching up with her.

"I'll just have a cup of coffee," Dale told Karen, "black."

"I'll be right back with that."

"What do you need to talk to me about?" Dale asked. "Something about a missing woman?"

"I recently came across a quilt with the name Fiona Hamill on it," Sarah said.

Dale's face turned grim. "I remember that. It was a bitter cold December too, so we searched to find her just in case she was lost somewhere in the woods behind her parents' house."

"What do you think happened to her?"

"I don't know what to think. No sign of forced entry, none of the guard dogs alerted, but she didn't take anything—no clothes, suitcases, duffel bags, or backpacks missing. I was a detective at the time—not in charge of the case, but we were all called in to help."

"Did you have any suspects?"

"Nothing substantial. The parents had alibis, the servants vouched for each other. At first we were looking at the chauffeur, an ex-junkie, but his brother came forward. He admitted he had been waiting for his older brother to return from driving the Hamills and the two of them talked for a couple of hours while the chauffeur was cleaning out the car."

"Roger Marstadt?"

Dale eyed her sharply. "Why don't you tell me what you know about him."

Sarah shrugged, hoping she looked innocent enough. "His company was a competitor with Hamill Shipping, and he was seen in Maple Hill often in the months before Fiona disappeared. And ..." She wondered if she should play this card, then decided to go for it. Dale wouldn't spread it around, and it might induce him to tell her more. "They were engaged. There were rumors it was part of a merger between the two companies that didn't happen when she went missing."

Dale shook his head. "How do you find the information you do?"

"It's not true?"

He sighed. "I suppose it doesn't matter anymore. Yes, it was true. At least, that's what one of the maids told us. The Hamills and the Marstadts refused to comment, saying that company business was highly confidential and we'd have to subpoena their lawyers. I could understand, because if word got out, it would have affected stock prices and someone could have made a killing. But the merger didn't go through after all, so I guess it didn't matter."

"The Hamills had an alibi for the night? I heard Mr. Hamill may not have been a very loving father."

"He wasn't, from what I heard, but his wife gave him an alibi for the night."

Was it true? Or was Clarissa Hamill simply obeying her husband?

"The Hamills were at a Christmas party until about midnight, and then they drove back to Maple Hill all the way from Boston. The chauffeur was up a couple of hours more, cleaning out the car and talking to his brother, but then he went to bed." Dale gave Sarah a look she couldn't interpret. "Mr. Hamill's wife said he didn't leave her side all night."

"Roger Marstadt had an alibi?"

"Watertight," Dale replied. "Both the younger and the older Mr. Marstadts were at a charity event in Boston and there were several photographers there. We saw them and Mrs. Marstadt too in candid shots that were taken from early in the evening up until the wee morning hours."

"And what about Peter Bickham?" Sarah held her breath.

"What about him?" Dale asked in a carefully neutral voice.

"He was pursuing Fiona at the time," Sarah said, "when she was possibly engaged to Roger. Do you think he might have been involved? A jealous quarrel?"

Dale sighed. "Let me guess. You talked to Les McLean, right?"

Sarah felt her cheeks start to burn.

"Sarah, your best qualities are that you're persistent and methodical, but you also have a tendency to give people more credit than you should. Even back then, Mr. McLean's memory wasn't the best."

But Les had remembered her engagement ring and the wedding bands. Sarah kept silent.

"He might have thought the man who bought that engagement ring and then returned it was Peter, but it wasn't. It must have been someone else who looked a bit like Peter."

Sarah noticed that Dale was calling him Peter and not Mr. Bickham. In contrast, he had referred to Mr. Marstadt and Mr. Hamill when speaking about the other two men. Curious. "Did you speak to Peter about it?" Sarah asked.

"I didn't, but the detective in charge did."

"And he had an alibi?"

"Yes. Sarah, you're barking up the wrong tree. Peter didn't have anything to do with Miss Hamill's disappearance. The only problem is we don't know who did."

There was something odd about the way Dale spoke about Peter—not just calling him by his first name, but his certainty about Peter's innocence.

"So there's nothing else you can tell me about Peter Bickham?" Sarah asked.

"Nothing. But if you find something that has to do with anything else in the case, be sure to tell me." He gave her a tight smile.

"Of course I will."

"Now, tell me how those rascally granddaughters of yours are doing." His smile this time was warmer and more genuine.

They chatted easily for another twenty minutes, and then Dale excused himself to go pick up his grandsons and play some basketball with them. "They like the fact that I'm old enough that they can beat me," he groused good-naturedly, and then said his good-byes before leaving the café.

Sarah stayed in her seat awhile longer, thinking about what Dale had and hadn't said about Fiona, Roger, and especially Peter. Dale had neglected to mention what Peter's alibi was, although he had spoken at length about Roger's alibi and the Hamills' iffy alibis. And his utter confidence in Peter Bickham surprised her, because as a police officer, wasn't he supposed to be objective? Maybe he himself was Peter's alibi, but he couldn't say so for some reason? Who was Peter Bickham?

Or maybe the question should be how did Peter Bickham get the Maple Hill Police Department to believe in his innocence?

It looked as if she had hit another dead end with Peter Bickham. But Les McLean had given her the name of someone else who might remember what had happened to

Fiona—Wayne Lessman, who had adjusted Fiona's neck-lace. She wasn't sure if he could give her any new informa-tion, but it wouldn't hurt to chat with him for a few minutes at church on Sunday. Like Mrs. Bitty and Les McLean, he might know something else that wasn't in the paper.

She paid for her drink and left the café. She found it cu-rious that while people knew both Roger and Peter were ro-mantically pursuing Fiona, only Angela and Mrs. Bitty had mentioned Liam being involved with her—no one else had mentioned him at all. And yet it was his name on the quilt with Fiona Hamill's.

What was Liam's connection with Fiona? Sarah was no closer to an answer.

Her cell phone rang as she reached her car, still parked in front of McLean Jewelers. "Hello?"

"Sarah, it's Irene."

"Hi, Irene." Doc McLean, Les's older brother, was walk-ing down the sidewalk and apparently making his way to his brother's store. He waved to her but didn't stop to chat.

"I called some friends at Boston newspaper offices today—they have indexes of their older editions that they searched for me. They found an article about Elysa Quin-ton ... sort of."

"Sort of?"

"Well, when I asked them to look, they couldn't find Elysa Quinton, so I had them do a search for just Quin-ton, and you wouldn't believe how many Quintons there are in Massachusetts, not to mention in Boston alone. Anyway, there was an article about the Quinton Auction House just outside of Boston, which burned down about five years go. It was vandalism—a few kids were caught who had broken in and started a fire in an antique stove in the warehouse to keep them warm while they spray-painted the inventory."

Irene sighed in dismay. Sarah could understand how she must feel about that.

"What caught my eye was that the article mentioned the owner, Elysa Sweeney. Elysa isn't a very common name and it seemed too coincidental, so I tried to look up Quinton Auction House. After the fire, they closed up shop, but I'm almost sure she's the same Elysa Quinton who went to Queen's Academy, and that means if she disappeared like Mrs. Gray said she did, then she didn't go far. I just don't know how to find her now."

But Sarah had an idea. "Irene, let me call you back in a few minutes, okay?"

"Do you know how to find her?"

"Maybe." Sarah hung up and called Chester Winslow at *Country Cottage* magazine.

"Hello, Sarah," Chester said pleasantly. "How are you? Do you have a new idea for your monthly column yet?"

Sarah hadn't even thought about a subject for her next quilting column for the magazine. She fleetingly thought about the Double Wedding Ring quilt, but knew she couldn't possibly write about it unless she got to the bottom of the mysterious names on it. "Maybe the combination of embroidery with quilts," she said, the idea coming to her.

"That sounds interesting," Chester said, "and it'll appeal to readers who embroider but don't quilt. Good idea."

"Chester, I'm calling to ask you if you know anything about the Quinton Auction House just outside of Boston."

"Yes, I purchased several pieces there before they closed down. Tragic thing, that fire. What do you need to know?"

"Do you know anything about the owner, Elysa Sweeney?"

"Very professional, great to work with. Really knew her stuff—her parents owned the auction house before she took over."

"Her parents were the Quintons?" Sarah asked, hope rising in her chest.

"Yes, George and Julie. Julie died of a stroke a few years ago, and George lasted only a year after she was gone. They were very devoted to each other."

"Do you know where Elysa Sweeney is now? I want to chat with her about a couple of boys she knew in high school."

"Looking up old flames?" Chester joked. "Elysa and I used to work together quite a bit, so I have her private cell phone number from before the fire. However, I'm not sure if she still has the same number."

"If it's her private number, I don't want you to give it to me without her permission. Would you do me a favor and call her and ask if she'd be willing to chat with me?"

"Certainly. I'll try the number and call you back."

"Thanks, Chester."

"Anything for you, Sarah." She could hear the smile in his voice before he hung up.

Sarah started driving home, but Chester called her back right away. She turned the wheel and pulled over to the side of the road so she could answer the call. "Hello?"

"Sarah, good news. She still has the same cell phone number."

"That's wonderful."

"I left her a voice mail message, and I'll call you as soon as I get in touch with her."

"Thanks so much, Chester."

Sarah started the car again and pulled out into the lane, intending to call Irene as soon as she got home.

So if Elysa Quinton Sweeney had indeed disappeared, she had apparently been found. Perhaps Mrs. Gray had been mistaken, and Peter and Roger hadn't been questioned about the disappearance. But then what had the police wanted with the two boys?

Or maybe this wasn't the same Elysa Quinton. While Elysa wasn't a common name, it wasn't completely unusual. What if this was just a coincidence?

Sarah turned into her driveway, realizing that all this speculation was fruitless until Chester called her back.

Sarah called Irene first, explaining how she had contacted Chester Winslow about the Quinton Auction House, and how he had left a message for Elysa Sweeney.

"Sarah, you're better than a private investigator," Irene said.

Sarah laughed. "I couldn't have found her if you hadn't gotten your contacts to pore through old Boston newspapers all day."

Sarah also called Jason, who was still at the office, to tell him about the bracelet.

"That's a great idea, Mom," he said. "Whew! I was wondering what to get her for Christmas this year and hoping it wouldn't be a disaster like the 'Learn to Knit' kit I bought her last year." Maggie had enjoyed learning to knit with the comprehensive kit, but she had also discovered she was allergic to the mohair fiber that was in much of the yarn in that particular kit.

Sarah had an early dinner of chicken vegetable soup that she thawed from the freezer, and she was about to go back to taking notes on Caitlin's quilt when the telephone rang. "Hello?" she answered absently, her mind already on the quilt. Then when the phone rang again, she realized her cell phone was ringing, not the house phone. She hurriedly grabbed her cell phone from her purse and answered the call, which had an unfamiliar number. "Hello?"

"Is this Sarah Hart?" asked a soft, low feminine voice.

"Yes."

"This is Elysa Sweeney," the woman said. "Chester said you wished to speak to me?"

"Thank you so much for calling me. Did you by any chance go to Queen's Academy in Boston for high school?"

"Yes, I did."

Sarah's heart began to pound. "Did you know both Roger Marstadt and Peter Bickham?"

There was the sound of a soft indrawn breath. "Oh my," she said. "I haven't thought of them in years."

"I wanted to ask you about them, what they were like in high school. Could I meet with you to talk?" Sarah wanted to see Elysa's expressions as she asked questions.

"Such a long time ago ... Chester mentioned you live near Pittsfield?"

"Yes, I'm only a few minutes away."

"I'm going to be in Springfield tomorrow at an auction," Elysa said. "Would you like to meet there in the afternoon? It's easier than your driving all the way to Worcester."

"That would be wonderful. Thank you."

Elysa gave her the name of a coffee shop in Springfield, and Sarah said good-bye and hung up. She then called Irene.

"How would you like to go to Springfield tomorrow?"

CHAPTER THIRTEEN

I can't believe you found her," Irene said as she pulled into a public parking space in Springfield the next day.

The coffee shop was large, with high ceilings and art deco paintings on the walls. It smelled pleasantly of coffee, chocolate, and the faintest hint of cinnamon. Sarah found out why when she saw that the coffee of the day was a Mexican coffee that had a cinnamon flavor to it. "I'll take one of those," she ordered at the front counter. She also bought Irene a mocha latte as a thank-you for driving them.

They had arrived a little early, but they didn't have long to wait for Elysa Sweeney. A tall, elegant woman dressed in an expensive gray pantsuit and a wool coat against the October wind walked in. Her hair was pulled back in smooth, gold-silver waves, and gold jewelry gleamed at her ears and throat. She smiled as she came up to the small table where they were sitting. "Sarah Hart?" she asked.

"Yes. You're Elysa Sweeney?"

"Nice to meet you." She shook Sarah's hand.

"Elysa, let me introduce you to Irene Stuart. She's the historian at the Maple Hill Historical Society and a good friend. We were searching for you and she's the one who discovered the article about your auction house in the newspaper."

"I have to admit, I don't really miss the auction house," Elysa said. "I was always so busy. Now, I'm doing contract auctions and I like it so much better. Let me go get some coffee and then I'll join you."

Once she had gotten a cappuccino, she sat with them and pulled some photos out of her handbag. "I found these last night and thought you might like to see them."

They were pictures of Roger and of Peter, and unlike in most of the pictures Sarah had seen of them, they were together in one photo, along with Elysa and another girl.

"I went to a basketball game," Elysa said. "This was in Peter's senior year and Roger's junior year, and they were both on the varsity team." She sighed. "I had brought a girl friend to try to get Roger interested in someone else, but he hardly looked at her."

In the photo, Peter was as Sarah had always seen him—that stunning smile, the intent eyes. He was taller than Roger by about four inches. Roger, on the other hand, was more serious than in the yearbook photos Sarah had seen of him, and even in some of the more recent pictures she had seen on the Internet. He almost glowered at the camera, saved only by a somewhat vain attempt at a smile, and he had subtly turned his shoulder away from Peter.

Elysa looked happy and full of life. Her golden wavy hair was thicker and more unruly than it was now, and without the silver.

"Peter's classmate mentioned that he and Roger both liked you," Sarah said.

"Actually, it was only Roger," Elysa said. "Peter was friends with my older brother, but we weren't attracted to each other. I was in love with someone else, but no matter what I did, I couldn't dampen Roger's crush on me, so I asked Peter to pretend to be my boyfriend. That backfired, though, because Peter and I didn't realize how competitive Roger was, and especially with Peter."

"Why with Peter?"

"I think it was pure jealousy." Elysa sipped her cappuccino. "Roger was the kind of boy who strutted around as if everyone knew who his father was and, what's more, as if everyone cared. But the only one who cared was Roger himself. He was supposedly the wealthiest boy in the school, although there were rumors that his father's business wasn't doing as well as he said it was.

"But despite Roger's money, people just liked Peter better. He was friendly and made people feel welcome, while Roger made people feel like they were his servants. Roger hated that Peter stole his thunder, especially because Peter's father wasn't very wealthy—he was an underpaid, overworked defense lawyer for the state. Peter went to Regency Academy because his maternal grandfather was an alumnus and had made a lot of money with some type of overseas investments."

"But Peter's mother wasn't wealthy?" Irene asked.

Elysa shook her head. "According to what Peter told me, his father refused the money for himself because he wanted to support his wife on his own, and he asked that the money be tied up in trust for Peter's education."

"I can understand that," Irene said.

"Were Roger and Peter outright enemies?" Sarah asked.

"No, not really. That's why I didn't realize how much Roger resented Peter until after I'd asked Peter to pose as my boyfriend. Roger was like a bulldog—he just wouldn't back down. Outwardly, he was always polite to Peter, and he never insulted him in any obvious way, but you could tell there was friction—at least on Roger's part. And Peter wasn't the kind of guy to cower before anyone."

"What happened to them, and you?" Sarah asked. She hoped Elysa would tell them about her disappearance and Sarah wouldn't have to ask her outright.

"Things went on with the three of us for several months," Elysa said. "I felt like a bone being fought over by two dogs. It was very uncomfortable. And then . . ." She hesitated, then said, "And then, I ran away."

"From home?" Sarah asked. When Elysa only nodded in reply, she added gently, "One of Peter's classmates said you had disappeared. I wondered if maybe she had been mistaken."

"I'm sure it seemed like I disappeared," Elysa said. "The truth is, I'm rather embarrassed by it all, but I suppose it was so long ago . . . " She sighed. "I tried to elope to Canada with a man."

"Earlier, you mentioned you were in love with someone else," Sarah said. "Was this the man?"

"Yes. He wanted to go to Canada to dodge the Vietnam draft, but then he took all my money and abandoned me as soon as he was safe. I had to call my parents to get them to help me get home. I finished my last year of high school under a tutor, and then I went to a business college in New York. That's where I met my husband, and we returned to Boston to help my parents run the auction house. He doesn't know about my little disappearing act." Elysa's cheeks glowed pink. "I suppose I could tell him now. It's been a long time, and to be honest, I hadn't even thought about it for years, until you mentioned Queen's Academy on the phone."

"Did you ever see Peter or Roger again?"

"I didn't want to see Roger," Elysa said. "I know he went on to work for his father at M&S Shipping, but all the money in the world isn't worth the hassle of pandering to Roger's ego.

"As for Peter . . . " Elysa's dark blue eyes took on a faraway look. "I wish I knew. I know he went to Boston University, but after that?" She shrugged. "My brother and I both lost touch with him."

"Do you know where his family lives?" Sarah asked.

"His parents died the year after he graduated college, although he graduated a year early. His mother died from cancer, and then his father died only a few months later from a heart attack."

Sarah did some addition in her head. That would have been in 1968, just two years before Peter came to Maple Hill.

"In fact," Elysa said, "that might have been the last time my brother and I saw Peter, at his father's funeral. He said he was going to sell his parents' house, but he wasn't sure what he was going to do with his life." Elysa's eyes seemed mournful. "The thing is, Peter was made for so much more than a desk job. He could have done anything. I wouldn't have been surprised if he decided to climb Mount Everest or dig wells in Africa or rescue orphans in Burma."

She shook her head. "At the funeral, he was so broken up we didn't push him too hard or ask too many questions. And then we never heard from him again."

That was why the Regency Academy alumni letters had been returned—Peter had sold his parents' house and hadn't bothered to leave a forwarding address with the new owners.

Irene said, "So you didn't disappear after all."

Elysa smiled ruefully. "No, sorry. It was a bit more embarrassing than a disappearance."

"Well, we're very glad you didn't disappear," Sarah said.

"My parents were, too, after they were done being furious at me," said Elysa.

"Is there anything else you can think of to tell us about Peter and Roger?" Sarah asked.

"I wish there were. I think I've told you everything I can remember."

"If you think of anything else, please be sure to call me," Sarah said. "Thank you so much for speaking to us about this."

"You're quite welcome. It's brought back so many memories."

They all rose to go, and after exchanging business cards with Elysa, Sarah and Irene left for the long drive back to Maple Hill.

Irene said, "It's like Peter's the one who disappeared."

"At least we've got a richer understanding of Peter's and Roger's characters," Sarah said thoughtfully. Elysa had mentioned Peter had been made for more than a desk job. Why had he lied about working for *New England Sunrises* magazine? What exactly had Peter been doing in Maple Hill?

It pointed to something "more than a desk job." It solidified Sarah's suspicions that Peter had a powerful ally who had somehow been able to buy the police department's cooperation or irrefutably convince them that Peter was innocent.

Sarah shook her head. She was probably just being fanciful. After all, how many secret, powerful people really came to a small, sleepy town like Maple Hill?

"Hey, stranger," Martha greeted Sarah as she slid into the pew on Sunday morning. "I saw Wayne and Julie Lessman just a few minutes ago. They sat near the back, where they always do, next to Sandra and Keith Pohlman." Since Sandra and Julie were closer than two peas in a pod, Sarah wasn't surprised.

The music started, and the two friends turned their attention to the service. Pastor John taught from the familiar passage in James, chapter two, about how faith without works is dead.

Sarah had heard the passage dozens of times before, but this time, she felt it had extra meaning. She had always been conscientious about serving at church, giving of her time to the community when she had the opportunity, but today, she could only think of Leland.

If she truly loved the Lord, she would love all his children—even Leland, and serve him in any way she could. She just didn't know what Leland wanted. He wasn't very forthcoming and he wasn't all that pleasant, either.

But what if he needed a friend? And what if God wanted Sarah to be that friend? Would she be willing to do that?

She didn't want to be Leland's friend. He was too prickly. She didn't understand him.

But if God asked her to, how could she say no?

She prayed, *Lord, help me to serve you the way you want me to. Give me wisdom and the words to say so I can serve Leland and help him to understand that he's not alone in this world. Amen.*

After the service, she excused herself to Martha and headed toward the back to try to catch Wayne Lessman. She found him and Julie still in their pew. Julie was talking animatedly to Sandra Pohlman, while Wayne and Keith were talking around their wives about the football game last weekend.

"Oh hi, Sarah," Julie said as she caught sight of her standing there.

"Hello," she said. "I was wondering if I could speak to Wayne for a moment?"

"Uh-oh, what did you do now?" Julie asked him in a mock-stern voice, fixing her brown eyes on her husband's laughing ones.

Wayne reached over to tweak one of Julie's silver locks and said, "Nothing worse than normal." He turned to Sarah and asked, "What do you need to talk about?"

"It's easier to show you." Sarah gave him the photo of Fiona and Frank.

But before she could ask him about Fiona, Wayne's white eyebrows sank low over his faded blue eyes. "Frank Shields," he growled. "He was quite a character."

"Frank?" Keith Pohlman looked over at him at the mention of the name. "What about him?"

Wayne showed him the photo, and Keith nodded. "Bad business, he was."

"What about Frank?" Wayne asked Sarah.

"Actually, I was hoping you might remember when that girl disappeared."

Wayne nodded. "I remember. Didn't the police say it was foul play?"

"No, they didn't," Julie said. "They said they didn't know if it was foul play. Your memory gets worse every day."

"You reach eighty-five and see how clear you're thinking, my girl," he said.

Sandra cackled. "She's almost there."

"Am not," Julie protested. "I'm only seventy-five."

"And I'm Bette Davis," Sandra fired back.

"Girls," Keith said in a gravelly voice, directing a stern glance at both women from beneath his straight, steel gray eyebrows. He looked at Sarah. "What else do you want to know?"

"I'm digging into her disappearance," Sarah said, "and was hoping some of you might remember things that weren't in the paper. Things people might have been saying or things you told the police."

Sandra shook her head. "We didn't know the Hamills at all. I don't even know where they lived."

"Somewhere outside Maple Hill," Julie said. "I know that much."

"The police didn't talk to any of us, Sarah," Wayne said. "Sorry about that."

Sarah had known it was a long shot, but she also knew it wouldn't hurt to ask. But she had one last question. "So none of you knew Peter Bickham or Roger Marstadt?"

Sandra and Julie shook their heads, but Wayne and Keith glanced at each other. Sarah waited for them to speak.

Finally, Wayne said, "You tell her, Keith."

He hesitated, then said, "About two weeks after Fiona disappeared, Frank Shields came back to Maple Hill."

"He did?" Sarah asked.

Keith sighed. "I should never have hired him."

"You hired him?" his wife asked. "Whatever for? You knew what kind of man he was. Always up to no good."

Keith explained to Sarah, "I used to own a construction company—I sold it when I retired—and Frank came looking for a job, so I hired him. He'd been away from Maple Hill for a while, and he said he'd changed and he only wanted to make an honest living. Well, I hadn't heard of him even applying for a job before, so I gave him the benefit of the doubt."

"Don't feel bad, Keith," Wayne said. "I would've done the same thing."

"Barely three days after I hired him, he up and disappeared. Just didn't show up at work. I waited a few hours, thinking maybe he'd had car trouble—his old Ford was in bad shape. But by noon, he still hadn't showed up. So I called his folks and they didn't know where he was. The thing is, I remember seeing Peter Bickham hanging around the construction site the day before."

"You think Peter had something to do with it?" Sarah asked.

"I don't know what to think," Keith said, "but when Frank disappeared from Maple Hill, well, Peter did too."

Sarah and Martha sat in Sarah's Grand Prix, enjoying the brief flashes of sunlight that occasionally peeked through the thick clouds as they drove out of Maple Hill to interview Frank Shields's mother on Monday morning. Sarah had invited Irene, but she had declined, saying she was headed to Boston that day and wouldn't be back until Wednesday night. She had also promised pictures of the Hamill letters from the Irish Historical Museum, which Sarah was looking forward to seeing, if only out of curiosity.

"I wish it would just rain or be sunny rather than this cloudy sunshine," Martha complained.

"At least it's not snowing." Sarah maneuvered the car around a turn, with maple leaves flying through the air before her car. The countryside was still and sleepy today, as if just about to nod off for the winter, and the recent winds had stripped the trees of any leaves not strong enough to hold fast.

When Sarah had looked for the Shields's telephone number, she hadn't found them listed at all, but Keith Pohlman had been able to give her directions to their house. When Frank hadn't shown up for work the rest of that week, a co-worker had told Keith where Frank lived. Keith had then driven out to the Shields's house to deliver Frank's partial paycheck for the two complete days he had worked.

The house stood back from the main road in a slight dip in the landscape, so it was partially hidden from view by trees and a few scraggly shrubs. The small one-story structure looked old and worn, with paint peeling in places and several shingles loose on the sloping roof.

The sun shone fitfully on Sarah's back as she approached the house, stepping carefully onto the front porch. The planks creaked dangerously under her weight, and Martha held back, eyeing them nervously. She stopped just short of the porch.

Sarah knocked on the weather-beaten gray door, which sounded flimsy and hollow. All around, the country-side was silent—Sarah couldn't even hear the chirping of birds. But the faint moan of the wind reached her ears every so often, giving everything a rather creepy feeling.

The door opened to a woman with black and gray hair pulled back in a severe bun. Her face was a mass of wrinkles, and she stood with a pronounced curve to her back. "What do you want?" she barked.

"My name is Sarah Hart—"

"I didn't ask your name, I asked what you wanted," the woman said.

Sarah wet her lips. "Are you Mrs. Shields?"

"Not anymore. Now I'm Mrs. Webb, and I'm widowed again."

"Mrs. Webb, I wanted to talk to you about your son and Peter Bickham."

The woman spat on the floor, missing Sarah's shoe by inches. Sarah jumped back a pace.

"The man's a hunter," Mrs. Webb said. "Except he hunts people instead of animals. *He* should be the one locked up, not my poor son."

"What do you mean he hunts people?"

"Are you stupid?" Mrs. Webb demanded. "The man was a U.S. Marshall. They're all bounty hunters with no conscience whatsoever."

A U.S. Marshall. Peter hadn't needed a powerful, rich ally, because he himself had been in law enforcement. He might have checked in with the police when he first came to town, or at the very least, he would have told the lead detective on Fiona's case who he was. "He was hunting your son?"

The woman's mouth curved down and tears filled her eyes. "My poor boy. He was on a bus on his way to prison for a crime he didn't commit. It was one of the other men who made the bus crash, and then he forced Frank to run or they'd kill him. He wouldn't hurt a fly, so he just did what they told him."

Sarah remembered Mrs. Bitty talking about Frank's crimes in Maple Hill, and assault had been one of his vices. She wasn't sure she believed Mrs. Webb's version of the story, but it still explained a lot.

"Meanwhile, that Peter Bickham killed that poor girl, and does he go to jail?" Mrs. Webb asked with venom.

"You mean Fiona Hamill?"

Mrs. Webb continued as if Sarah hadn't spoken. "No, he doesn't. That U.S. Marshall was here in Maple Hill when she went missing. He even went to Ireland to befriend that girl, and he followed her back here, and then he killed her, probably just to spite Frank. The only reason my son came back to Maple Hill was because of Fiona, but she was already gone by the time he got here."

Suddenly the pieces fit. Frank had dated Fiona about a year before she went to Ireland. Mrs. Bitty had said he was completely obsessed with Fiona. Sarah could see how Peter, knowing how important Fiona was to Frank, would go to Ireland to find her, get into her confidence, and see if Frank would seek her out again. And he had, but Fiona had already gone missing.

He had probably been camping out here in Maple Hill just waiting for Frank Shields to turn up, whether to see his parents or Fiona. But while here, he'd fallen in love with Fiona, and if Les McLean was to be believed, Peter had proposed to her and been rejected. And then she had disappeared.

But Peter's job had forced him to stay in Maple Hill, because he still had to find Frank. When Frank turned up, he took him and left Maple Hill, which was why Frank had abandoned his job so suddenly, and why Peter had disappeared at the same time.

"I know Peter took her because I saw it with my own eyes," Mrs. Webb said, widening her watery blue eyes at Sarah.

"What did you see?" Sarah asked. The woman was a bit hard to follow at times.

"That night she disappeared? I saw her."

Sarah blinked. "You did?"

Mrs. Webb nodded fiercely. "It was a little after four. I'd just gotten up to feed the chickens and I saw her with that Bickham guy, in a pickup truck driving south." Mrs. Webb pointed to the road Sarah and Martha had driven on, which would lead south and then east toward a small village a few miles down the road.

"You saw Peter Bickham driving with Fiona Hamill down that road?" Sarah asked, astonished. "Are you sure it was the night she disappeared?"

"Why else would she be driving here? This is the back end of nowhere."

Why would Fiona be driving in this remote part of the county? It wasn't on the way to any major towns, or airports.

"Are you sure it was Fiona Hamill?" Sarah asked doubt-fully.

"Of course it was her. She dated Frank for months. I think I'd know what she looked like. She was kidnapped, I tell you. Why else would she be riding with a man in that ratty old truck with one headlight out?"

"Did you tell the police?" Martha asked from beyond the porch, and it was obvious she didn't believe Mrs. Webb for a moment.

"Of course I didn't," Mrs. Webb snapped at her. "They're all on Bickham's side. They'd probably find a way to pin it on Frank, but it was Bickham driving that truck, I tell you."

"Are you sure you saw it clearly?" Sarah glanced back at the road, which had no street lamps.

"Another car was passing them, so I saw her and that Bickham guy. And the pickup was a big blue and red pile of junk with one headlight out."

Sarah felt as if her entire body had been plunged into ice water. "Blue and red?" she asked.

"Red hood, blue fender," Mrs. Webb said.

Sarah sucked in a breath. It couldn't be. Mrs. Webb was confused, she had to be mistaken.

Because Liam had always boasted that his first car in Maple Hill had been a blue and red pickup truck with one headlight out.

CHAPTER FOURTEEN

Despite her less than welcoming greeting, Mrs. Webb wanted to keep talking to them about her wonderful son, and Sarah and Martha had to make repeated attempts to leave before they could do so without being rude.

As they were finally able to walk back to their car, Martha gasped, "Sarah, Liam had a pickup truck like that."

"I know."

"Do you think he had something to do with Fiona's disappearance?"

"I don't know what to think," Sarah said.

They got to the car and slipped inside to escape the chill wind that swept down the road. They sat in stunned silence for a long moment.

"Maybe Peter Bickham *did* have something to do with Fiona's disappearance after all, even if he *was* a U.S. Marshall," Martha said.

"But wouldn't the police have thought of that? Dale Wexler was very confident in Peter. He said Peter had an alibi for that night, but he didn't say what it was. It made me think that Peter's alibi was that he was with police officers at the time."

"Maybe it wasn't Fiona."

"Maybe it wasn't." Sarah thought a moment. "Mrs. Webb must be mistaken."

"Are you sure you don't simply *want* her to be mistaken?" Martha asked.

"No, hear me out. This road is several miles south of Maple Hill. The Hamills' estate is all the way at the northern outskirts of Maple Hill. Fiona and Liam would have had to drive directly through Maple Hill to get to that road, which meant other people besides Mrs. Webb would have seen Liam in his distinctive pickup truck and Fiona in the passenger seat. And if no one else saw them, well, maybe Mrs. Webb is mistaken."

Martha thought a moment. "Are you sure there's no other road they could have taken around town to get to this road?"

"We can check on a map later, but I'm pretty sure. If the Hamill estate had been on, say, the west side of town, there's a remote road that bypasses Maple Hill and intersects with this highway. But from the northern part of town? They'd have had to go directly through Maple Hill."

"Maybe absolutely no one saw Liam's red and blue pickup going through town that morning," Martha said. "Is that possible?"

"Stores wouldn't have been open at that hour, but when the truck passed through residential areas, people would be getting up or leaving to commute to work. I think Mrs. Webb really is mistaken and it wasn't Fiona in that truck. Chuck Blodgett and Ivan Hillman interviewed a lot of Maple Hill residents about that night. Wouldn't they have found at least one other witness?"

"That's true," Martha said. "Also, why would she be out on this road, at night? It only leads to Teesdale."

Then Sarah remembered. "There's a major bus depot in Teesdale."

They sat in silence for a moment.

"So on the remote chance Mrs. Webb really did see them, maybe Liam was helping Fiona to run away," Sarah said.

"What else would be in Teesdale?" Martha replied.

She had a point.

Sarah couldn't decide whether to be ashamed or proud that she had been shown up by her granddaughters.

While she had been struggling in church to obey God and serve Leland however God wanted her to, the twins had baked cookies for him.

"I'm very impressed," Sarah said as she drove them toward Bradford Manor, "but I'm curious. What made you decide to bake cookies for him?"

Audrey answered from the backseat of the car. "Well, we figured that in case he sat there and didn't say anything like last time, we could at least eat."

Sarah smiled.

"We couldn't decide what kind to bake." Amy sat in the passenger seat and held up two open plastic containers so Sarah could see as she drove. "So we made two kinds— oatmeal cranberry and a carrot cookie with cream cheese frosting."

Sarah glanced at a puffy carrot cookie. "It looks like a muffin top more than a cookie."

"But it tastes amazing," Amy said.

"Don't believe her, Grandma," Audrey said. "It tastes like carrot cake."

"Who doesn't like carrot cake?" Amy asked.

With her eyes wide for emphasis, Audrey pointed to herself.

"Well, you're just weird," Amy said with a grin.

"You're weirder—" Audrey retaliated, but Sarah cut off the impending bicker.

"I'm sure Leland will like *both* cookies," she said firmly as she pulled into the gravel driveway of the nursing home.

Truthfully, she wasn't sure if he would like either of them. It might depend on what mood he was in. Would he be friendlier? Or would he revert to the closed old man he had been over a week ago?

As they entered Bradford Manor, the first people they saw were Olive Cavanaugh and Chuck Blodgett, who were sitting near the front door and chatting.

"What're you telling Chuck now, Olive?" Sarah teased them. "Reading him another laundry list?"

"Don't tempt me. He's not entirely deaf, but he still can't hear very well, anyway," Olive said.

"What?" Chuck barked.

Biting back a smile, Sarah said, "How are you doing, Mr. Blodgett?"

"Fine. Mrs. Russo told me another gruesome story about her mafia relations, but I'm starting to wonder if she knows I can hear her, because those tales are getting taller by the day." With a more serious expression, Chuck asked, "Did you find out anything more about Fiona Hamill?"

"Fiona Hamill?" Olive said. "That name sounds familiar."

Sarah glanced at the twins, but they were looking at her with solemn expressions. She had asked them and Justin not to tell anyone about the photo they had found of Liam and Fiona until she talked to him about it. She hadn't told the twins much about Fiona's disappearance, but they kept their silence even now at the mention of her name.

"Fiona disappeared from her home in 1970," Chuck told Olive.

"Oh, that's right, I remember now. She didn't take anything, right? So the police don't know for sure if she was kidnapped or if she ran away."

"Did you know her, Olive?" Sarah asked.

Olive shook her head. "Not personally."

"Did you find anything?" Chuck asked Sarah.

"Nothing solid," Sarah said. "Just more speculation and more questions."

"Ah, well," Chuck said. "It happened forty years ago, anyway."

Tiffany Henderson came up to them. "Hi, Mrs. Hart, Amy, Audrey."

"Hey, Miss Henderson," the girls replied.

Audrey took a fortifying breath, then said, "We have cookies for Mr. Mercer."

"Can he eat cookies?" Amy asked. "He's not diabetic, is he?"

"No, he's not," Tiffany said. "Although he shouldn't eat too many cookies, I'm sure he'll be very happy to see you. Let me take you to his room."

Sarah didn't mention that she already knew which room was his. Instead, she said good-bye to Olive and Chuck—who was mock-moaning about how he didn't get any cookies—and followed Tiffany down the hallway.

As they walked, Tiffany said, "I heard you talking to Mrs. Maplethorpe at Caitlin's shower. Did you find a dress for the wedding yet?"

Sarah waffled. "I did, sort of."

"Sort of?"

"I bought a black skirt and blue gray blouse, and I look fine in them, but they're a bit...uninspiring. I don't intend to outshine the bride, but I wonder if I'm just going to look the way I do when I go to the church's Christmas Eve service."

"Do you have anything that can spice it up?" Tiffany asked.

"I searched my closet and found a gray scarf with black threaded stripes," Sarah said, "but it just doesn't have a lot of pizzazz."

"You should look for something with pizzazz, Grandma," Audrey said sagely.

"When you come to my wedding, I want you to have pizzazz," Amy added.

They had reached Leland's room at this point, and the three Hart women paused outside the open doorway.

Tiffany's eyes crinkled in humor. "I'm sure you'll find something, Mrs. Hart. I went to Concord with Caitlin, not even looking for anything since I'll be wearing the bridesmaid's dress, but I found a cute green dress that's perfect to wear to a winter wedding. And it's a classic sheath style so it'll last a few years."

"Maybe I'll have to go to Concord too," Sarah said. "I really wanted something pretty to wear to Caitlin's wedding."

"Don't wait too long. If you leave it to the last minute, desperation will make you buy something you may not really like later."

"I think I already did that," Sarah said, thinking of the black skirt and blue gray top.

"Well, this is Mr. Mercer's room." Tiffany gestured to the open door. "Have fun." She headed back down the hall to the nurse's station.

Sarah saw Leland looking at them from inside his room. She couldn't tell if he was annoyed to see them or not, but he didn't seem terribly happy, maybe because they had been talking outside his room for a little while.

Sarah expected Audrey to enter the room first, but it was Amy who walked through the doorway with a polite, "Hello, Mr. Mercer. Do you remember us? It's Amy and Audrey Hart."

Leland's mouth was in a tight line, but he nodded and grunted something that may have been "Hello."

"We, uh . . ." Audrey opened the plastic container she carried. "We made cookies for you."

Leland's face went completely slack. As he stared down into the container at the cookies, his cheeks and neck darkened, and his brows started to pull together. Sarah took a step forward.

Then he raised his eyes to Audrey's anxious face. The color faded from his skin and he glanced down, muttering, "Thanks."

Sarah stepped in and surveyed his room. It was still as cluttered as it had been before, but this time Sarah noticed that the walls were cream, and everything personalized was in a shade of blue—his puffy slate-blue comforter, the Colonial blue knitted blanket thrown over a chair, a blue signed Patriots jersey in a dark blue frame on the wall. Leland sat in a chair next to a chess game table.

"Can we move this?" Amy asked, reaching for the chess game.

Leland nodded, and Amy took it and placed it gently on top of his dresser. The two girls then set the containers of cookies on top of the table. They had included napkins inside the containers and soon had one of each on a napkin in front of him.

He watched them with an inscrutable expression on his face, almost as if he didn't want to watch them, and yet he couldn't help it.

"So which cookie will you eat first?" Audrey asked him. "This one's oatmeal-cranberry, and—"

"This one," Amy interrupted, "is a carrot cookie with *cream cheese frosting*."

A sardonic gleam shone out of his eyes, making him look ten years younger. "I'm not dumb. I wouldn't choose between two women's cooking if my life depended on it."

Sarah laughed.

Leland stacked the two cookies on top of each other and took a bite out of both at the same time.

He wasn't smiling at the twins, but he wasn't ignoring them or treating them like annoyances either.

"The only thing I'm missing is coffee," he said with a significant glance at the twins.

"I'll get it." Amy went outside to get him a cup.

And true to his word, he alternated bites from each cookie in between sips of coffee so neither girl felt slighted. However, he didn't initiate conversation.

Audrey looked at Sarah, who gave her an encouraging nod. Then Audrey said, "We had a mock trial at school today."

Leland looked at her from under gray brows, but didn't say anything.

"I made a brilliant, heartrending plea for the defendant," Audrey said with dramatic flair.

"She did," Amy said. "Half the girls were crying by the end...but just because they were dying for her to finally stop talking."

Leland's lips might have twitched.

Valiantly ignoring the dig, Audrey said, "Amy was head juror, but Cole kept throwing paper airplanes at her head when the teacher wasn't looking. I think he likes her."

"No he doesn't," Amy said.

"Yes he does."

Before Sarah could step in to nip the bickering in the bud, Leland cleared his throat. "I think your sister's right."

"Who's right?" Amy asked.

"Take it from me, a boy. Paper airplanes are a sure sign he thinks you're cute."

Amy rolled her eyes, but said nothing.

However, encouraged by Leland's responses, the twins recounted more stories from school. Sometimes Leland responded, sometimes he didn't. It was as if he was relearning how to talk to people. The twins prattled on the way thirteen-year-old girls do, and he seemed to become more comfortable. His brown eyes seemed to lighten to amber, and his shoulders relaxed. He might have even cracked a smile at Audrey's wild exaggerations about how *vile* the history teacher was to his students.

Finally, he had finished his cookies and his coffee, and the girls had started to repeat themselves. "We should go," Sarah told them. "We still need to pack up Grandpa's stuff, and you need to get home to do homework."

At mention of her great-grandpa's things, Audrey turned to Leland. "Mr. Mercer, do you have Grandpa's quilt?"

Leland's eyes darkened.

Not noticing, Audrey went on, "Because Grandma really wants to send it to our uncle. He's living in Italy."

They must have overheard Sarah speaking to Jason about the quilt, wanting it back and mentioning what she wanted to do with it. They were only trying to help her, but Sarah's stomach clenched against the bubble of panic that began to rise.

Emboldened by her sister, Amy added, "We helped Grandma find that quilt, did you know that? In the walls of our house—"

"That's all you wanted?" Leland growled. "The quilt?"

"No, of course not," Sarah hastened to tell him, trying to get him to look at her and not the twins. "The girls just wanted to bake you cookies."

He spat out one word: "Vultures."

Then he turned his chair toward the window and looked out.

"Leland?"

"Go away."

In the tense atmosphere, Audrey's eyes filled with tears. Amy, on the other hand, looked stony. Both girls collected their cookie containers in silence.

At the door, Audrey sniffled, "Good-bye," but Amy sailed through without a backward look.

Sarah took a last hard look at Leland's figure, still staring out the window. Then she turned and left him.

CHAPTER FIFTEEN

Sarah maneuvered the car toward Bridge Street Church, Martha sitting beside her. She had a basket of cranberry orange bread—Gerry's mother's famous recipe—in the backseat. They were going to park at the church and walk again to Mrs. Bitty's house because her driveway was very shallow, and Sarah didn't want to attempt to reverse back out onto Bridge Street, where it narrowed at the curve.

"Don't blame yourself," Martha told her.

"I do. I shouldn't have brought the girls with me. I shouldn't have made them be polite to a man too caught up in his own misery to be considerate to those around him."

"Sarah."

"I'm sorry." It was a bit harsh. But when it came to her granddaughters, she grew as fiercely protective as she had been with Jason and Jenna growing up.

"Maybe God brought Leland into your life for a reason," Martha said. "After all, he did know your father."

"What would God want me to do with a man like Leland?"

Martha shrugged. "Beats me. I guess it's between you and God."

When they knocked on Mrs. Bitty's door, there was a faint "Come in!" so they opened the door and stepped inside the small living room.

"Sorry I couldn't open the door," Mrs. Bitty called from the kitchen. "I saw you walking up and got in the middle of pouring hot water for tea."

Sarah entered the small kitchen. "I brought cranberry orange bread. Do you have a knife I could use?"

"Don't stand on ceremony, just grab a knife and a cutting board from there." Mrs. Bitty gestured to a corner where a cutting board rested against the wall and a block of knives sat next to it.

After slicing the bread and making tea, the three women settled into the living room. "You're looking much better," Martha said to Mrs. Bitty.

"I'm still pretty stiff," the old woman admitted, "but at least I can walk and sit up. Doctor says I need to take it easy for a few weeks, but I do miss my daily walks."

"I'm sure you'll be back out there soon," Sarah said.

"I may not get out again this winter," Mrs. Bitty said. "Once bitten, twice shy—I'm still afraid of slipping again."

"One of us can come walk with you if you'd like," Martha said.

Sarah nodded agreement.

Mrs. Bitty's brown eyes shone. "I'd appreciate that so much. I won't feel half so nervous if I have someone's arm to hold on to. You're being awfully good to a poor old widow."

The Bible passage on helping widows and orphans flashed through Sarah's mind again. *Lord, I think you're setting things up so that I can serve you in this way. Thank you for this opportunity to help out Mrs. Bitty.*

But then came the errant thought—*what about helping Leland?*

"So did you ever find out more about Fiona Hamill?" Mrs. Bitty asked.

Sarah didn't want to keep Mrs. Bitty in the dark about what she had found, since Mrs. Bitty had helped her by telling her about Fiona. But Sarah also didn't want to mention Liam, so she told her everything she could, but not about the pickup truck or the photo of Liam and Fiona.

As Sarah recounted what they had learned, she had the sinking feeling she hadn't really uncovered much about this mystery after all—and definitely not the deeper core of it. She was missing something. She could feel it.

"To think Peter was a U.S. Marshall," Mrs. Bitty said. "Goodness gracious." She gave a little sigh. "If Fiona had married that boy, maybe she wouldn't have felt she had to leave."

This was the second time Mrs. Bitty seemed certain Fiona had run away, not been kidnapped or killed. "Mrs. Bitty, you think Fiona might be alive?" Sarah asked.

She moved her mouth as if to say no, but no sound came from her lips. She was still a long moment, staring into space, then she said, "I know Fiona's alive. I saw her ten years after she disappeared."

Sarah could only sit speechless. Martha, too, was gaping at Mrs. Bitty.

"It was in Pittsfield," Mrs. Bitty said. "My husband and I had married, and he had already gotten that new position as office manager. I was in the process of moving our things to our new apartment. And I remember the day exactly because the Hamills had died a few months before. The Hamills' lawyer contacted me and said the Hamill estate had left me a small monetary gift. I gave him the name of a lawyer friend I knew in Pittsfield, and I went to his office to pick up the check."

Mrs. Bitty sighed, and suddenly she looked older. "I saw her across the street when I walked out of the lawyer's offices. I thought at first I was seeing things, but I kept staring. It was Fiona. She was walking along the sidewalk, and she looked so sad and lonely."

"Are you sure it was her?" Sarah asked.

"I saw her nearly every day for five years—it was Fiona."

But Mrs. Bitty herself had said her eyesight was never very good. Had she really seen Fiona?

"Did you talk to her?" Martha asked.

"I called her name, but she didn't respond, maybe she didn't hear me. I tried to cross the street to catch up to her, but by the time I crossed, she was gone."

"Alive," Martha breathed. "Ten years later, you said?"

"The police had all said it looked like foul play because nothing was taken from her room. She didn't take clothes," Mrs. Bitty said slowly, "but as I told you before, I think she did take her favorite camera."

"You told the police?"

"I told them over and over, but Mr. Hamill could be so persuasive. Who were the police going to believe, a confident businessman or a young housemaid? And then later, I was glad they hadn't believed me. If Fiona did run away, she didn't want to be found, and I didn't want to be the one who helped her father find her."

"And he didn't?"

"Despite all the private investigators he hired. I think he hired them more to make it look like he cared about his daughter than because he really did miss her."

"I can't imagine having a father like that," Martha said.

"I thought about telling the Maple Hill police I'd seen Fiona, but I didn't. After all, Fiona obviously didn't want to be found."

"When you saw Fiona in Pittsfield," Sarah said, "do you remember what day it was?"

"It was August third, and a pretty muggy August it was, too."

"What was she wearing?" Sarah asked.

"Red lipstick," Mrs. Bitty said. "Brighter than I was used to seeing on her. And her hair was pulled back in a bun-like thing."

That was a different look for Fiona. At least, it was very different from how she appeared in the photos Sarah had seen.

"And a blue dress," Mrs. Bitty pronounced. "Blue was Fiona's favorite color, but she'd never worn a dress as bright as this one was—it was Easter egg blue. Long, and she wore camel-colored boots. She also had a camel-colored jacket."

Mrs. Bitty frowned as she stared at her cup. "Or it could have been a white coat. Now that I think back on it, it might have been white."

Martha gave Sarah a quick glance. Sarah wasn't sure if she could believe Mrs. Bitty's memory.

"I know I sound like an old fool," Mrs. Bitty said, "but it was Fiona. I'm sure of it."

"I hope she is alive," Sarah said. She hoped Liam hadn't had anything to do with her disappearance, or at the very least, that he'd had good reason to be involved.

"And here's more proof," Mrs. Bitty said. "I had always told Fiona I wanted a gold charm bracelet, but that I couldn't justify spending money on a bracelet and charms. When I picked up that check at the lawyer's office in Pittsfield, not only had the Hamills left me something, but I got a jeweler's box with a gold charm bracelet inside."

Sarah sat up. "You did?"

"Let me show it to you." Mrs. Bitty got up and went to her bedroom, returning with the box and a business card. She handed the box to Sarah. It held a beautiful gold charm bracelet, populated with lovely charms.

"There was a note that said for me to use the check to buy charms for that bracelet." Mrs. Bitty's eyes filled with tears. "So I did. I bought a camera charm in honor of Fiona."

Sarah fingered the tiny gold camera on the bracelet. "It's beautiful."

"The Hamills didn't know about my wanting a charm bracelet," Mrs. Bitty said. "Only Fiona knew, so it could only have been Fiona who gave me that check and the bracelet."

Sarah returned the bracelet to Mrs. Bitty, and the old woman handed her the business card.

"This is the card I got when I picked up the check," she said. "It's the name of the Hamills' lawyer who contacted me about everything."

Sarah glanced at the card: Richard Asher, with a Boston address.

"You contact that lawyer," Mrs. Bitty said. "Contact him and see. I know I'm right. He knows that Fiona is still alive."

"I figured that was the case," Sarah told Jason over the phone, "but I figured I ought to call you to ask, just the same."

"No problem, Mom," he said. "Oh, and I remembered who Leland reminded me of."

Leland's name made her neck tense, but she said, "Oh?"

"He reminds me of a client I have," Jason said. "He's in a bad place, Mom—he lost everything. His wife and daughter died in a car accident, then his brother died overseas a few months later, then he got laid off from his job right after that and he couldn't keep up his mortgage payments."

"My goodness. And Leland reminds you of him?"

"His features don't look like Leland's, but the expression on his face reminds me of him."

Jason's words stirred Sarah's heart. All the pain in that man's life, probably etched in his face. Did Leland have a similar heartache?

"Well, I just wanted to tell you, Mom."

"I'm glad you did. Thanks, honey." He hung up, but Sarah held on to the phone for a moment, thinking about what he had said. And she realized she would need more time later to think it over.

Sarah turned to Martha, who was crocheting at the kitchen table.

"Well?" Martha asked. "Can you get the lawyer to tell us about Fiona?"

"No, Jason confirmed it. Even if Fiona was alive, her lawyer wouldn't be able to tell me because of lawyer-client privilege. In fact, he'd probably laugh me out of his office if I went there to ask."

Martha sighed. "Well, it was worth a shot. Do you think Fiona's still alive?"

Sarah hesitated before answering. "I'm not sure what to think. Mrs. Bitty was pretty certain about seeing Fiona in Pittsfield, and there is that charm bracelet."

"Mrs. Bitty's memory isn't great."

"But she was thirty years younger when she saw Fiona."
Martha nodded thoughtfully. "True."

"But if Fiona did run away, why didn't she take anything with her? She had to have had help—someone to give her money if she didn't have some cash already on hand."

"She might have. After all, the Hamills were rich at the time. I'm sure her allowance would have made our mothers laugh themselves silly."

"Maybe Liam helped her run away."

"Do you think he loved her after all?"

"If he did love her, why didn't he go with her? He didn't have ties to Maple Hill yet." Sarah shook her head. "I feel like I'm just going around and around in circles."

A knock at the door made her turn. "I wonder who that could be?"

She opened the door to her neighbor, Imogene Dowling, dressed in a turquoise muumuu-style dress. Imogene gave a smile and a hug, as usual, but her face looked tight and anxious.

"I'm sorry to bother you, Sarah, but I wondered if today or anytime this week, you accidentally got a package I'm expecting. Oh, hi, Martha," Imogene said as she saw Martha wandering out from the kitchen.

Sarah shook her head. "I'm sorry, I didn't get any packages in the mail today. If I'd gotten something this week, I'd have walked it over to you."

"That's what I figured." Imogene exhaled on a short, hard breath. "She's not going to be happy about this."

"What happened?" Martha asked.

"An old schoolmate got in touch with me online," Imogene said. "She had found out I do embroidery work and asked if I'd repair an embroidery picture her mother had made. Before I could e-mail her back to tell her yes or no, she e-mailed to say she'd gotten my mailing address from a friend and had sent me her mother's picture!"

"Uh-oh," Martha said.

"That was a week ago. She's just e-mailed me again to ask if I've gotten the package yet, which I haven't. I asked her what address she used, and for some reason she put your house number on the package, not mine."

"Well, we're neighbors, so a number mix-up isn't too bad," Sarah said.

"But what's even worse is that she addressed it to the wrong name—Harriet Smythe rather than Imogene Dowling." Imogene shook her head. "I bet the package was 'returned to sender.' It's happened to me before—people mail something addressed to Harriet Smythe, and the post office sends it back because they think it isn't addressed to the right person."

"Harriet?" Sarah was confused. "I know Smythe was your maiden name, but ..."

Imogene groaned. "Harriet is my real first name. I hate it, I always have. When I was in high school, I started asking people to call me by my middle name, Imogene, instead, and I would sign my name, 'H. Imogene Smythe.'"

Sarah experienced a sudden shock of recognition and sucked in her breath. H. Imogene Smythe. Could the M. in M. Fiona Hamill refer to a name rather than "married?"

"Mabina," Sarah whispered.

"What?" Imogene asked.

"Er...nothing. I was just thinking out loud."

"Well, if that package ever shows up..." Imogene turned to go.

"I'll be sure to rush it over to you," Sarah said.

Imogene turned to give her a wink. "Don't get injured doing it." She laughed heartily and then left.

"You've got that 'look,'" Martha said. "What did you figure out?"

"In the letter Angela showed me from Fiona, I think she mentioned an Aunt Mabina."

"I think you mentioned that when you told me about it."

"I think Fiona stayed with her Aunt Mabina in Ireland. Some distant great-aunt or something like that. But I need to know Mabina's full name."

Martha looked at the time. "Maybe Angela knows. She might be home for the day by now."

"Good idea." Sarah picked up the phone and dialed Angela's home phone number, and luckily she answered.

"Hello?"

"Hi, Angela, it's Sarah Hart."

"Hi, Sarah. What can I do for you?"

"I wanted to know about that letter from Fiona that you showed to me."

"I looked for the other letters, but still can't find them, I'm afraid."

"That's okay. I was wondering if you might scan that letter and e-mail it to me. I wanted to look at it again."

"Oh, no problem." There were bustling sounds as Angela seemed to be rummaging around on her desk.

"Do you remember Fiona's Aunt Mabina mentioned in the letter? Do you know what her full name was?"

"I'm afraid not. I don't think it's in the letter, either. Do you still want me to send a copy?"

"Yes, please, if it's not too much trouble."

"Oh, no trouble at all." There was a humming sound, and then Angela said, "I just e-mailed it to you."

"Thanks so much, Angela."

"You can thank me by taking my Sunday school class again the next time I need a substitute," Angela said with a smile in her voice.

"I always love taking your class. The six- and seven-year-olds say the most interesting things."

"I'll see you at church on Sunday."

"Bye."

Sarah fired up her laptop and opened the e-mail from Angela, with the .jpg file of the letter. She skimmed it again. "Listen to this, Martha. *'Aunt Mabina has taken out her fabrics and is separating all the purple prints and solids.*

She's threatening to make a skirt for me with the scraps left over.'"

"From the scraps left over?" Martha said.

"Meaning she was going to make something else with the fabric first?" Sarah said. "Like maybe a quilt?"

"Wasn't there a purple ring on Caitlin's quilt?" Martha said.

"I'm wondering if 'M. Fiona Hamill' is the *signature* of the quilter," Sarah said. "Is it possible that Fiona's Aunt Mabina made Caitlin's quilt?"

CHAPTER SIXTEEN

Early the next morning, Sarah awoke to the sound of thunder and saw that the blustery skies were finally unloading rain on Maple Hill. It was the perfect sort of day to stay at home with a good book and a pot of tea.

She sat with her Bible open for a long time before she started reading. She enjoyed diving straight into the Word, but this morning, Leland was on her mind, so she started off her time with God with a prayer.

Lord, I don't understand why Leland came into my life. Is he supposed to stay?

She remembered Audrey's tears and Amy's stony hurt. It wasn't worth their pain. She would simply let Leland have the quilt. She didn't want to fight with him anymore.

She opened her devotional, and the passage was from Corinthians I, chapter thirteen:

"If I give all I possess to the poor and surrender my body to the flames, but have not love, I gain nothing. Love is patient, love is kind. It does not envy, it does not boast, it is

not proud. It is not rude, it is not self-seeking, it is not easily angered, it keeps no record of wrongs. It always protects,
always trusts, always hopes, always perseveres."

And she realized that despite everything he had done, Leland was worth loving anyway.

It didn't make any sense. Leland wasn't easy to get to
know. He seemed to want to hold everyone at arm's length,
and he went to extremes to do it. Most people would look at
him and assume that there was nothing lovable about him.
And yet Sarah felt God reminding her of His most basic
command—to love one another.

Even when it didn't make sense.

She remembered the passage from Samuel I, chapter sixteen, and flipped to it:

"The Lord does not look at the things man looks at. Man
looks at the outward appearance, but the Lord looks at the
heart."

All she could see was Leland's outward actions, but
maybe God wanted her to trust him and try to look beneath
the surface. To love Leland the way God loved him.

She bowed her head. *Lord, forgive me for not wanting to
do your will and open my heart to Leland. Only you can help
me to do this for you, so please help me. Amen.*

She had finished her breakfast of egg on toast when the
telephone rang. "Hello?"

"Hi, Sarah, it's Irene. Did you get my e-mail?"

"I'm afraid I haven't opened my e-mail yet this morning,"
Sarah said, holding back her smile at Irene's eagerness.

"Oh. Well, I'll stay on the line while you do."

Sarah fired up her computer. "How was your trip to Boston?"

"Same as usual—a lot of fun, but I'm glad to be home. A history professor at Boston College wanted my opinion on a Civil War artifact he had found. Before I left Boston though, I stopped in at the Irish Historical Museum and got them to let me take pictures of those letters Robert Hamill donated."

Sarah pulled up her e-mail, seeing that Irene had sent her three picture files. They were of three letters, each addressed to Riona Hamill, sent to her in Boston, all the way from Ireland. The paper was old and yellowed, the edges badly cracked, and the writing slanted and flowed across the page. The letters were dated 1899, 1902, and 1905, but it was the 1905 letter that caught her eye.

April 8, 1905
Pomeroy, Tyrone, Ireland
Dear Riona,

We're pleased to announce the birth of Mabina Fiona, born at seven o'clock in the morning today. Briana went into labor almost twenty-four hours earlier, so the sweet girl took her time in entering this world. She's got a gusty set of lungs guaranteed to wake the neighbors all the way on the other side of the stream. Her hair is black as coal and her face as red as a beet, but my sister assures me that will go away as she grows.

Niall recovered from his cold only to break his arm while playing around with his hooligan friends. He is imprisoned at home with a stack of reading as penance for breaking Mr. Martin's window with a ball. I am anxious for his mother to come fetch him next month. I am not the doting auntie I was a month ago, as Niall keeps telling me.

Thank you for the Lattice Chain quilting pattern in your last letter. As soon as I finish the chain quilt I'm working on, I want to make the Lattice pattern. It uses so many little pieces of fabric, and it is something I can start right quickly.

Thank you also for the money you sent to Mam last month. She bought a chicken and a pig with it.

Yours,

Shannon Hamill

The birth of Mabina Fiona Hamill.

M. Fiona Hamill. Yes, now some things about the quilt were starting to make more sense.

Irene said, "The letters are dated seventy years before Fiona Hamill's disappearance, but they're fascinating, aren't they?"

"They're very interesting," Sarah said in a carefully mild voice.

"Did you see the one that mentions the quilting pattern? Do you know what it looks like?"

"Patterns often have different names in different regions, so it's hard to know which pattern this is, but I'll look it up."

"I figured you'd have fun figuring out what it is," Irene said.

"Thank you so much for getting these photos for me," Sarah said.

"Oh, don't mention it. It was interesting. I'll talk to you later." Irene hung up.

Sarah stared at the picture of the letter. If Fiona's Aunt Mabina had made Caitlin's quilt, that would explain the polyester batting, which would have been readily available in 1969, when Fiona spent that year with her aunt in Ireland. The fabrics used in the quilt could have been old fabrics from Mabina's stash, passed down from generation to generation, explaining why they were old-fashioned and heavy.

Was there a way to investigate whether the fabrics were from Ireland or Great Britain as opposed to the United States? She would have to show the quilt again to Vanessa at Wild Goose Chase. Because Vanessa dealt in fabrics, she might be able to tell Sarah whether it was possible to determine if a particular fabric was from the U.S. or overseas.

Even if the quilt had indeed been made by Mabina Hamill in Ireland, that still didn't explain why Liam's name was on it and how he had ended up with the quilt. It also didn't shed any light on Fiona's mysterious disappearance two months after returning from Ireland.

Then a thought made Sarah sit back in her chair in amazement. She had been going down a rabbit hole when she should have already known it wasn't the right one.

She had naturally thought the quilt belonged to Liam, but Caitlin had said it herself—she had recognized it as her mom's quilt. It was Jeannie's quilt, not Liam's.

Mabina's quilt had probably been given to Fiona in Ireland. Then somehow, it had come into *Jeannie's* possession, and *Liam's* name had been written on it.

Liam had said Jeannie didn't know Fiona. What was the connection linking the three of them?

Early Friday morning found Sarah outside Wild Goose Chase a full hour before opening time. She felt like a criminal when Vanessa arrived a few minutes after she did and let the two of them into the dark store, looking around to see if anyone could see them entering.

Vanessa locked the front door behind them. "I know that the last thing you want is for someone to see the names on that quilt. I hope no one sees me here, thinks I'm open, and knocks to be let in."

"We'd have to throw a sheet over the quilt," Sarah joked. "Or maybe drop one from the ceiling at the touch of a button."

Vanessa led the way to the cutting table in the middle of the store. She turned on the light directly above the table, but the rest of the store remained dark. "I'm sorry I couldn't look at it yesterday when you called."

"Don't be silly," Sarah said. "You're running a business, and I didn't want to take you away from your family after you closed shop yesterday. How are things with Drew?"

Vanessa smiled. "The kids are happy. We played Apples to Apples last night and they had more fun than I've seen them have in years." Her smile faltered a little. "I won't lie to you, it's not all smooth sailing, but we're trying so hard. I hope it works out."

"I'll be praying for you," Sarah promised. She had already been praying for Vanessa during her morning time with God.

"I appreciate that." Vanessa put her hands on her petite waist. "Let's see the quilt. I'm raring to go."

Sarah took the quilt out of the plastic bin and laid it out on the cutting table, top side up. As she caught sight of the amateur stitches on the melon pieces, she suddenly wondered if Fiona had sewn them. In her letter to Angela, she had mentioned her aunt making her practice sewing stitches. When she read the letter, Sarah had assumed they were embroidery stitches, but what if they had been running stitches for quilting? Had Aunt Mabina made Fiona help her quilt this beautiful piece?

Sarah had already told Vanessa about her suspicion that Mabina had made the quilt. "I was hoping you'd be able to tell me if there's a way to know whether the fabric was made in Ireland or England," Sarah said.

Vanessa ran a hand absently through her dark, cropped hair. She turned the quilt over and stared hard at the backing fabric, then shook her head. "I don't know. Let's flip it over again."

They did so, and Vanessa scrutinized each tiny piece of fabric. "Many of these fabrics are unfamiliar to me," she said, "but that could be because they're old, not necessarily because they're from England." She carefully examined every ring in the quilt until she got to the bright red ring near the center. She stared at it for an extra long time, then said, "Wait while I look something up."

She left and then came back with a heavy volume that looked like a coffee-table book. The book was about fabric dyes, and Vanessa checked the index in back before flipping to the chapter titled "Turkey Red."

"Turkey red dye comes from madder root, but to get this fiery red color, there was a special process that involved many steps and many months. The technique was imported from the Mediterranean to France and then to England. Because the process was so complicated, it wasn't done commercially in the United States. This piece"—Vanessa pointed to a bright solid fabric in an odd shade of red—"might be Turkey red."

"Is there a way to know for sure?" Sarah asked.

"Let me e-mail a chemist I've worked with in Atlanta," she said. "I once bought some fabric at a garage sale that looked like it had silver threads in it, but I began to suspect the threads were nickel instead. I sent him some of it to test and sure enough, the threads were nickel. He does general chemical testing, but I don't know if he can test for dyes."

Sarah looked at the tiny square of fabric. "How much would he need in order to test the dye?"

"I'll ask."

Sarah hoped he didn't need too much. While she would like to know if the dye was indeed from England, she would rather preserve the integrity of the quilt and this beautiful, difficult design.

"Another thing," Vanessa said. "The Double Wedding Ring quilt pattern is supposedly an American pattern, not an English pattern. If Mabina did make it, how did she get it?"

"I saw an old letter from one of the Hamills' relatives in Ireland," Sarah said. "Dated 1905. She talks about a 'Lattice Chain' pattern one of the American Hamills had apparently sent to her."

Vanessa stared at the quilt. "The Double Wedding Ring does look a bit like a lattice."

"I think the Lattice Chain pattern in the letter was the Double Wedding Ring pattern. I did some Internet research, and the pattern wasn't named 'Double Wedding Ring' until it was published in 1928."

"I just thought of something else," Vanessa said, turning over the edge of the quilt to look at the names again. "If Mabina did make this quilt, and this embroidered name is her signature, how did Liam's name get on the quilt?"

"I've been thinking about that too," Sarah said, "and I'm out of ideas."

"Why don't you try to figure out *when* his name was put on the quilt," Vanessa said.

"When?" Sarah realized Vanessa might be on to something. "Meaning, see if his name was on the quilt when he or Jeannie got it?"

"Exactly. Maybe it was accidentally written on the quilt after they were married, or something like that. But if Liam's name was already on the quilt when they got it—and Jeannie's wasn't—perhaps you can figure out why."

"So you're thinking his name might have been put on there by mistake somehow?"

Vanessa nodded. "*If* Mabina made this quilt, and *if* it belonged to Jeannie."

Sarah's heart beat fast as she answered the phone. "Hi, Liam."

"Hello, Sarah. It's good to hear your voice."

"Me too." His gentle brogue strummed on her heart in a comforting, familiar way. "I mean, it's good to hear your voice too. Are you still at that booksellers' event at that publishing house, or are you at the book expo?"

"The booksellers' event ended a few days ago—it went very well. I rented a car and drove to the book expo, and it's been an exhausting couple of days. Right now I'm in my hotel room, taking the opportunity to rest a bit." There was a pause, then he asked, "How are things going?"

He sounded almost as cheerful as normal, but Sarah thought she detected a brassiness to his bright voice, as if he were trying hard to hide some anxiety. She wondered if he was tired from his traveling, or if their last awkward conversation was on his mind. It was certainly on hers.

The problem with answering his question was that most of what she had been doing lately had involved looking into Fiona Hamill's disappearance.

So she said, "I've been getting to know this very prickly old man at Bradford Manor. In fact, he has my father's quilt and won't give it back to me. But the strangest thing is that I feel God telling me to befriend this man." She sighed. "I'm not sure yet how to go about it. He doesn't seem to want any friends."

"If you feel God is nudging you, then probably he'll help you know what to do," Liam said.

"You're right. I just can't help thinking about it."

There was a pause. Sarah's mind worked frantically to come up with something else to talk about except the one thing she had been doing for the past few weeks.

"So . . . anything else interesting happening?" Liam finally asked.

Was it just an idle question or was he fishing for something? Would he be upset that she had been investigating Fiona?

Or would he be interested in what she had discovered? He had known Peter Bickham and Roger Marstadt.

So she tentatively asked, "Would you like to know what I've found out about Fiona Hamill's disappearance?"

There was a long moment of silence on the line, and Sarah's heartbeat pulsed in her ears.

Finally Liam said, "What did you find out?"

She picked the safest bit of news first. "Peter Bickham was a U.S. Marshall."

"Was he really?" The surprise in his voice was genuine. "I never knew that. He never let on."

"He had apparently been after Frank Shields, who used to date Fiona. Frank was obsessed with Fiona, and Peter befriended Fiona, waiting for Frank to seek her out."

Liam gave a short burst of laughter. "I knew his job as a journalist seemed strange, but I never thought he was an undercover federal agent."

"I think Peter fell in love with her."

There was a softness in his deep voice as he replied, "He never said as much, but I think you're right. I felt sorry for him."

"I guess Fiona didn't love him back?"

"Fiona had … other things she was passionate about, like her photography. Marriage wasn't on her list."

Yet there had been the photo, with their names written on the back and encircled with a heart.

Then it occurred to Sarah that perhaps Liam didn't know about that photo. Perhaps he didn't even know about Fiona's feelings for him. After all, the photo had been carefully hidden in a box in Fiona's yard. What if it had been her secret?

Sarah obviously couldn't ask Liam about it. She would have to tread carefully, since she didn't want to jeopardize their friendship in any way. She cared about Liam, and she wanted to trust him.

But Sarah wasn't sure what to do about the fact that she knew he hadn't told her the entire truth. When she had last spoken to him, he had clearly said, twice, that he had been given the quilt. But Caitlin had said it was her mom's quilt. Was it just a slip of the tongue? Did he mean he and Jeannie had received the quilt as a gift, or had he really wanted to stress that the quilt had been given to him alone?

"I've been cleaning the quilt you gave to Caitlin," she said. "It's very beautiful."

"Even though it says I married Fiona Hamill?" he said, his words a little sharp-edged.

"Liam, you mentioned that when you got the quilt, you didn't notice those names on the backing?"

He gusted out a breath. "Sarah, it's a *quilt*. When Jeannie showed it to me, I barely registered anything about it besides the fact it was colorful."

When Jeannie showed it to him? "So the quilt was given to Jeannie?"

There was a pause on the line, then he said, almost reluctantly, "Yes, which makes it even more confusing why my name and Fiona's would be on it."

"It may not be Fiona's name," Sarah said. "It might be her aunt, Mabina Fiona Hamill. I think she might have been the one to make the quilt, and her name is on there as a signature."

"Fiona's aunt? You mean, from Ireland? I met Mabina Hamill when I first met Fiona."

"Did she quilt?"

"Yes, she had quilts all over her house. I didn't notice much about them, but I could see she had a lot of them."

"I don't understand why, but it's looking more and more likely that Mabina made that quilt."

Liam released a confounded gust of air. "But if Fiona's aunt made it, why is my name on it?"

"You can't think of a reason why?"

"Jeannie didn't get that quilt until years after Fiona had disappeared."

"When did she get it? And from whom?"

Liam sighed heavily. "I don't know from whom, but it was a few weeks before our wedding."

In 1975 then. Five years after Fiona went missing. "Jeannie didn't say who gave it to her?"

"No, it was given to her privately."

"Privately?" Sarah frowned at the phone, remembering the spectacle Roseanna had made at Caitlin's shower. "She didn't receive it at her bridal shower or the reception?"

"Jeannie showed it to me one day and said it was from a relative. I admit I wasn't interested enough to ask her who it was from."

That didn't really surprise Sarah. There weren't many grooms who would care who had given their bride a quilt. "Did she show it to anyone else? Maybe we can ask some of Jeannie's relatives if they saw it, or if they noticed the names on the backing."

"I don't know if she showed it to anyone else, but if they saw the names, I would think they'd have said something."

That was true. "Do you have any photos of the quilt? Caitlin mentioned it was on your bed in your old house. Do you have any old pictures that might have the quilt in the background?"

"There are a couple of boxes of old photos in the attic in my house." There was a brief pause, then he said, "Why don't you go to my house and look for them?"

"I can wait until you get back," Sarah said.

"No need." Liam cleared his throat. "I trust you, Sarah."

The words wrapped around her. He wasn't just telling her that he trusted her, he was telling her that she should trust him, too, even if he wasn't quite ready to tell her everything about that time in his life. She had to trust in the Liam she knew.

"Thank you, Liam."

"There's a spare key in a lockbox in the garage," Liam said. He gave her the combination to the lock so she could open the lockbox and retrieve the house key, and also told her where the attic door was.

"Thanks," she said.

"I'll be back the day after tomorrow, in the morning," Liam said.

"I can't wait to see you again, Liam."

"Me too."

As she hung up the phone, Sarah wondered what secrets she might uncover, and if Liam would be okay with her uncovering them.

CHAPTER SEVENTEEN

The Connolly home was a beautiful two-story house on the northwest side of Maple Hill, surrounded by other houses built around the same time, about fifteen to twenty years ago. It had a wide, deep porch with a swing and a table and a set of chairs, and Jeannie's favorite daffodils bloomed in the front garden in the springtime. Now there were only a few sparse rosebushes near the front steps, as the earth started to sink into winter sleep.

Sarah retrieved the spare key from the lockbox and unlocked the front door. She entered the spacious foyer, peeking into the large front room with warm, honey-colored wood paneling the walls.

She climbed the stairs that led up from the front foyer to the landing above. The attic door was in the ceiling of the landing. Sarah easily reached up to pull the door down, and the clink-clank of metal rang through the high-ceilinged foyer as metal steps slid down from the door panel.

Sarah climbed the steep steps.

She turned on the light switch on the wall and the attic flooded with light. A faint whistling sounded where the wind was blowing through a crack in the roof, and the attic was chilly after the warmth of the heated house. There were some small pieces of furniture, a couple of trunks, and several boxes. Sarah found that the steepled ceiling was high enough that she could stand upright in the middle.

"Where to begin?" she murmured to herself, then simply grabbed a box and started looking.

Since she was looking for photographs of the Connollys' old house, when Sarah found a box of old children's books, she quickly set it aside. She didn't think Liam would put old photos in with Caitlin's *I Can Read* books.

Sarah found the next box full of desk items, but they looked rather feminine—there was a letter opener with fancy scrollwork on the handle, a pen cup with Victorian roses painted on the outside, and a packet of different colored paper clips. Perhaps all from Jeannie's desk?

Sarah hesitated as she looked into the box. She felt as though she shouldn't be pawing through Jeannie's things. Sarah hadn't known her well when she was alive, and had only gotten closer to Liam over the past few years. This was a piece of his past—and Jeannie's—that Sarah hadn't been a part of.

But Liam had said he trusted her. He hadn't wanted her to wait until he came home before going through these things. He must have known what she would find since he had put these boxes up here in the attic.

She took a deep breath, then looked through Jeannie's desk items carefully, hoping to find some photos of the old house, but no luck.

At the bottom, Sarah found a box about the size of a telephone book and almost as heavy. She lifted it out and set it on a small table nearby. Inside were papers—a few old receipts for some large book orders for the bookstore, a book of stubs for a paid-off loan from the bank, and in Jeannie's slanted handwriting, a list of repairs that needed to be made around the house. "Fix the whistling in the roof in the attic" was on there, and Sarah smiled.

She looked through the box carefully, in case Jeannie had put some photographs in there for safekeeping, although she didn't hold out hope. These looked like mostly business papers.

Then at the very bottom of the box, Sarah found a copy of a canceled check for fifty thousand dollars, made out to Jeannie Connolly.

From the Hamill estate.

Sarah could only stare at the check. Fifty thousand dollars! And why in the world would the Hamills pay Jeannie that kind of money?

She immediately looked for the date: July 15, 1980. Just around the time Mrs. Bitty received her money from the Hamills' will.

Why would the Hamills leave Jeannie fifty thousand dollars? The check very clearly said Jeannie Connolly, not Jeannie and Liam Connolly.

Sarah ran through possible explanations. Then she thought back to when Liam and Jeannie had opened the bookstore. Caitlin had said it had been in December 1980.

Sarah had assumed Liam had saved up money from his years working in Boston before he married Jeannie, or that maybe they had applied for a small business loan.

She never would have guessed that they had opened The Spotted Dog because they had received a check for fifty thousand dollars.

Had Liam known about this? Or was this something Jeannie wouldn't have wanted anyone to know? The check *was* in her private papers.

Up until this point, there hadn't been any connection between Jeannie and the Hamills except for the fact that Liam had known them both, and the even stranger fact that Mabina's quilt had been given to Jeannie. But this . . .

Sarah needed to figure out if Fiona had been friends with Jeannie as well as Liam. Liam had firmly denied it, but he had also tried to make Sarah think the quilt had been given to him and not to Jeannie.

She would ask Mrs. Bitty about Fiona's relationship with Jeannie. Somehow, she had to figure out why Jeannie had received this check.

The next morning, Sarah again drove to Liam's house, ready to work.

She had called Mrs. Bitty the day before, but the older woman had said she had never noticed that Fiona was special friends with Jeannie. She had noticed Fiona was friends with Angela and Roseanna, but Mrs. Bitty mentioned that Fiona had a tendency to go out a lot and she didn't know with whom. Most of the time it was with Peter or Roger, or sometimes with Liam.

Sarah had gone through most of the boxes yesterday, but stopped when her back muscles ached from hunching over for so many hours. She hoped to finish going through the boxes today.

She was finally rewarded when she found three boxes filled with old picture albums, and she took them downstairs to the living room to spend an hour poring through them. She found several pictures in Liam and Jeannie's first house—a few parties they had given, some fun pictures of the two of them as newlyweds.

She also found several pictures that had been taken in their bedroom, with the Double Wedding Ring quilt in the background on their bed: a picture of Jeannie dressed up, ready to go to a fancy party or a wedding; Liam dressed in a Halloween costume as a swashbuckling pirate; a loving shot of Jeannie curled up on the bed, a sleeping infant Caitlin in her arms.

There were a few pictures where the bed in the background was rumpled or unmade, and Sarah searched eagerly, using the magnifying glass she had brought from home, to see if the backing corner with the names was visible. While the quilt was flipped over in several shots, none of the pictures showed the corner that Sarah was interested in seeing.

In the bottom of the last box, Sarah found a small memory box filled with things from Jeannie's thirtieth birthday, when Liam had surprised her with a trip to Hawaii. This had been before Caitlin was born, but Liam had once told Sarah about how he had woken Jeannie up at five in the morning, groggy and grouchy, with a birthday cake and candles, and two plane tickets.

Sarah had already seen the photos of the trip in one of the albums she had found. The memory box seemed to have more Hawaii photos.

But then she discovered other mementos that Jeannie hadn't been able to put in the photo album, like a shell lei, some other loose shells they must have collected from the beach, a blue and brown Hawaiian print short-sleeved shirt, and a pink and white bikini.

Sarah smiled as she looked at the bikini. She had only seen Jeannie in neat, comfortable clothing—nothing as fanciful as this!

And then she came across Jeannie's thirtieth birthday card, featuring a crocodile on the front, and inside ...

A picture of Jeannie, laughing, on the bed, with the Double Wedding Ring quilt rumpled up around her.

Liam must have taken the photo when he woke her up that morning, because a small cake sat next to her on top of the quilt with the blown-out candles still smoking slightly in the picture. Sarah got out the magnifying glass and held the picture up to the light streaming through the living room windows.

On the corner of the bed, the quilt had been turned over where Jeannie had thrown back the covers. Sarah squinted, and it looked like the edge of some name was visible. Was that Mabina's signature? Or Liam's name?

Sarah squinted some more. The picture was a little grainy, so she wasn't sure, but it looked like there was the edge of a patch above the writing on the quilt.

If there had been a patch above Mabina's signature, where had it gone? And what had been on it?

And suddenly Sarah knew. Of course! How could she have been so stupid? But how to determine if her hunch was correct?

She needed to look at the quilt under a black light.

Sarah didn't often use a black light for her work with quilts. Sometimes ultraviolet light could be used to help determine a quilt's age, but it didn't help her repair a quilt because UV light showed stains on fabric, and antique quilts tended to have many of those. Also, even if the fabric was old, if it had come into contact with any detergents made after World War II, the detergent residue would fluoresce.

But in this situation, it might show her exactly what she expected to see.

Jason and Maggie had a black light they had used to see stains left on the wood floor of their house that weren't otherwise visible. She called Jason at his law office.

"Hi, Mom," he said.

"Jason, where's your black light?"

"You need to use it? It's in the hall closet. There's a box with the stuff I use for the home remodel."

"Thanks," Sarah said, and hung up just as Jason started to say something.

She drove to Jason's house, used the spare key he had given her to let herself in, and went straight to the hall closet. Retrieving the black light, she turned it on and off to make sure it worked, then raced out to the car and back home.

The quilt was laid out on the dining room table, where she had put it after showing it to Vanessa. She closed the drapes, moved the quilt around, and flipped over the corner where the names were. The only light came through the open doorway.

Sarah turned on the black light and shone it on the quilt. Immediately she saw three lines she hadn't seen before.

"March 1, 1976" was the top line, then "Jeannie Crofter" appeared beneath it. Then there was an "and" on the next line. "Liam Connolly" was below that. Under Liam's name was Mabina's embroidered signature, "M. Fiona Hamill," but it didn't glow under the black light the way the other names did. The date and names fluoresced faintly, pointing to a modern ink that had ingredients that reacted to UV light.

A thin line that fluoresced a bright blue color formed a square that wrapped around Jeannie's and Liam's names but above Mabina's. Sarah guessed it was glue. She traced the square with her finger, and thought she felt roughness, but wasn't sure if it was just her imagination.

The patch she thought she had seen in the photo had been *glued* to the quilt above Mabina's name.

It made sense. Often people wanted to put a patch on a wedding quilt with the couple's names and the wedding date. Caitlin had mentioned that none of Jeannie's family sewed except for Jeannie's great-aunt. So if Jeannie or someone else had wanted to put a patch on the quilt, she might have glued it on.

It also meant she might have written their names on the patch since she couldn't embroider them, and the ink had seeped through.

Sarah herself had shuddered at more than one antique quilt to which a patch had been glued by a current owner who didn't know how to sew. And, in each case, the names on the patch had been written in dark ink.

Sarah had also seen one antique friendship quilt which had patches with people's names and addresses written on them, like an address book on the quilt so the bride could keep in touch with friends and family. Some of the names in ink had seeped through the patches and stained the fabric underneath.

If the corner of this quilt got wet at some point in the past, it was possible that Liam's name got wet, but not the date or Jeannie's name. So Liam's name stained through to the backing underneath the patch more than Jeannie's name or the date.

She should have realized that the ink on the back of Caitlin's quilt could have been transferred from something that lay on top of it, and had not necessarily been written directly on the quilt fabric. At some point, the patch must have fallen off because it had only been glued on—perhaps it had loosened when the quilt got wet and Liam's name was transferred to the backing.

She wondered if she could find the patch. If she was right, it would show Jeannie's name and the wedding date in addition to Liam's name. Or it might simply be lost.

Regardless, these names appearing under the black light proved that Liam's name on the quilt was simply...a mistake.

But they didn't explain why Jeannie, of all people, had been given Mabina's quilt.

Sarah rang the doorbell to Roseanna Walsh's front door and saw Roseanna approach through the glass panes in the door. She paused as she caught sight of Sarah, then reluctantly opened the door.

"Hello, Sarah," Roseanna said in a cool voice.

"May I come in?"

"I'm afraid I'm rather busy—"

"Roseanna, I found out how Liam's name got on the quilt."

Her face remained as smooth as glass. "I don't know what you're—"

"It was a mistake," Sarah said. "It wasn't Fiona's name, it was her aunt's."

Roseanna's brow wrinkled. "Her aunt?"

"And Liam's name was on the quilt because there used to be an old patch with Liam's and Jeannie's names written on it, and the ink bled through."

Roseanna's lips parted, and she could only stare at Sarah for a moment. Then she closed her mouth and stepped back. "Come in."

Sarah dutifully gave Roseanna her coat so she could put it in her hallway closet. Then Roseanna led the way to the living room and sat on a chair. "Now, what's this you say about it not being Fiona?" she asked.

Sarah explained what she had learned, about Angela's letter from Fiona, about how the "M. Fiona Hamill" had referred to Fiona's Aunt Mabina, who had made the quilt, and also about the names on the patch that had been glued to the quilt.

"Glued?" Roseanna's voice rose in horror at *glue* being used on a quilt.

"I used a black light and saw residue in the outline of a square patch," Sarah said. "I've seen glued patches before. Since it was only glued, I'm guessing the patch fell off at some point, maybe when Jeannie and Liam moved to their new house when Caitlin was five."

"So it was all a mistake," Roseanna repeated in a hushed voice. "I can't believe it."

"You didn't see the loose patch when you got the quilt from Liam, did you?"

"No." She emphatically shook her head. "Otherwise, I'd have known and not..." Her eyes flickered away from Sarah as her voice trailed off.

"Roseanna," Sarah said, "can you tell me why you were so desperate to hide the names?"

"Well, isn't it obvious? It looked like he'd married Fiona. I knew that wasn't possible, but I didn't want to bring up the old scandal of Fiona's disappearance and make the police wonder if Liam had anything to do with it. He's going to be Travis's father-in-law. Even if it came to nothing, I didn't want there to be any kind of trouble for him that might affect Travis and Caitlin."

Sarah could understand that. Roseanna was fiercely loyal and protective of her only son and the oldest of all her children. "But they were only friends," Sarah said. "There was no other connection between them."

Roseanna looked out the window for a moment, lost in memories. "I knew Fiona loved him, but he didn't love her."

Sarah's breath froze in her throat. Liam hadn't loved Fiona.

"I don't think Angela knew," Roseanna continued. "Fiona never said anything to us. But I'm pretty observant. There were times I saw Fiona looking at Liam, and it was so clear from the expression in her eyes. And I saw how Liam looked at Jeannie Crofter with the same type of look. I knew he didn't love Fiona. And I think Fiona knew too."

"How sad," Sarah said.

"So when I saw his name with Fiona's on the quilt, I wanted to hide it. I didn't think anyone else knew that she'd been in love with Liam, and since the police hadn't found *any* clues, they might look to Liam if they saw the quilt."

"Well, you can rest easy now," Sarah said.

"What are you going to do with the quilt now?"

"Maybe try to clean the glue off of it, although no one can see it, so it may not make a difference. Why?"

Roseanna straightened her shoulders, her mouth primly set. "Because while I appreciate your taking my patch off and cleaning it, I'd really like to sew it back on myself."

Jason's presence strengthened Sarah as they went to visit Leland again on Sunday afternoon. Strangely, the twins had wanted to come with them, mumbling something about a Bible verse in Sunday school that morning.

Their support gave Sarah a little more peace in her heart about what she was going to do.

Sarah and her granddaughters approached Leland's room with careful steps, mindful of their last conversation with him. But while Jason had been told about Leland's fierce reaction, he didn't hesitate to knock on Leland's door.

There was a shuffling sound, and then Leland opened the door to them.

He seemed to have grown a little older in the few days since they had last seen him, or maybe he was more tired. But his scowl was fierce as he caught sight of Sarah. "What do you want?"

Sarah took a deep breath to try to still the frantic fluttering in her rib cage. Then she held up her portable sewing kit and said, "I'm here to embroider your initials on Dad's quilt."

Leland stared at her for a full ten seconds. Sarah counted as he simply stood in his doorway. Finally he said, "Why are you going to do that?"

"Because Dad wanted you to have that quilt, and you should also have your initials on it, just like Dad's initials are embroidered on the corner patch." Dad's mother, Molly Harrison Drayton, had embroidered the initials W.J.H. in the corner patch of the baby quilt: William James Harrison. Sarah could think of only one way to show Leland that she wanted him to have her Dad's quilt—and with her blessing—and that was to truly make it his, with his initials next to his friend's.

Sarah couldn't quite explain it, but something in Leland's expression...cracked.

And then he was opening the door with a gruff, "Come in."

Amy and Audrey followed Sarah and Jason into the tiny room with a bit of trepidation, but they too must have seen something different in Leland's manner. They perched on Leland's bed with much less tension than before.

Leland reached into the bottom drawer of his dresser and pulled out Sarah's father's baby quilt.

The diagonal pattern leapt out at her as the diamonds in deep blues and yellows radiated out from the center of the blanket. She hadn't seen the quilt in several months, and she had forgotten how painstakingly her grandmother had pieced and quilted it.

Sarah sat on one of the two chairs in the room, and Leland sat in the other, so Jason wandered around the cramped space, looking at pictures and knickknacks tucked into corners and onto shelves.

Sarah found the corner block with her father's initials embroidered on it, and she opened her sewing kit. Her father's initials had been embroidered in dark blue floss on the yellow square, so she would embroider Leland's initials in the same color. "What are your initials?" she asked him.

"Leland Montgomery Mercer the Second," he replied. His voice caught on the last part of it.

Jason looked up from a photo he was peering at. "The Second? Is your son Leland Montgomery Mercer the Third?" He pointed to a man a little younger than Sarah in a picture on a bookshelf.

Leland's gaze moved to the photo, and it was as if he tried to look away but couldn't. And then Sarah saw the pain behind his eyes as he stared at his son's photo. She remembered what Jason had said, how Leland reminded him of a client who had gone through so much loss and suffering.

Lord, give me the words to say to him. "Where is your son now?" she asked.

"Dead," he croaked.

Sarah closed her eyes briefly, because she could only imagine his pain.

"Monty died only a few months ago from a stroke," Leland said softly. He cleared his throat. "My daughter-in-law died in a drunk driving accident only a couple of years ago. With both Monty and his wife gone, and no grandchildren to take care of me, I moved back to Maple Hill and became a resident here."

"It must have been so hard," Sarah said.

"Your dad . . ." Leland exhaled slowly. "Your dad would talk to me. At first we just caught up with each other's lives since we last saw one another."

"How did you know my dad?"

"We went to school together, but we were a few years apart and didn't become friends until he got married and had you."

"I don't remember you, growing up," Sarah said.

"I moved away from Maple Hill when you were barely two," Leland said. "I got a new job in Concord. Didn't keep up with your dad much—wish I had. We met up again when I came here a couple of months ago." The lines of sadness around his mouth deepened. "William was helping me learn how to move on."

And then he had died.

Sarah understood now why he had been so determined to stay aloof. He had lost his family and his friend within such a short space of time. How he must have been hurting.

"I'm glad you knew Grandpa," Amy suddenly said. "He liked talking to people."

Leland looked at the twins, sitting on the bed, and the corner of his mouth turned up in a half smile. Their youth was like a fresh breeze in this room, filled with Leland's old life. Sarah realized the room was so crowded because he didn't have anyone to store his belongings, so he must have brought everything with him.

Jason shifted away from the bookcase. "We like talking to people too," he said. "Why don't we pick you up and take you to our house for dinner tonight?"

Leland's eyes were wary. "You don't need to entertain an old man."

"I want to hear more about my grandfather," Jason said. "What kinds of fishing lures he liked best. How he disciplined his children." He winked at the twins.

"Da-ad..." Audrey said, while Amy giggled.

Leland nodded to Jason. "Sure, I can tell you that. Crickets in their beds, that's how."

While Leland talked with Jason and teased the girls, Sarah completed the initials on the quilt. It was even more fitting now that he have this memento from his close friend.

As she cut the last thread and shook out the quilt, Leland leaned over the table to talk to her. "Do you still need a dress for a wedding?"

Sarah started. He must have overheard her talking to Tiffany about it. "Yes, although it's next weekend."

Leland looked down for a moment, then said, "Look in the bottom drawer of that dresser."

Amy jumped off the bed and went to go look, and she came out with a paper-wrapped parcel. She laid it on the table to open it, and inside was a dark blue dress.

"My daughter-in-law was working on that when she died," Leland said. "I found it when I was cleaning out my son's house. It might fit you, and, well..." He shrugged, not looking at Sarah. "If you think you could finish it, and if you want it..."

Sarah held up the dress. It was almost completed. The dress was made of a soft rayon-cotton-blend fabric that had a nice drape but also stood up well to the shaping of the seams and the embroidery. It had a shallow scoop neckline and an A-line skirt, and long sleeves.

It still needed an invisible zipper sewn in, but that was because Leland's daughter-in-law had spent her time embroidering a lovely one-inch-wide maple leaf design in blue embroidery floss on the fabric on either side of the placket. She had also already completed the even more laborious job of making a beautiful row of embroidery along the bottom hem, about five inches wide, again in a maple leaf pattern. She had embroidered the cuff of one sleeve, a three-inch-wide circle of embroidery, and obviously intended to do the other. It also looked as though she had intended to embroider the neckline.

"Oh, Leland, it's lovely," Sarah breathed. It might even fit her, and the design was simple and classic. "But are you sure?"

He shrugged again. "Take it, if you want it," he said in a deceptively careless tone that didn't fool Sarah at all.

The embroidery, while beautiful, looked fairly straightforward. And while Sarah was better at quilts than embroidery, Imogene Dowling had often told her that if she needed any embroidery projects done, she would be happy to do them. Perhaps she would be able to finish the embroidery on this dress by next Saturday.

This dress had pizzazz, that was for sure. And yet it was elegant and classic in design, and it entirely suited her taste.

"Wow, Grandma," Amy said. "You're going to look like a princess."

"Then it's a good thing I have a prince, isn't it?"

"Liam's a nice prince," Audrey said. "But I want my prince to have raven black hair and piercing cerulean blue eyes."

Sarah looked at Jason with a silent *Where does she get this?* expression. Jason returned it with a shrug that said, I dunno.

A nurse knocked on Leland's door a few minutes later to take him to his physical therapy session. After arranging to pick him up for dinner later, Jason left with Sarah and the two girls.

As they were walking through the front common room, a voice interrupted her thoughts.

"Sarah! Yoohoo!"

Sarah saw Olive Cavanaugh waving at her. Tiffany Henderson was just pushing her wheelchair into the common room, and Olive's wildly flapping hand nearly swiped the nurse in the eye.

Olive's excited air had Sarah approaching with a curious smile. "Hi, Olive."

"I'm so glad you're here. I need to tell you something."

"What is it?"

"The last time you were here, you mentioned Fiona Hamill. I told you I knew about her disappearance but I hadn't known her personally, but after you left, I remembered something that you might be interested in."

"Something about Fiona?"

"Not quite. My brother Walter used to be head over heels in love with a girl named Margo Edghill," Olive said, her blue eyes bright. "She was a little younger than me, and all the boys were after her because she was gorgeous—hair like a waterfall of chocolate, eyes like dark roasted coffee. She was feisty too. A little like me." Olive grinned, and Sarah chuckled.

Olive continued, "Margo was perhaps the only girl who reduced Walter to a blathering fool anytime she came near, which I thought was hilarious. So naturally I'd try to drag him with me to talk to her just to embarrass him."

"Olive!" Sarah said with a grin.

"But I liked Margo, too—she was a lot of fun to talk to. Because I was such a devoted sister, interested in furthering my brother's love life, I got to know Margo quite well."

"Did Walter ever ask her out?"

"Actually, he did, and she turned him down because she had started dating Theodore Woltherstorf."

"Oh, poor Walter."

"He eventually got her to go out with him on a date to the movies a few weeks later when she realized Theodore Woltherstorf was a bore."

"So how long did he date Margo?"

"Oh, just that once. She found out Walter was a bore too," Olive said.

Sarah laughed. "Olive! And your own brother too."

"Anyway, fast-forward a few years," Olive said. "Margo and I had both grown up, and I saw her in Concord. I asked, 'What are you up to now?' She said, 'Why, I'm the secretary to Robert Hamill at Hamill Shipping.'"

Sarah was speechless for a second. "Robert Hamill?"

"That was Fiona's father, wasn't it?" Olive said.

"Yes, that was Fiona's father."

"I know Fiona's parents died quite a few years ago, and Fiona disappeared, but I thought you might want to look up Margo to see if she's still around. She might remember something about Fiona."

"Thank you so much, Olive," Sarah said. "I'll definitely try to find her."

Olive gave a triumphant look. "I told you you'd want to hear this story."

CHAPTER EIGHTEEN

Sarah felt a bit guilty as she rang Liam's doorbell. If his flight had arrived on time, then he had returned to Maple Hill only a scant hour before, and here she was bothering him. The man probably hadn't even unpacked yet.

He opened the door with a look of pleased surprise. "Now this is a bonny sight." He reached out to give her a hug.

She relaxed against him, feeling his warmth and strength. "I'm so sorry to come over when you've only just gotten home."

"Sarah, don't you realize that when I'm with you, I feel at home?"

She couldn't help smiling at his blarney.

He released her. "Come in. Still looking for photos?"

"Actually, I found one, and I wanted to ask you if you still had the box the quilt was stored in."

"I think so." He led the way to the back of the house. "I gave the quilt to Roseanna a couple of weeks before I left, but the box was torn and dusty. She took the quilt out and left the box, and I never got around to throwing it out. It should be on the back porch. Why do you need it?"

"I'm looking for a patch that was glued onto the quilt."

They headed out the backdoor and stepped out onto the porch that wrapped around the back of the house. A few feet from the door sat a sagging cardboard box with a water stain on a corner.

"A patch?" Liam asked.

"With your name and Jeannie's written on it, and the date of your wedding. I think the ink seeped through onto the quilt backing right above Mabina's signature." Sarah peered inside the box at the sheets of tissue paper lying there. Several pieces were horribly stained and damaged from the same water that had stained the outside of the box. She sifted through them, and near the bottom, she saw a faded blue piece of cloth.

It was the patch, with wrinkled edges stiff with dried glue and light brown waves of water stains on the fabric. And written in faded blue black ink: "March 1, 1976, Jeannie Crofter and Liam Connolly." Liam's name was more faded and more stained than the rest of the patch.

"I was right," Sarah said.

"Well, that's a relief." His voice had a lightness she hadn't heard since she first told him about the names on the quilt. "I was beginning to think I'd completely forgotten a wedding I'd been in." He took the patch from her, and faint lines of tightness around his eyes relaxed as he looked at it.

"There's something else I found out today," Sarah said. "Do you have an old picture of Jeannie?"

"How old?"

"One where she's in her twenties?"

"I have our wedding photo." Liam led the way back into the house and into the living room, gingerly placing the patch on the coffee table. He retrieved a framed photo from the bookshelf. "Jeannie was about twenty-eight."

From out of her purse Sarah pulled the photo she had printed off the Internet and held it up side by side with Jeannie's wedding photo.

Liam froze. "That woman looks exactly like Jeannie."

"This woman," Sarah said, holding up the printed picture, "was Margo Edghill, Robert Hamill's secretary."

"How did you find her?"

"Olive Cavanaugh. I had asked her about Fiona Hamill before, and she said she hadn't known Fiona, but then later she remembered a girl she knew, Margo Edghill, who had been Robert Hamill's secretary."

"I never met her."

"I looked her up on the Internet and found an obituary for Margo Edghill Bennett. She died in 2000, but the obituary showed a younger photo of her. As soon as I saw her, I knew I had to come to tell you."

"And you think they're related?"

"I think Margo Edghill was Jeannie's biological mother, not Jane Crofter," Sarah said. "I'm guessing that Margo got pregnant with Robert Hamill's baby and gave her up when she was born."

"Robert Hamill? Are you sure?"

"When I first saw pictures of Robert Hamill and Fiona," Sarah said, "something about them struck me, but I didn't know what it was. Now I realize it was that Jeannie has some similar features—and Caitlin too. Caitlin has your coloring, but she looks very much like her mother. Jeannie looks most like Margo, but she also has some of Robert Hamill's features. Did Jeannie or her parents ever say she was adopted?"

"No."

Liam took Margo's photo from Sarah and sank into a chair, staring at it and reading the obituary. "She was born in 1925. She would have been twenty-three when Jeannie was born."

"I never met Jeannie's parents, but I'm guessing they don't look like her?"

Liam rose and took another photo from the bookshelf, showing it to Sarah. "Jeannie's parents."

Jeannie didn't look like either of her parents. Her mother had a long face and wide smile while her father's face was round and florid.

Liam sighed and sat back down on the chair. "Jeannie was adopted. I can't believe it. Did she know?"

"I think she did." Sarah sat in a chair across from him.

"Then why didn't she tell me?"

"I think she didn't tell you because the Crofters didn't tell her she was adopted. I think she found out from Fiona, her half sister."

"Fiona." Liam's voice was quiet, and his eyes skirted away from Sarah's gaze. "I lied to you before, Sarah. Fiona and Jeannie were very close, but when you started asking questions, all I could think of was that I needed to keep Jeannie's involvement a secret."

Sarah's brow wrinkled. "What do you mean?"

"The night Fiona disappeared, I knew something strange had happened. I was renting a room in a house nearby the Crofters, so my truck was only a little way down the road from Jeannie, and she knew where my keys were kept in the garage. The morning Fiona went missing, I noticed the gas gauge had gone down on my truck. When I saw Jeannie later that day, I could tell she'd been upset, but when I asked her about it, she refused to tell me."

"You mean Jeannie borrowed your truck to help Fiona run away?"

"Jeannie never kept any secrets from me except about that one night. I didn't know what to think, but I kept her secret all these years. I wanted to know the truth, but I trusted Jeannie and didn't want to implicate her in Fiona's disappearance, so I never said anything. I left Maple Hill a few weeks later to work in Boston."

Sarah sat back in her chair, then said slowly, "That explains about your truck."

"Explains what?"

"The night Fiona disappeared, Frank Shields's mother saw Fiona in your truck heading south on the road to Teesdale, but no one in Maple Hill saw her, so I thought Mrs. Webb must be mistaken. But if Fiona managed to get from her house to the Crofters' house on the south side of town, then she and Jeannie could have taken your truck and headed to the bus depot in Teesdale, where no one would know Fiona. And no one in Maple Hill would have seen the truck."

"That means Fiona is alive." Liam looked a little shell-shocked. "All these years wondering what really happened to her, but she's alive."

"One of the Hamill servants, Mrs. Bitty, insisted she saw Fiona in Pittsfield a few months after the Hamills died. But Mrs. Bitty is getting older, and I wasn't sure if I could trust her memory."

"So you think Jeannie helped Fiona run away, because they knew they were sisters."

"I think it makes a lot of sense. It also explains about the check."

"What check?"

"When I was looking for photos of the quilt in the attic, I found a box from Jeannie's desk. Mostly receipts and lists, but also a cancelled check for fifty thousand dollars made out to Jeannie from the Hamill estate."

Liam closed his eyes and leaned back in his seat. "That's where she got it from. Jeannie told me she'd received an inheritance from a distant aunt," Liam said. "I had no reason to doubt her. I was too excited about the money to ask who it was, especially when Jeannie said I hadn't ever met her. We used the money to open The Spotted Dog that December."

"I thought so."

"So Fiona came back to Maple Hill that year."

"It was a few months after her parents died. She would have inherited everything. She apparently gave several gifts, including that one to her sister."

"Her sister." Liam looked again at the picture of Margo. "So Fiona gave Jeannie that quilt."

"Yes. Mabina was Jeannie's aunt, too. Fiona might have given the quilt to Jeannie the night she disappeared, but Jeannie didn't show it to you until just before the wedding. Or maybe Fiona mailed it to Jeannie."

"Mailed?" Liam frowned as he stared at the coffee table. "Now that would explain a lot."

"What do you mean?"

"After Jeannie died, I found a box filled with letters she'd received. She loved corresponding with people—family, friends from school—so I didn't look through all the letters because there were a lot of them. But I saw a few letters from Fiona in which she referred to Jeannie as her sister. I knew they were close, so I thought she was speaking figuratively."

Sarah straightened in her chair. "Do you still have those letters?"

"Let me get them." He rose and disappeared down the hallway toward his office. He came back carrying a large hat-box covered in flowery blue paper.

He placed the box on the coffee table and opened it. Then immediately his face turned red and he snatched at a large, ribbon-tied packet of letters. "Er ... best not see those."

"Why?"

"They're from me to Jeannie during the years I was working in Boston."

Sarah couldn't help but laugh at his embarrassment.

They sifted through the letters, and finally Liam said, "Here's one."

Sarah immediately recognized the same thin, international airmail paper that Fiona had used for the letter to Angela from Ireland.

December 12, 1969
Pomeroy, Tyrone, Ireland
Dear Jeannie,
I'm especially missing you this Christmas. Do you remember last year how we snuck out and then got lost driving to Pittsfield to see that show? This year, I have no sweet sister to be naughty with. I am dull, respectable, and full of holiday festivities.

Fiona went on to describe the holiday shopping she had done, trying to buy presents for her cousins without them knowing about it, and she ended the letter with:

Missing you dreadfully,
Your sister,
Fiona

Sarah read through the letter again. "Fiona and Jeannie knew they were half sisters, even before Fiona went to Ireland."

"I wonder how they found out?" Liam mused.

"Maybe the answer is here, in these letters. Did Fiona write to Jeannie after she left?"

They searched through the letters, finally finding one dated December 20, 1970, in Fiona's handwriting.

Dear Jeannie,

I landed in Heathrow without problems. I considered calling one of my cousins who I know would keep her mouth shut, but decided not to. I think it best that only you and I know what happened.

I checked into a hotel, flung open the windows to my room, and breathed deep of the London fog. It smelled like freedom to me.

Tomorrow I will think more sensibly about what I will do with the money. But tonight I write to you and thank you from the bottom of my heart. Tonight I also take on the new me, and try it out on you.

Yours,

Mabina Fredericks

"She took on the name Mabina," Sarah said.

They continued searching through the letters. Except for Liam's letters, Jeannie hadn't grouped the other letters together, so Liam and Sarah had to sift through letters from cousins and high school friends, among others. Eventually they found several from Fiona, the oldest dated a year before she left for Ireland. Apparently they had kept their relationship secret by writing letters to each other, even though they lived in the same town. Fiona wrote to Jeannie when she was in Ireland, and they also found a few letters from Mabina. She was an indifferent letter writer as the years passed and she grew busier, but there was at least one letter a year from her.

They kept searching until they reached the last letter in the box, a small envelope, which was strange since the other letters had been removed from their envelopes. As Sarah tried to pick it up, she realized it had been glued to the bottom of the box.

"I wonder what this is?" She opened the flap and took out two sheets of paper, the top one addressed to Jeannie in handwriting that was different from any of the others. Sarah started when she saw the name at the bottom: Margo Bennett.

"Liam," Sarah said, and read him the letter.

July 12, 1968
Dear Jeannie,
In a way, I'm relieved your parents told you about me. I've been good friends with your mother Jane for years, and so when I found myself unexpectedly pregnant, they were more than happy to adopt you as their own, and they have always kept me informed about how you are doing.

I am enclosing your birth certificate, but I must warn you that your biological father will deny all of it. I think it for the best. You are the best parts of him, and none of the bad.

You are welcome to come visit me in Boston at some point. My husband knows about you and will welcome you into our home. Because of complications with the pregnancy, I am no longer able to have children, and I would love to get to know you more. Your parents have approved of all of this.

Let me know if you are open to visiting us.

Yours,

Margo Bennett

Sarah looked at the birth certificate, and saw Robert Hamill listed as the father.

She gave both papers to Liam. "Jeannie might have approached Fiona, or maybe they were friends already and Jeannie knew how Fiona would react to this news."

It amazed and touched her that the two sisters had remained so close, despite the fact that both of them had loved Liam.

He looked at the letters they had scattered over the table and even the floor. "Is that it, then?"

"It might be worth it to look through the attic. I found that box of things that looked like they were from Jeannie's desk. Maybe she had more letters squirreled away." Sarah glanced at the small pile they had made of Fiona's letters. "At least we found Fiona."

"There's one more place we can look." Liam jumped up to bring his laptop computer into the living room. "Mabina's letters talked about her photography winning awards. Maybe we can find out about her on the Internet. If she's still alive and taking pictures, surely there would be articles about her."

They did even better than that. They found Mabina Fredericks's Web site showcasing her wonderful photographs—images that captured emotions like the photos Mrs. Bitty had shown Sarah.

There was a small head shot of Mabina, with the same clear blue eyes, calm demeanor, and core of steel, but her face was wreathed in more wrinkles than before and deeply tanned, probably from the time she spent outdoors taking photographs.

Liam stared at the computer screen. "That's Fiona," he said.

"Caitlin's aunt," Sarah added.

Liam looked at her. "Did you tell Caitlin about any of this?"

She shook her head emphatically. "Absolutely not. She thinks I'm just cleaning her quilt. Do you want me to sew Jeannie's patch back on?" Sarah saw a corner of the blue patch peeking out from under a stack of letters. "Except...do I hide Mabina's signature again?"

Liam's normally cheerful, easygoing face had become terribly grave. "No. No more secrets. Not about Jeannie and Fiona. And...not about me."

"You don't owe me an explanation," Sarah said. "I'm so sorry I pushed. I shouldn't have."

"Yes, you should have. And yes, I do," Liam replied. "And thank you for keeping this secret from others while you've been looking into it.

"The real reason I left Ireland with Fiona and Peter was because my father killed a man in a hit-and-run, while driving my car."

Sarah took a sharp breath.

"He was drunk as a lord," Liam said with a trace of bitterness in his voice. "He'd been drinking more and more ever since he left the British Secret Service. I was questioned about the man's death but never charged or arrested. But our neighbors all thought I'd killed the man.

"A few months later, I met Fiona and Peter. Fiona was leaving Ireland in a few weeks, and Peter was going with her, and I thought, 'Why not?' So I left too. I tried to get me Mam to come with me, but she wouldn't leave him. She died only a few months later. I never spoke to my father after I left, up to the day he died, several years after my mother, of liver failure."

"Oh, Liam."

"I never went back to Ireland. I couldn't. And when I arrived in Maple Hill, I realized I didn't want to. I met Jeannie." He hesitated. "But when Fiona disappeared, I wondered if something I had done had made her run away."

"Fiona was in love with you," Sarah said.

Liam nodded heavily. "I tried to let Fiona down easy, but I'd already taken one look at Jeannie and fallen in love. Fiona was hurt, which I think is why she was more encouraging to Peter than she should have been. She became even more wild when she returned home to Maple Hill—they went out to parties at night and Fiona tried to get me to go with them, but I always refused. We argued about it."

"In the library, once?" Sarah guessed. "Mrs. Bitty saw you."

Liam nodded. "That was our worst argument. She wanted me to take her to a party—Peter and Roger couldn't go, they were both in Boston that weekend—and I told her no. She got more and more angry. I tried to get her to calm down, but she was too riled up. Then she disappeared only a few days later. I thought it might have been my fault, but then the newspaper said nothing had been taken from her room, and I thought she might have been kidnapped."

"You must be glad to know she's alive." Sarah reached out and took his hand. "Thank you for sharing that with me, Liam. I know that wasn't easy for you."

"Thank you for finding Fiona. Now I have answers to give when I explain the quilt to Caitlin."

"She'll be excited to know she has an aunt," Sarah said, remembering the girl's wistfulness about her Irish relatives.

"I wonder . . ." Liam looked at his laptop, still open on the table, crushing the letters they had piled on the surface. "I wonder if Fiona would want to come to Caitlin's wedding."

"I don't know if she'd come, but Caitlin is her only niece."

Liam nodded in decision. "I'll e-mail her through her Web site, though I have no idea how I'll start." He suddenly looked up at Sarah, his smile bright. "Speaking of the wedding, I almost forgot. I talked to Caitlin when she picked me up from the airport this morning, and she wanted me to ask you if you'd read a poem during the wedding ceremony."

At first, Sarah was too flattered to say a word. Then she said, "I'd be honored."

Irene could only stare dumbfounded at Sarah. "And that's the truth?" she said.

"That's the truth," Sarah said.

Irene sat back in her chair. "It's not very flattering to the Hamills, or the Marstadts."

"But I wanted you to know," Sarah said.

"Do you think Fiona will come to Caitlin's wedding? I'd love to meet her, finally."

"Liam e-mailed her, but she hasn't responded, so I don't think she's coming. After all, she left Maple Hill forty years ago and never looked back. She had good reason to go."

"True." Irene stared at her office computer. "Call me a romantic, but I wish this had a happier ending. I like the stories from history where there's some sense of closure and acceptance and contentment. Where people can feel good about the world for a little while."

"The happy ending here has to be Caitlin's wedding and the Double Wedding Ring quilt," Sarah said. "I cleaned up Jeannie's patch and sewed it on, and Roseanna put her embroidered patch back on—not covering Mabina's name, this time—and it'll be displayed at the wedding reception." Sarah smiled. "The wedding ring symbolizes unity, and Caitlin and Travis will form their own family."

CHAPTER NINETEEN

The Congregational Church echoed pleasantly as the young people laughed and chattered at their places in front of the stage. Caitlin stood in a green dress that matched her eyes, ready to go to the rehearsal dinner after they were done here in the church, rehearsing the wedding ceremony.

Sarah sat in a pew, watching the bride and groom figure out where they were supposed to stand, while the bridesmaids held fake bouquets and the groomsmen stood looking a little bored. Sarah had already gone up to pretend to read the poem at the podium and then had returned to her seat.

A cough tickled her throat, so she rose to go to the restrooms, which were at the back of the sanctuary. She was looking right at the doors when they opened to reveal a tall, elegant woman wandering into the church.

Her gray hair was up in a French twist, contrasting dramatically with her deeply tanned face. She wore an expensive suit in brown with bold lime green trim.

Her gaze fell on the bridal party at the front of the church, or perhaps just on the bride. No one else had seen the woman enter the sanctuary.

Sarah stepped forward. "Mabina Fredericks?" she asked. She smiled and held out a hand. "I'm Sarah Hart. Welcome to Maple Hill."

Mabina looked startled for a moment, but then she shook Sarah's hand. "Pleased to meet you," she said. "Liam mentioned you in his e-mail to me. Is that Caitlin?"

Sarah nodded. "Would you like to speak to Liam first?"

A flash of some emotion crossed Mabina's face, but then she smiled, looking exactly like Caitlin. "I'd like th—"

"Fiona?" Liam had apparently seen them from his seat near the front of the church and now approached them.

"It's Mabina now," she said, and gave him her hand with a smile.

He returned the smile, but bent to buss her cheek as he clasped her hand with both of his. "It's good to see you again. When you didn't e-mail me back, I didn't think you'd come."

"I didn't decide to come until yesterday," Mabina said. "I was in the middle of a wildlife photo shoot, but something made me hop on a plane, and here I am."

The three of them sat in a pew near the back while the rehearsal continued up front.

"I hear you're a famous photographer now," Liam said.

"Not quite famous, but I make enough not to starve," Mabina said with dry humor.

They sat and watched the rehearsal for a while, and Mabina said softly, "She's a beautiful girl, Liam. Jeannie would be so proud."

"I wish you'd told me," he said.

Mabina shook her head. "No, you don't. Jeannie thought you shouldn't know, and I trusted her, even more than I trusted you."

"But why did you leave like that?"

"Luck landed in my lap, so I took it," Mabina said with a touch of fierceness. "While I was in Ireland, an uncle died and left me—left all his nephews and nieces—a tidy legacy. I knew if I brought the money back to Maple Hill, my father would take it, and I suddenly saw a way to escape him. You didn't know what he was like, Liam."

Sarah remembered Mrs. Bitty's words about Robert Hamill, and shivered.

"So I asked Jeannie to help me, and she did. And I ran."

"Why did you leave everything?" Sarah asked her.

"I left my old life behind," Mabina said. "I was no longer Fiona, I had become Mabina. The only things I took were my camera and Aunt Mabina's quilt, which I gave to Jeannie. She gave me a suitcase full of clothes and a wad of cash, and she drove me to the bus depot. Once I got to England, I could use the inheritance from my uncle, and I could live the life of excitement that I wanted."

And apparently she had, to the fullest.

"Could I ask you a question?" Sarah said.

"Certainly."

"Did Peter Bickham propose to you?"

Mabina smiled suddenly. "Peter. I haven't thought of him in so long. Yes, he did, but I didn't love him. He told me he was a U.S. Marshall, you know. His life was certainly exciting, full of traveling, but not the kind I wanted to do."

"Did your Aunt Mabina make the quilt for you while you were in Ireland?"

"Yes, did you see it? I stitched some of it myself."

"Caitlin has it now," Sarah said.

"I'd like to see it again," Mabina said wistfully. "I stared at it until I was sick of it that year in Ireland, but after I gave it to Jeannie, I missed it every so often. But I would remember it was with her, and that made me happy."

Mabina's eyes shone with unshed tears. "I didn't know Jeannie had died until I sent a letter to her, and Liam, you sent it back unopened with a note telling me she was gone."

"I didn't know who you were."

"I know. At the time, I thought about telling you, but then I decided not to, after all these years."

"You still own the Hamill estate?" Sarah asked.

"Yes. It'll go to Caitlin and her children someday." Mabina smiled. "But not just yet. I have lots of living to do first."

"I hope you'll come back to Maple Hill more often than once every forty years," Liam said.

"Maybe I will." Mabina looked at Caitlin, seeing her sister Jeannie, and the happy memories played in the expressions on her face.

Sarah had originally thought the only connection between Liam and Fiona had been that quilt, but now she realized it wasn't the quilt. It was love: Fiona's love for Liam, Liam's love for Jeannie, and Jeannie's and Fiona's love for each other.

And now the quilt stood for a new love: Caitlin and Travis, and Caitlin and Mabina.

Sarah couldn't think of a better quilt to celebrate that love than the Double Wedding Ring quilt.

About the Author

Camy Tang grew up in Hawaii and now lives in San Jose, California, with her engineer husband and rambunctious dog Snickers. She graduated from Stanford University and worked as a biologist researcher for nine years, but now she writes full time. She is a staff worker for her church youth group, and she leads one of the worship teams for Sunday service. On her blog, www.camytang.com, she ponders knitting, spinning wool, dogs, running, the Never-Ending Diet, and other tantalizing things.

CHAPTER ONE

Sarah Hart loved weddings. They wrapped around you like a warm quilt and promised a golden future.

She sat in the third row of the padded church pews, with her daughter-in-law Maggie on her right and her twin granddaughters just next to Maggie. Beyond Amy and Audrey, Sarah's son Jason sat on the aisle, chatting quietly over the back of his seat with Ernie Maplethorpe, her best friend Martha's husband. Maggie sat serenely with a wistful smile on her face. Sarah wondered if her daughter-in-law was recalling her own wedding day.

Sarah herself had a packet of tissues in her purse for the inevitable tears of joy, but she wouldn't willingly have been anywhere else on earth today.

As the organ music swelled into the prelude, Sarah's stomach fluttered. This wedding would unite Liam Connolly's daughter Caitlin with her fiancé, Travis Walsh. Sarah liked both young people enormously, and her feelings for Liam had lately grown to a warmth beyond friendship. Because of that, this day was doubly special.

She would soon get up to fulfill Caitlin's request that she read a poem. Sarah was glad to do it, but as usual when she had to speak before a large group, her nerves niggled at her. She reached up and touched her hair. Did she look all right? Would she mess up the reading and embarrass Caitlin? She had brought a copy of the poem along, just in case she needed it. She made herself lower her hand and sit still.

The processional began, and the bridesmaids entered, smiling and gorgeous as they glided down the aisle in lush green gowns. When the bride's march began, Sarah and all the others stood and faced the church door.

Caitlin beamed as she started down the aisle with her father. Her red hair framed her face, and her green eyes glistened with a sheen that might be tears. Tiny, pale green beads sparkled in the embroidery on the bodice of her white gown. She carried a bouquet of white roses and greenery that offered the only other color against the shimmery white folds.

Liam's pride was evident when he walked his daughter the length of the sanctuary with his shoulders back and his head high. Sarah had never seen him look so handsome. His green eyes appeared to be a bit misty as he left Caitlin in Travis's care and took his seat in the front pew with other family members, including Caitlin's aunt, Mabina Fredericks, who had flown in from Ireland for the wedding.

Sarah had been flattered when Liam had invited her to join him up front with the family, but she had gently declined. This special day belonged to the Connollys. She would perform with joy the small part Caitlin had asked her to play, but she didn't want the spotlight to shine too long on her.

A harpist began to play a traditional Irish song that pulled at Sarah's heart. Caitlin and Travis stood, hands clasped, gazing at each other. Sarah couldn't remember seeing a more beautiful bride since her daughter Jenna's wedding day. She closed her eyes and let the haunting music take her back in memory.

All too soon, the music ended and Sarah's moment had arrived. At the minister's nod, she rose, smoothed down the skirt of her cobalt blue dress—a gift from her new friend, Leland Mercer. His daughter-in-law had made it shortly before her death, and had embroidered a lovely border of blue maple leaves at the hem, neck, and cuffs. Sarah's friend and neighbor Imogene Dowling had finished the dress for Sarah, and she loved it. She had wondered if it was too elegant, but both Maggie and Martha had assured her it suited her well and hung on her frame well. Sarah found that she liked the dress more each time she looked at it.

She walked to the front and stood behind a lectern at one side of the platform. Her pulse ran a little fast, but that would pass as soon as she had finished this reading.

Looking out over the sea of faces, Sarah inhaled deeply. Half the town had turned out for this wedding, it seemed, and more than thirty guests had come from out of town. Sarah had met most of Caitlin's relatives at yesterday's rehearsal. Even so, the crowd was dotted with several people she didn't know.

She lowered her gaze to the parchment lying on the lectern. She had copied out the poem on decorative paper just in case. For hours she had practiced it, muttering the lines under her breath as she quilted or vacuumed, and she knew it all by heart, but even so, she was nervous.

The poem was "To My Dear and Loving Husband," by the colonial poet Anne Bradstreet. Sarah took a deep breath and began, "If ever two were one, then surely we. If ever man were lov'd by wife, then thee." She never uttered the lines without thinking of her late husband Gerry. She was glad Caitlin had chosen this, one of her favorites verses by an early Massachusetts writer, but it made her voice catch every time.

She focused on her granddaughters in the third row. Both were watching her and listening avidly. By zeroing in on Amy and Audrey, Sarah was able to go on without her eyes tearing up. That morning she had reminded herself not to look at Liam while reciting. She hoped he wouldn't mind, but if his direct, piercing gaze caught hers in the middle of the emotional piece, she wasn't sure what would happen.

As she reached the last lines, she dared to lift her gaze farther afield, to the back rows of the church.

"Then while we live, in love let's so persever, That when we live no more, we may live ever." That line usually tripped her up, between the thoughts of Gerry already "living no more," and the awkward pronunciation of "persevere," to rhyme with "ever." But today something quite unrelated to Bradstreet's rhyme scheme made Sarah almost flub her recitation.

Through the tiny windows of glass in the double doors at the back of the sanctuary, she saw Ernie Maplethorpe, her friend Martha's husband, about to enter. He had been in the sanctuary earlier, sitting just behind the Hart family and next to Martha, Sarah was sure. He must have stepped out during the music.

Ernie hesitated and turned to speak to someone—a woman wearing a wide-brimmed, dark hat. That in itself was unusual these days—only two other women in the church wore hats, and they were elderly ladies. But this woman looked like someone Sarah knew and hadn't seen for many years. Her brain searched her memory and told her the woman was Ruby Sears. But it couldn't be. Not after all these years.

She lowered the paper with the poem on it and walked down the steps off the platform, and the minister took over to perform the ceremony. As she headed for the pew where

Jason, Maggie, and the twins sat, Sarah looked toward the doors again.

Ernie still stood just outside, turned away from her, apparently in quiet conversation with the woman in the hat. As Sarah watched, the woman turned for a moment and looked in through the glass. Sarah caught her breath. The hat bore a cluster of light blue silk flowers on one side of the crown, bringing out the color, even at a distance, of her vivid blue eyes. Her cheekbones, her rosebud mouth. Even though she hadn't seen the woman in almost forty years, Sarah knew that distinctive face.

What on earth was Ruby Sears doing back in Maple Hill?

The reception was held in the church hall at Congregational Church, and Sarah made her way through the crowd as quickly as she could with Jason, Maggie, and the twins trailing after her. This was not her home church, but she had been in it many times over the years. The bridal party was forming a receiving line at one side of the hall. Sarah got in line with Maggie and the others. As they waited to congratulate the bride and groom, she kept her eye on the other guests entering the hall, but she saw no sign of Ruby.

When Sarah got to the head of the line, she expressed her appreciation to each of Caitlin and Travis's attendants and complimented the bridesmaids on how lovely they looked.

The maid of honor, Tiffany Henderson, greeted Sarah with a big smile. "Hello, Mrs. Hart. That was a beautiful poem."

"Thank you. It's a favorite of mine." Tiffany was a nurse at Bradford Manor, the nursing home where her father had spent his last several years. "That dress suits you to a T."

"Better than scrubs," Tiffany said with a chuckle.

When Sarah reached the bride, she gave Caitlin a big hug.

"Sarah, thank you so much—for everything!" Tears glistened in Caitlin's eyes.

"I'm glad I could be a part of your special day. And congratulations, Travis."

Travis bent down and kissed her cheek. "Thank you, Mrs. Hart." He winked and she knew he was referring to the family mystery she had recently helped unravel.

"You are most welcome."

Caitlin had laid aside her sheaf of pristine white roses. Sarah glanced over at the table where they lay. "Your bouquet is exquisite."

"Thanks! Aren't they amazing? I'm so happy with all the flowers—with everything. Today's been wonderful."

Next to her, Liam waited with gleaming green eyes. "Sarah, darlin'." He drew her into his embrace for a lingering moment.

Sarah gave him a squeeze. "That was a beautiful ceremony."

"It was." Liam gave an exaggerated sigh. "I'm getting old, Sarah. My baby is all grown up."

Sarah chuckled. "Welcome to the empty-nest club."

"Your poem was almost as lovely as the woman reading it."

"Well, it wasn't *my* poem." Sarah teased. "But thank you. You clean up pretty well yourself." She looked down the line, searching the faces of those waiting to greet the wedding party.

"Looking for someone?" Liam asked.

"Yes, I thought I spotted an acquaintance I haven't seen in a good many years." She patted his arm. "I don't want to hold up the line. I'll catch up with you later."

She walked over to the table where Karen Bancroft, a waitress in Liam's café, was pouring punch.

"Hello, Karen. Lovely ceremony, wasn't it?" Sarah picked up a paper cup of punch.

"Absolutely. I admit I shed some tears." Karen looked past Sarah. "Oh, hello, Pastor John."

Sarah turned to greet the pastor of Bridge Street Church, where she was a member. More people came along to get punch, and one of them drew the pastor into conversation, so Sarah drifted about the edges of the large room, scanning for Ruby Sears.

Had she been mistaken? Ruby had left town so long ago, and in a hurry. It would cause quite a stir if she showed up in Maple Hill again. She had probably glimpsed a stranger— one of Caitlin's relatives, perhaps—whose facial structure was similar to Ruby's.

Far across the hall, close to the door, Ernie Maplethorpe stood next to Martha, holding a punch cup, while Martha talked to Maggie. Ernie could tell Sarah what she wanted to know. She made her way between the tables and clusters of chatting people. She almost bumped into Irene Stuart, the historian who managed the local historical society's collection.

"Sarah, what a beautiful dress."

"Oh, thank you. Did you get to meet Caitlin's aunt Mabina?"

"Yes, I did. She's delightful." Irene's eyes sparkled. She had helped Sarah solve a mystery involving Mabina Fredericks, and had anticipated meeting the Irish lady.

Sarah glanced beyond Irene, glimpsing Ernie once more. "Excuse me, Irene. I'll talk to you later." She hurried toward her target.

"Oh, Sarah, there you are," Martha said.

She smiled. "Hi, Martha."

"Wasn't that the sweetest wedding you ever saw? And Caitlin looks so beautiful."

"Yes, she certainly does. She and Travis look extremely happy."

"Sarah, your reading was perfect," Maggie said.

"Thank you."

"I don't think I've ever heard that poem before," Martha told her. "It was beautiful."

"I've always loved it, ever since I discovered it in my college literature class." Sarah looked around again. Jason was talking to their pastor a short distance away. "Weren't you and Jason going to bring Leland to the wedding?" Jason and Maggie's family had "adopted" the elderly man, who lived at Bradford Manor, the nursing home where Sarah's father William had lived until his death just a few short months ago.

"Yes, but he came down with a cold. We're going to take him a slice of cake later. He'll be sorry he didn't see you wearing that dress today." Maggie looked toward the buffet. "I see the girls are loading their plates already. I'd better go supervise."

Sarah turned to Ernie. He nodded to her and took a sip of his punch, holding it with both hands. The tremors from his Parkinson's seemed under control today. Sarah smiled at him. "Ernie, who was that woman you were talking to?"

Ernie's neatly trimmed mustache twitched. "Woman?"

"Yes. Outside the sanctuary doors during the wedding— the one in the hat." Sarah looked around again. "I don't see her now. Where is she?"

Ernie frowned. "I'm not sure who you mean."

Sarah squinted at him. This was not like Ernie. "You left the sanctuary during the ceremony. As I was giving my reading, I saw you outside the doors. And a woman was talking to you. Dark hat, blue flowers. Ring a bell?"

"Oh?" Ernie peered about innocently, as though he meant to help her find the person she sought. "What's her name?"

"That's what I was going to ask you. She looked like someone I used to know."

Ernie raised his chin. "Oh, excuse me. Harry Butler is waving me over." Ernie set his punch cup on a nearby table and walked away.

Sarah stared after him. "Can you believe that?"

Martha chuckled. "Can't tell a lie to save his life. Don't worry about it. I'll ask him later."

Sarah sighed. A quick survey of the hall failed to turn up anyone wearing the large hat she had seen earlier. She had about decided that the woman had gone. Maybe she had even slipped out after talking to Ernie. Sarah wished she had walked on out there at the time and satisfied her curiosity. She scanned the room again, in case the woman had removed her headgear, but no one remotely resembling Ruby Sears came within her view.

The receiving line was dwindling. Sarah decided to go ask Liam if Ruby Sears had been invited to the wedding.

"Will you excuse me, Martha? I need to speak to Liam, and I think I'll get in line again. But I'll be back in a few minutes."

"All right. I'll find our table."

Martha looked slightly baffled, and Sarah hoped she wasn't being rude, but her curiosity was piqued. She hurried across the room and slid in at the end of the line.

"I don't recall that name," Liam said when she reached him again. Sarah described the woman she had seen and asked if he had seen her come through the receiving line. He smiled and shook his head. "I've been hugged by more people I didn't know I didn't know. But let me ask Caitlin."

He leaned forward and touched Caitlin's sleeve. "Caitlin, dear—"

Caitlin scrunched up her face. "I know, I know. It's time for us to go to the head table. I'll catch up with you later, Dad."

Liam shrugged at Sarah. "Sorry. Who was she?"

Sarah hesitated. "I thought she looked like someone I knew way back when Gerry and I were first married." She looked up at Liam. "Did you know Ruby Sears?"

"I don't think so. Did she live here in town?"

"Yes. Her family used to own the furniture factory—well, the building, that is. They didn't make furniture. It was a textile mill back then. They made woolens, I think."

"Dad," Caitlin called from five yards away.

Sarah smiled apologetically. "We can talk about this later. The bride needs you."

Liam nodded with a knowing look. "Yes, and this is her day. But don't you go too far, will you?" He gave her hand a squeeze.

Sarah couldn't stop thinking about Ruby and the Sears family. When Ruby's father, Matthew Sears, had died, Ruby was barely out of her teens. She had inherited the Sears Textiles factory, and she had hired Gerry to go over the company's books. Shortly afterward, Ruby had shut down the textile operation, sold the factory, and moved away.

Sarah made a complete circuit of the hall, during which she greeted dozens of people—but not Ruby. Next she moseyed over to the buffet table, where Martha and Ernie stood at the end of the line. She slipped in next to them. Ernie was talking to the man ahead of him, and it seemed a good time to question Martha.

"So Martha, did you see Ruby Sears?"

Martha blinked. "Who?"

"Ruby Sears. The woman I saw talking to Ernie was either Ruby or someone who looked an awful lot like her."

"Are you still thinking about that?"

"Yes. If it wasn't Ruby, that's fine, but if it was, I'd love to talk to her."

"But Ruby Sears hasn't been around here for forty years or so," Martha said.

"I know. That's why I was so surprised when I saw her."

"Well, Ernie went out to the restroom during the harp solo, and I was upset that he didn't get back in time to hear you recite. But he didn't say anything about meeting anyone out in the narthex." Martha tapped Ernie on the back, and he turned around. "So, tell us, who were you talking to out in the entry during the wedding? Sarah thinks it was Ruby Sears."

Ernie frowned. "Who's that?"

"Don't you remember the family who owned the textile factory?" Sarah asked. "Their daughter Ruby went to our school. She was a few years behind Martha and me. I don't suppose you knew her well."

"Wait a minute," Martha said to Ernie. "Didn't your sister Anna work at the woolen mill for a while?"

"That's right, she did," Ernie said.

"And you think Ruby is here," Martha prodded.

Sarah shrugged. "I've been looking for her, but I can't find her. Unless that was someone else you were talking to." She gazed pointedly at Ernie.

His cheeks grew pink, and he avoided looking at Sarah. "Can't think who you mean. Must've been one of Liam's Irish relatives."

Sarah sighed. No use trying to get more out of Ernie. "I guess it wasn't her then." Sarah tried to think of a way to change the subject. "So, Martha, don't forget we're supposed to vote on Tuesday."

Martha had reached the corner of the buffet, and she took a plate. "I wouldn't miss it. Mostly local issues this year, though."

"Do you want to go together?" Sarah reached for a plate and a fork. "Then if we have to wait, at least we'll have someone to talk to."

"Sure," Martha said.

Sarah gave up trying to change the subject and looked around again, still hoping to spot Ruby—or whomever she had thought was Ruby. If she could only find the woman, she could settle the question once and for all. "I suppose if Ruby Sears were in town, she'd be staying with relatives."

"Or at a hotel," Martha said.

"That's a thought," Sarah said. "I'll ask around tomorrow. I guess she didn't stay for the reception."

"I'm trying to remember her," Martha said. "I didn't know her well. When did that factory shut down?"

"It must have been around 1972 that it closed." Sarah said. That was about a year after she and Gerry were married. Forty years ago!

She felt old and suddenly doubted her earlier impressions. Would she recognize a woman she hadn't seen in forty years? Ruby would have aged and changed.

"I guess it wasn't really her," she said again and placed a small sandwich and a few cookies on her plate.

Ernie looked relieved. He took a big bite from a finger sandwich.

Martha watched her husband closely. "Let me know if you find out anything."

Sarah nodded. "I will."

Liam stepped to the center of the hall and raised his hands. "Folks," he called, "Caitlin and Travis are going to cut the cake."

The bride and groom were making their way toward the table where the cake was set up, pausing to speak to a few friends along the way.

"I want to get a picture." Sarah handed Martha her plate, pulled her small digital camera from her pocket, and hurried toward the bride and groom. The woman she had seen Ernie talking to probably wasn't Ruby Sears at all. But why Ernie would care if anyone knew, she couldn't fathom. Still, it bothered her. She wanted to know, one way or the other: had Ruby Sears come back to Maple Hill, and if so, why?

A NOTE FROM THE EDITORS

We hope you enjoyed Patchwork Mysteries, published by the Books and Inspirational Media Division of Guideposts, a nonprofit organization that touches millions of lives every day through products and services that inspire, encourage, help you grow in your faith, and celebrate God's love.

Thank you for making a difference with your purchase of this book, which helps fund our many outreach programs to military personnel, prisons, hospitals, nursing homes, and educational institutions.

We also create many useful and uplifting online resources. Visit Guideposts.org to read true stories of hope and inspiration, access OurPrayer network, sign up for free newsletters, download free e-books, join our Facebook community, and follow our stimulating blogs.

To learn about other Guideposts publications, including the best-selling devotional *Daily Guideposts*, go to Guideposts .org/Shop, call (800) 932-2145, or write to Guideposts, PO Box 5815, Harlan, Iowa 51593.

Sign up for the
Guideposts Fiction Newsletter
and stay up-to-date on the books you love!

You'll get sneak peeks of new releases, recommendations from other Guideposts readers, and special offers just for you . . .
and it's FREE!

Just go to Guideposts.org/Newsletters today to sign up.

Guideposts®

Visit Guideposts.org/Shop
or call (800) 932-2145